CAPITOL
OFFENSE

ALSO BY MIKE DOOGAN

Lost Angel

G. P. Putnam's Sons   New York

CAPITOL
OFFENSE

A NIK KANE ALASKA MYSTERY

MIKE DOOGAN

G. P. PUTNAM'S SONS
Publishers Since 1838
Published by the Penguin Group
Penguin Group (USA) Inc., 375 Hudson Street, New York, New York 10014, USA •
Penguin Group (Canada), 90 Eglinton Avenue East, Suite 700,
Toronto, Ontario M4P 2Y3, Canada (a division of Pearson Penguin Canada Inc.) •
Penguin Books Ltd, 80 Strand, London WC2R 0RL, England • Penguin Ireland,
25 St Stephen's Green, Dublin 2, Ireland (a division of Penguin Books Ltd) •
Penguin Group (Australia), 250 Camberwell Road, Camberwell, Victoria 3124,
Australia (a division of Pearson Australia Group Pty Ltd) •
Penguin Books India Pvt Ltd, 11 Community Centre, Panchsheel Park,
New Delhi–110 017, India • Penguin Group (NZ), 67 Apollo Drive,
Rosedale, North Shore 0745, Auckland, New Zealand (a division of Pearson
New Zealand Ltd) • Penguin Books (South Africa) (Pty) Ltd, 24 Sturdee Avenue,
Rosebank, Johannesburg 2196, South Africa

Penguin Books Ltd, Registered Offices:
80 Strand, London WC2R 0RL, England

Library of Congress Cataloging-in-Publication Data

Doogan, Mike.
Capitol offense : Nik Kane Alaska mystery / Mike Doogan.
p.   cm.
ISBN 978-0-399-15431-7
1. Private investigators—Alaska—Fiction.   2. Alaska—Fiction.   I. Title.
PS3604.O5675C37   2007   2007008804
813'.6—dc22

Printed in the United States of America
1   3   5   7   9   10   8   6   4   2

BOOK DESIGN BY MEIGHAN CAVANAUGH

This is a work of fiction. Names, characters, places, and incidents either are the product of the author's imagination or are used fictitiously, and any resemblance to actual persons, living or dead, businesses, companies, events, or locales is entirely coincidental.

While the author has made every effort to provide accurate telephone numbers and Internet addresses at the time of publication, neither the publisher nor the author assumes any responsibility for errors, or for changes that occur after publication. Further, the publisher does not have any control over and does not assume any responsibility for author or third-party websites or their content.

For my father, Jim Doogan,

who believed that politics could make

the world a better place

ACKNOWLEDGMENTS

I want to thank the usual suspects—my agent, Marcy Posner; my editor, Tom Colgan; and most of all my wife, Kathy—and some unusual ones, the generations of Alaska politicians whose exploits and antics were the inspiration for this book.

CAPITOL OFFENSE

PROLOGUE

Baby Santos got off the elevator on the fifth floor of the Alaska State Capitol. He pushed his cleaning cart to the right, down the hall, around the corner, and through the propped-open door to the House Finance Committee hearing room. At just after 10 p.m., the room, like all of the offices he'd passed, was empty.

Baby had been cleaning offices here for many years. He knew that if it had been May instead of March, the rooms would be brightly lit and full of people. He was glad it wasn't the end of the legislative session yet, because working around all those people talk-talk-talking made his job much harder. And the wastepaper they made. Holy Mother!

He took his CD player from the shoe box that held his music. The CD player was old and heavy and his sons, with their iPod Nanos, made fun of him for using it. But the CD player still worked and he saw no reason to get rid of a perfectly good piece of equipment just because there was a newer one.

Baby put the player into a pouch he'd made from canvas and clipped it to his belt. Then he put on his earphones, inserted the new One Vo1ce CD into the player, and hit Play. If Corazon, his wife, found out he was listening to these young girls, he'd never hear the end of it. But he liked the bright, R&B stylings. And the girls. Aiee. Even a man as old as Baby could dream.

He took the thirty-three-gallon plastic garbage can off the cart and started emptying wastebaskets. When he was finished, he took down his vacuum cleaner and ran it over the carpet. He knew some of the other janitors didn't vacuum every night, but this was his floor and he wanted it just so. Besides, they had spent so much time and money remodeling these offices, it would be a shame to let the carpet get dirty.

When Baby finished that room, he worked his way from office to office, around the corner, along the hallway, and past the elevator to the women's restroom. He knocked on the door. When no one answered, he snapped on a pair of disposable rubber gloves, picked up the cleaner and some rags, and, leaving his cart in the hall, scrubbed the pedestal toilets and the big, square sinks of thick porcelain. When he was finished, he returned all the cleaning materials, hefted his mop and bucket, and scrubbed the floor. Then he moved on to the wing that belonged to the Senate, going in and out of offices with his garbage can and vacuum. One Vo1ce gave way to Rachel Alejandro, then Rachelle Ann Go. These young women could sing, and, aiee, did they look good.

Baby liked his job, liked being able to listen to music and move along the floor in an orderly fashion. The older he got, the more he liked everything just so. He even liked being able to work during the day on the weekends, because it gave him time to be with his family on some evenings. His boys were teenagers now and needed watching. Once he had been their hero. Now they clashed all the time. Fathers and sons. It was the way of the world.

Baby reached the men's restroom and looked for his cleaner. It was not in its usual place, with the rags and brushes, but on the bottom of the cart on the opposite side. Odd. Had he put it there? Baby shrugged. As he got older, he forgot many things.

When he was finished with the restroom, he put a Sugar Pie DeSanto CD into his player. She might not have the shape of the young women, but she had twice the voice. Baby had every CD she'd ever made.

Baby pushed his cart around the corner. The doors of the Senate Finance Committee room were propped open, too. In one of the offices at the far end, Baby saw a light. He switched off his CD player, removed his earphones, left his cart where it was, and walked softly through the committee room. The room was Baby's favorite, a big room that had been a federal courtroom when the building was young, carefully restored, and, since Baby had been doing the cleaning, carefully kept up, too.

Baby's sneakers made no noise on the thick carpet. He was glad; he wanted to see why the light was on before revealing himself. Once, years before, he'd blundered into that office and found a man, a senator, on top of a woman half his age, on the office's big, leather couch. How embarrassed everyone was. Holy Mother! Baby didn't want that to happen again.

He went through the reception area and peeked into the chairman's office next door. There was a young woman there, but she wasn't underneath anybody. She lay on the floor beside the desk.

She is wearing no clothes, or not many, Baby thought. Where are her clothes? And what is that pool around her head? Water?

Standing over her, holding something in his hand, was a slim, dark-skinned, dark-haired young man. The young man looked up from the woman's body, his face contorted in a horrible grimace.

Baby Santos turned and ran out of the office, around the corner and down the hall, screaming with all his might.

3

Politics are as exciting as war and almost as dangerous.
In war you can only be killed once, but in politics many times.

WINSTON CHURCHILL

Tom Jeffords leveled the Glock .45 and pulled the trigger. The automatic tried to kick upward, but Jeffords was a big man and held it level with ease as he fired again. When he'd run through thirteen rounds, he ejected the clip and laid it and the automatic on the counter in front of him. He removed his big hearing protectors and motioned to Nik Kane to do the same. The last shot still echoed in the big room, empty except for the two of them. Jeffords pushed a button on a pole next to his shooting station and a motor began to whir.

While he waited for his target to arrive, he said, "So you want to go out on your own."

His tone made it sound as if Kane intended to do something distasteful.

"Yes, I do," Kane said. "I'm bored."

Jeffords nodded and examined the target. It was an outline of a man with a gun. All thirteen holes were within the kill zone. Jeffords might be a desk-bound bureaucrat who was pushing sixty-five, but he could still shoot.

The Glock .45 was the Anchorage Police Department's standard-issue side arm, but the version lying in front of Jeffords was anything but standard issue. It was chrome-plated and had honest-to-God pearl handles with *TSJ* inlaid in ebony. A grateful salesman had given Jeffords the automatic after the department selected the Glock .45, and it went well with his $1,000-a-copy tailored uniform, his full head of well-barbered white hair, and his Maui tan.

It's easy to mistake Jeffords for a show horse and his automatic for a show gun, Kane thought. But not if you watch him on the firing range.

Jeffords clipped a new target to the line and hit the button again.

"I'd think boredom would be preferable to the life you've been leading for the past several years," he said. "I'd think you'd welcome some peace and quiet."

Ah, Kane thought. The oblique reference. A Jeffords specialty. So much more elegant than using words like *drunkenness, killing,* and *prison.*

"And if your life were more . . . exciting . . . you would be forced to carry a firearm," the chief said.

Kane hadn't carried a gun of any sort since the night he'd answered an officer needs assistance call on his way home from a bar and shot and killed a twelve-year-old. Of course, for seven of those eight years he'd been in prison, where they sort of frowned on inmates packing. He'd finally been exonerated when a witness recanted and admitted the dead boy had been aiming a gun at Kane, but he'd tried to steer clear of firearms since he'd gotten out anyway. Jeffords seemed to regard that as a form of weakness.

Jeffords put a fresh clip in the .45.

"A man in your line of work needs to carry a firearm for self-defense," he said, as he waited for his target to reach the proper position, "even if his assignments are boring."

The chief put the hearing protectors back on before Kane could reply. Kane did the same, then watched as Jeffords put another thirteen rounds right where he wanted them.

When Kane had gotten out of prison a little more than a year before, he had wanted to go back to his old job as a detective lieutenant with the Anchorage Police Department. Jeffords had put the kibosh on that, but had seen to it that Kane was hired by 49th Star Security, a firm in which he was a silent partner. Kane had had an interesting case or two, but mostly he'd been doing corporate background checks, some divorce work, a few pilfering cases, the kind of thing they'd left to the newbies when he'd been with the police department.

When his target returned, Jeffords regarded it for a moment.

If he had any emotions, Kane thought, that look might be satisfaction.

Jeffords took the targets up to the range master's stand, returned with a handful of supplies, and began breaking down the automatic.

"Aren't you a little old to be chasing after excitement?" he asked.

Kane laughed.

"I'm, what, seven years younger than you," he said. "Are you too old to be bossing cops and politicians around?"

Jeffords shot Kane a look that said age wasn't his favorite topic of discussion, then shrugged.

"If you are really thinking about going out on your own," he said, "then this is a happy coincidence. I have a job offer for you."

Kane laughed.

"And here I thought you just wanted to see my smiling face," Kane said. "I'm heartbroken."

"Very amusing," the chief said, in a tone that made it clear he wasn't amused. "There's a woman in town named Mrs. Richard Foster. She has some work that needs to be done. I'd like you to do it."

Kane had so many questions, he wasn't sure where to start.

"You'd like me to do it?" he said. "You mean, this isn't an order?"

"You aren't with the department anymore, Nik," Jeffords said. "I can't give you orders."

Just like Jeffords, Kane thought. We both know he owns the security firm, but he won't admit it even to me. In an empty room, no less.

"Why am I hearing this from you instead of someone at 49th Star?" he asked.

"I'm told the firm can't take this job," the chief said.

He's told, Kane thought. That's rich.

"Why not?" he asked.

Jeffords was slow to reply.

"The reasons are . . . complicated," he said at last.

Great, Kane thought. Now we're in the world of Jeffordsisms, answers that don't answer anything. Kane had known the chief for more than thirty years. They'd come up through the ranks of the police department together. Jeffords, who had joined the department sooner and had a much better grasp of politics, was always a couple of rungs above him on the career ladder. Since he'd often worked under Jeffords, Kane had had plenty of reason to study him. He had watched the chief become the man he was, each year growing a little more devious and a little less human.

"You want me to take a job the firm won't take, for 'complicated' reasons?" Kane said.

"Can't take," the chief said.

"Why not?" Kane asked.

Jeffords looked around to make sure no one had entered the firing range.

He probably arranged for this place to be empty, Kane thought. He didn't want anyone else to hear this conversation, and he's still not saying anything. I wonder who he thinks might be listening.

"The case involves a politician," Jeffords said. "It would be . . . incongruent . . . for me, or the firm, to be involved with this."

And that's as close to an admission that he owns the firm as I'm likely to get, Kane thought.

"Incongruent," Kane said. "I guess those word-a-day calendars really do pay off."

He was silent for a moment.

"If you're trying to lay low on this, why send me?" he asked. "All your political pals will figure you're involved the minute they see me anyway."

Jeffords's job title was chief of police, but for the past decade or more he'd actually run Anchorage, stage-managing the elections of mayors and assembly members who did what they were told. Because so much of the money that made the city go came from the state and federal governments, he had made himself a force in state and federal politics as well.

"I'm not responsible for what people may think," Jeffords said. "But if anyone asks, you can truthfully tell them that I am not involved in this case."

Kane decided to let that go.

"This politician have a name?" he asked.

"His name is Matthew Hope," Jeffords said. "He's a member of the Alaska State Senate."

Kane was silent as he thought about what Jeffords had said. Matthew Hope's name had been all over the news in the past couple of days. He'd been arrested for the murder of a young woman in the state Capitol. The victim had been beautiful and "scantily clad," as the newspapers and the TV newsreaders put it. She'd also been white, and Hope was an Alaska Native. The story had everything needed to crank up the media—sex, politics, violence, and race. The crime had even been given a tabloidy nickname—The White Rose Murder, for the flower embroidered on the front of the garter belt the victim had been wearing.

Maybe that's why Jeffords is being so careful, Kane thought. A case this hot could burn anybody involved. Or even anybody in the wrong place at the wrong time.

"The White Rose Murder case is a lollapalooza," Kane said. "Is Hope one of yours?"

The chief smiled.

"One of mine?" Jeffords said. "What do you think, Nik, that I have a stable of politicians who jump when I snap my fingers?"

Actually, that's exactly what Kane thought, but he couldn't see that saying so would get him anything but a lecture on how representative democracy worked. Instead, he asked, "Is he a friend of yours or not?"

Jeffords was silent for a moment.

"I think it's fair to say that Senator Hope and I don't see eye-to-eye on some things," he said.

Jeffords was clearly not going to tell him anything useful about his relationship with Matthew Hope, so Kane changed the subject.

"What do you know about the case?" he asked.

Jeffords looked around the firing range, as if expecting to see a grand jury sitting in it somewhere.

"The newspapers have given it extensive coverage," he said.

So he wants to be able to tell people he never discussed the case with me, Kane thought.

"If you don't like this guy's politics, why get involved?" he asked.

"I'm not getting involved," Jeffords said with a thin smile. "You're getting involved."

Kane opened his mouth, but Jeffords spoke again.

"I really can't tell you any more, " he said.

Can't, or won't, Kane thought. Either way, he knew trying to pry information out of the chief was useless.

Kane thought about what Jeffords was offering. He wouldn't put it past the chief to dump him into a sticky situation just to show him that he'd be better off staying with the security firm. But the chief had too much at stake to send Kane blundering into the political world just to teach him a lesson. So this was probably a legitimate job, and it did sound more interesting than what he'd been doing. Of course, watching paint dry sounded more interesting, too. As long as Jeffords didn't want him to do anything he just wouldn't do. He watched as Jeffords's fingers, nimble despite his age, danced just above the counter, reassembling the Glock. Then he began feeding rounds into an empty clip.

"So do you want me to try to get this guy out of the trouble he's in or not?" Kane asked.

Jeffords's thin smile became a grin. I'll be damned, Kane thought. He might still be human after all.

"You know I'd never ask you to do anything but what you thought was right, Nik," the chief said. "We both know that wouldn't do any good. What I'd like you to do is go and talk with Mrs. Foster and, if you find it agreeable, work for her."

He snapped the last round into the clip.

"I believe she's prepared to offer you quite a lot of money," he said. "You do need money, don't you, Nik?"

"Everybody needs money," Kane said.

The truth was that Kane was doing pretty well financially. He was drawing a salary from the security firm and a pension from the police department, and since he wasn't drinking he didn't have any expensive habits. But wanting to go out on his own was part of an effort to gain greater control of his life. Working, as he saw it, was a matter of trading his time for money and, as he got older, time got to be more and more important. More money would buy him more time to do what he wanted. If he could just figure out what that was.

"I'll have to hand off my part of a surveillance," Kane said. "Then I'll go see this Mrs. Richard Foster and I'll try really hard to take the job."

"Good," Jeffords said. He slapped the clip into the automatic and holstered it. "Wait here."

He went back to the range master's stand, returning with a much plainer automatic, a couple of clips, and a black fabric belt holster. He laid them all on the firing table.

"You should have a little practice," Jeffords said.

Kane looked at the gun for a long moment, then shook his head.

"I don't think so," he said.

Jeffords blew air through his lips in exasperation.

"Then at least take the weapon with you," he said. "It's a gift from me."

Kane could see that saying no would start an argument. It was easier just to take the gun.

"Okay," he said, picking up the automatic and accessories from the stand and stowing them in various pockets. "But I don't see why you're so concerned. If this case is political, what's the worst that could happen? A nasty campaign ad?"

Jeffords gave him another real smile.

"You have no idea," he said.

Politics is the art of human happiness.

HERBERT ALBERT LAURENS FISHER

Kane was sitting at his computer, reading up on the White Rose Murder, when his cell phone rang.

"You have to come and get your things out of the house," his ex-wife, Laurie, said.

"I'm fine, thanks for asking," Kane said. "How are you?"

He could hear her take a deep breath and exhale with a sigh.

Great, he thought. Just ten seconds on the telephone, I'm pissed off and she's long-suffering.

"Nik," she said with obvious patience, "we've talked about this. We're not married anymore and it's time to make the separation complete. We'll both be better off."

"I haven't got anyplace to put that stuff," he said.

Oh, that's good, he thought. Be childish. That's appealing.

13

"Don't be like that, Nik," she said. "You're making good money now. Get out of that crappy apartment and get a house big enough for your things. Build that cabin in the woods you always used to talk about. Rent a storage locker. Move on with your life, and let me move on with mine."

Kane bit back a smart-ass remark and waited. He still didn't understand what had happened between them. For twenty-five years Laurie had been, in addition to everything else, his best friend. She'd stood behind him during his trial and his years in prison, raising their kids, visiting him every week, toughing it out. Then, less than a month after he'd gotten out, she'd announced that she wanted a divorce.

She'd gone out and gotten one, too. Kane couldn't bring himself to fight it, couldn't see rewarding her for all she'd done by being a jerk about it. But he'd dragged his feet, not signing the final papers until she'd gone off on him like a nuclear explosion. And, for some reason, he was unable to clear out of the house and finish the job.

The house, their house, where they'd fought and sat companionably and made love and raised children, was just hers now, and she wanted him to remove his camping gear and guns and tools and everything else that reminded her of him, of them. She'd already removed everything inside the house, the gifts he'd given her and the photographs he was in, even the dishes they'd eaten off of. She'd covered the floors with new carpet and the walls with new paint. Laurie had erased him from her life, except for those few belongings still in the garage.

He didn't think she was being unreasonable, really, to want him out, to remove the last of his clutter from her life, but he couldn't bring himself to do it. And he didn't understand why.

"My analyst says you're trying to hold on to me," Laurie said. After all their years together, she had a spooky ability to tell what he was thinking. "She says leaving things here is an attempt to exercise control over me and our relationship."

Kane laughed.

"Well, that's really working, isn't it?" he said. He could hear the self-pity in his voice and it made him disgusted with himself.

"Nik, please," Laurie said. "You're just making this harder for me. And for yourself."

Kane sighed. She was right, of course. And she was entitled to the life she wanted, even if it was without him. He knew that he couldn't keep them together on his own. He knew that the right thing, the honorable thing, was to wish her luck and let her go. He thought of himself as a pragmatist, was proud of his ability to face facts without wincing, and yet . . . and yet he just wasn't able to do the pragmatic thing here.

Maybe I am a control freak, he thought, just like Laurie and her goddamn analyst say.

"Okay," he said. "I may be going out of town on a case, but if I do I'll come and get that stuff first thing when I get back."

"Do you think it will be long?" Laurie asked.

"I don't know," Kane said. "I'm going to Juneau. It's that case of murder in the legislature, the young woman who was killed there a few days ago. It could be a while."

"Oh," Laurie said. "I read about that in the newspaper. The White Rose Murder, they're calling it." She paused. "Are you sure you want to get mixed up in all that?"

Kane heard trouble in her voice.

"What is it, Laurie?" he asked. "What's wrong?"

"Nothing, Nik," she said. "Nothing's wrong."

Kane waited. She'd tell him. She was too honest not to.

"Dylan's down there," she said.

It took Kane a moment to make sense of what she'd said.

"Dylan?" he said. "Our son, Dylan? He's in Juneau?"

Dylan was the youngest of their three children, the only boy. He'd been twelve when Kane went off to prison, and he'd taken his father's departure hard. He was at college when Kane got out, and when the boy returned for the summer he'd refused to even speak to Kane. As a child Dylan had been mercurial, happy one minute and weeping the next, full of enthusiasms that died out as quickly as they were born. In his father's case, though, he seemed to have settled on hatred.

Kane hadn't been surprised. He knew all about hating your father. He'd planned to try to get through to his son during the summer, but Dylan had taken a job at an arts camp at the university in Fairbanks and Kane hadn't seen him again.

"What's he doing there?" Kane said. "Shouldn't he be in school?"

Laurie's voice was sharp with exasperation.

"I told you all about this, remember?" she said. "His school has a junior-year sabbatical, where the students go out for a semester and work. Dylan's working for a member of the House of Representatives. Tom Jeffords helped him get the job."

I suppose she did tell me, Kane thought, but I was probably thinking about something more important. That's the kind of father I always was and, apparently, still am.

"Well," Kane said, "I'll look him up when I get there, maybe buy him dinner."

Laurie was silent, then said, "Hmm."

"Hmm?" Kane said. "What's that supposed to mean?"

Laurie sighed again.

"What that means is that you should be careful with Dylan," she said. "He's still got a lot of anger at you for leaving us."

Kane could feel his self-control slipping away.

"Leaving you?" he said. "I didn't leave anybody. They put me in fucking prison. It wasn't my choice."

"You made choices," Laurie said, her voice rising, "and your choices led to prison."

Kane gripped the cell phone so hard his hand hurt.

"I don't need any secondhand analysis from you and that quack you're seeing, Laurie," he said. "Or any advice on how to get along with my kids."

He could hear her taking deep breaths.

"Fine," she said in a calmer voice. "Just come and get your things. I'll give you two weeks. If you haven't picked them up by then, I'm giving them to the Salvation Army."

"Don't you dare," Kane began, but the click of her hanging up stopped him. He closed his cell phone with great gentleness and put it into his shirt pocket. He sat thinking about the conversation, about how poorly he'd handled it.

When he'd first gotten out of prison, Kane was in many ways still institutionalized. He wasn't used to having choices, so he wore the same clothes every day. Large spaces made him nervous. The world was dangerously unpredictable, full of people doing whatever they wanted.

Intellectually, he knew that these were responses conditioned by his years in prison. He knew that, with work, he could overcome them. But emotionally, he didn't want to have to work at it. He wanted them to go away on their own. He wanted to just step back into his old life, back into his job on the police force, back into his marriage, and pretend that he'd never been in prison.

That didn't happen. Jeffords had refused to take him back on the force. Laurie had divorced him, saying he was not the man she had married. His children were strangers to him. He was fifty-six years old and living in a furnished apartment, without any significant ties to another human being. Whenever he was in the grip of self-pity, he even felt that life was better in prison, where he'd known everyone and they'd known him. He supposed that blighted sense of community was what kept some cons coming back behind the walls.

He fought the self-pity and all the other feelings—shame and anger and uncertainty—that tried to take control of him. He wore different clothes and went into crowds and tried to relate to the people at work.

But his job and his family had been his identity. His job and his family and, if he were to tell the truth, drinking. And now he had none of them, and that left a big hole where his life should be. He was having a hard time figuring out how to fill it. All he'd decided so far was that he needed to take control of himself and his life, and stop trying to crawl back into the dark hole of passivity that, even today, beckoned to him.

If I can just get my feet firmly planted, he thought, I can try to make up for my mistakes, to both Laurie and the kids. Maybe he could start with Dylan.

It wasn't any surprise that his son was mad at him, and he had every right to be. What was it the Bible said? "The fathers have eaten sour grapes, and the children's teeth are set on edge."

Kane shook his head and looked at his watch. If he left now, he could make it to his gym, have dinner, and still get to his surveillance on time.

He might be an aging, isolated, dry alcoholic, and a sorry excuse for a husband and father, he thought with a wry grin, but he could still beat the crap out of a heavy bag.

Never take anything for granted.

BENJAMIN DISRAELI

You got to hand it to the guy," Winslow said as he watched their subject's car weave into his driveway, narrowly missing a beater pickup on big tires that was parked to the side. "He's been to, what, three bars? No, four. And he's still able to navigate home."

Kane snorted. He'd been within an inch of dropping a dime on the guy—a big, boring accountant named Robert Bland he'd been watching for eleven nights now—but didn't want the complications that might arise from an arrest.

No, tonight his job was to hand off to Craig Winslow, a new hire in his twenties, a southern boy straight out of the military police with, as far as Kane could tell, no training in anything but shooting, saluting, and busting heads. Winslow, who was driving, had been far too obvious in following the subject, but with Bland as drunk as a Kennedy, Kane didn't think it made much difference.

"Like I said," Kane said, "this is aberrant behavior for the subject. Until tonight, he has been as exciting as American cheese."

The case was more of the agency's usual. Bland's wife had decided she liked women better than men—or a particular woman better than Bland, anyway—moved out, and filed for divorce. She and her lawyer were convinced that they had to catch Bland at something—hookers, hidden assets, kiddie porn—to offset in court Mrs. Bland's sudden change of sexual identity. So they'd hired 49th Star Security to find something. But a records search had come up dry and neither Kane nor the day surveillance guy had seen Bland do anything interesting, let alone suspicious. Tonight's drunk driving was it for bad behavior.

"Can't really blame the guy for having a few drinks," Winslow said. "If your wife decided she liked muff diving better than what you got, you'd drink, too. If you didn't do something worse. It's a man's worst nightmare, isn't it?"

Oh, good, Kane thought. A moral philosopher. Between Mississippi, or wherever he was from, and the United States Army, Winslow would be amazing indeed if his ideas about the world were as advanced as, say, the 1900s.

"We're not here to make judgments about the subject," he said, wincing at his own pompousness. "We're here to catch him at something, or to be able to say with certainty that he isn't up to something."

The night was typical for Anchorage in early March: overcast, dark, and cold enough that Winslow had left the agency's nondescript midsize running so the windows wouldn't fog. The only light was from a streetlamp at the corner. Kane watched Bland lurch from his car and start for the house that was all his at the moment, since his wife had moved in with her girlfriend. Bland entered a patch of shadows and didn't reappear at his door.

"What the hell?" Winslow said. "Did he fall down?"

"I don't think so," Kane said.

"Why not?" Winslow asked. "It's icy enough."

Kane's reply was drowned out by an earsplitting metallic racket. Blue smoke erupted from the exhaust pipe of the beater pickup.

"What the hell?" Winslow said again.

The pickup lurched, then shot out into the street, skidding and sliding through a 180-degree turn to point right at their car. The engine sounded like a blender full of nails, but it ran. Above the hood, Kane could make out Bland's face, split by a maniacal grin.

"Oh, jeez," Winslow said. "Oh, jeez."

The pickup bolted forward. Winslow slammed the midsize into gear and stomped on the gas.

If it had been summer, or Winslow had known more about driving on the ice, they would have made it. But when Winslow tromped on the accelerator, the tires spun before biting. The car surged forward, but not quickly enough. The pickup smashed into the left rear quarter panel, sending the midsize spinning. By the time Winslow got it under control again, their car was slewed across Bland's driveway.

Kane's airbag was trying to smother him.

"Muef furf," Winslow said, his voice strangled by his air bag.

Kane could smell burned rubber from where the left rear wheel had rubbed against the damaged bodywork, and hear the grinding of the pickup's starter as Bland tried to get going again.

Got to get out of here, Kane thought. The air bag, which was supposed to deflate after deployment, clearly wasn't going to. He dug into his pocket for his Buck knife. His left arm was trapped by the air bag, so he sat on the knife handle, pried the blade open one-handed, and stabbed the air bag repeatedly. Air hissed from the holes as it began to deflate. When he had clearance, he flipped the knife to his left hand and attacked Winslow's air bag. It began to deflate, too.

Kane tried his door handle. Stuck. The impact had torqued the car's frame, he thought. He heard the pickup's engine catch, then roar. He reared back and smashed his shoulder into the door. It popped open. Winslow was wrestling with his seat belt. Kane jumped out of the car, grabbed Winslow by the collar, and pulled. Winslow's seat belt popped open and he came out of the midsize like a cork out of a bottle. The two men stumbled and fell away from the car.

The pickup T-boned the midsize with a noise like the end of the world. The car bounded in their direction. They threw themselves behind a tree. The midsize glanced off the tree and hopped away.

"Mother jumper," Winslow said, "the crazy bastard's trying to kill us."

The beater pickup sat there, its bumper pushed in where it had hit the midsize, roaring like some prehistoric beast as Bland fed it gas to keep the engine from dying. Kane looked over at Winslow. The younger man had his left palm flat against the tree and was using his forearm as a rest for a revolver as he sighted along the barrel. Kane reached over, grabbed Winslow's gun hand, and wrenched it so that the barrel pointed straight up.

"What do you think you're doing?" he rasped.

"Defending myself," Winslow said, trying to pull the gun away.

Kane slid his grip to Winslow's thumb and pried it back.

"Give me the gun, kid," he said.

Winslow grunted and let go of the gun. Kane took it, uncocked it, and laid it on the ground.

"We're going to take enough guff for having been made," he said to the younger man, "and the paperwork on the car alone is going to be a nightmare. What do you think the agency would do if you shot somebody you were supposed to be following?"

Winslow shrugged.

"So what we going to do?" he asked.

"You go for the passenger's door, I'll go for the driver's," Kane said. He bolted from behind the tree and ran for the truck. Bland sawed the wheel toward him and popped the clutch. The pickup died. Kane pulled the door open, reached up, grabbed Bland's arm, and jerked. Bland was held in place by a lap belt and shoulder belt. His right hand scrabbled for something. Using his grip on Bland's arm, Kane hoisted himself up and flopped into the cab, putting his momentum behind a right hand to Bland's jaw. Bland's head snapped back and his right hand came up clutching a tire iron. Kane reached across Bland's body and grabbed his wrist to pin the tire iron.

"I'll fucking kill you," Bland screamed. "I'll fucking kill both of you and that no-good whore I married and the dyke she's with. I'll kill you all. Kill you all."

He tried to hit Kane with his left hand, but the shoulder harness got in the way. Kane could hear Winslow wrenching the handle of the pickup's other door. Bland threw his head forward and tried to bite Kane's face. His breath smelled like the inside of a whiskey barrel. Kane head-butted him and felt Bland's lips split. Bland's head snapped back. Both men were breathing hard. Bland was repeating "kill you all" over and over.

Bland had the strength of a madman and it was all Kane could do to hang on. He heard the passenger's door open and felt the truck shift as Winslow climbed into the cab.

"Duck," Winslow yelled.

Kane buried his face in Bland's midsection. He heard the unmistakable sound of flesh hitting flesh and felt Bland jerk. He heard the sound again and Bland went slack. Without letting go of Bland's wrist, Kane reached across his body and took the tire iron from his limp hand.

"Let's get him out of here," Kane said.

The two of them got Bland's seat belt undone and lowered him to the ground. Kane sat in the snow next to him, took out his cell phone, and called the police. Winslow leaned against the truck. For several minutes they did nothing but breathe. Then Kane reached over and rubbed snow in Bland's face. He groaned and tried to sit up.

"I knew you were following me," Bland said. His lips were puffy from Kane's head butt and he was hard to understand. "Bitch told me."

"What?" Winslow said. "Our client told our subject she was having him followed? Why would she do that?"

"Who knows?" Kane said, shaking his head. "Human beings are unpredictable. The same heart that was full of love can be full of hate. Even mild-mannered accountants can turn violent."

That sounds profound, he thought, but what do I know? I'm the one who thought this job was too boring.

Nothing in politics is ever so good
or so bad as it first appears.

EDWARD BOYLE

Kane walked up the short flight of steps and rang the doorbell. The wind that always blew down by the lagoon cut at his face. March, coming in like a lion. He buried his hands in the pockets of his overcoat and waited.

The house was big and built of pale wood, a collection of rectangular boxes pointing this way and that, all with large windows that looked out over the lagoon, the railroad tracks, and the Inlet beyond. It was clearly a house that had been designed by an architect, but Kane couldn't tell what effect the architect had hoped to achieve. Pik-Up Stiks? Driftwood stacked up on the beach? A structural metaphor for the anarchy of modern life?

The front door was opened by a brown-skinned man the size of a small car. His black hair was cut to stubble and he had surprising blue eyes in his round, strong face. He wore a black suit with a fine blue stripe, a shirt as white as new snow, and a neatly knotted black tie. He looked Kane over carefully from head to foot, his gaze moving neither faster nor slower over the scar that ran the length of Kane's face. He gave Kane a half-smile and cocked one eyebrow quizzically.

"Aleut?" Kane said.

"Eskimo," the man said.

"Yupik?" Kane said.

"Inupiat," the man said.

"You can tell I know my Natives," Kane said with a laugh. "You're big for an Inupiat."

"Swede in the woodpile," the man said, and they both laughed.

"I'm here to see Mrs. Foster," Kane said. "She's expecting me. I'm Nik Kane."

The man stepped back to let Kane enter and motioned for him to hang his coat on a wrought-iron coatrack. Kane did, then sat to remove his overshoes. No Alaskan would track snow and dirt through a house as ritzy as this.

"If you are armed, I'm afraid I must ask for your weapon," the man said when Kane stood up. His voice was deep and rich, almost a stage voice.

"I'm not," Kane said, raising his arms, "but you'll want to check for yourself."

After patting him down, the man led Kane back into the house. Although he was a good four inches taller than Kane and a hundred pounds heavier, he moved with the grace of a ballet dancer. After they'd passed through several large rooms, he opened a set of double doors and motioned Kane through.

"That suit's a good fit," Kane said as he passed the man. "You can hardly see a bulge from your shoulder holster."

The man gave Kane a smile, showing teeth as white as his shirt.

"That's Mrs. Foster, by the fireplace," he said, and pulled the doors shut behind him.

Kane advanced toward a fireplace big enough to roast a moose in. A woman sat next to it in a high-backed, soft, rose-colored chair. The veil hanging from her small, black hat hid her face, but her long, black dress couldn't hide the suppleness of her body as she rose to greet him.

"Sergeant Kane, how nice to see you again," she said, offering a black-gloved hand.

"We know each other?" Kane asked, trying to see through the veil's black mesh. He wasn't sure what to do with the hand, so he held it lightly.

The woman gave a musical laugh.

"You men," she said in a teasing tone. "How soon you forget."

Withdrawing her hand, she resumed her seat with a motion so smooth and liquid it was like she was being poured into the chair. She waved Kane to a gray leather sofa that faced the fireplace.

Kane sat and looked around the room. It was expensively furnished and dimly lit, soft spotlights illuminating paintings here and there. A Sydney Laurence McKinley took up most of one wall, a couple of bucks' worth of canvas and oil paint that was probably worth $100,000 now. He turned his attention back to the woman.

"If I'm starting to forget women like you," he said, "I'd better check myself into the Pioneer Home."

The woman laughed again and shifted in her chair, her body doing interesting things beneath the material of her dress.

"That's very gallant," she said, giving the last word a French pronunciation. "I hope you'll forgive me for not removing my veil. I'm still in mourning."

Kane was surprised; Rip Foster had been dead for nearly a year now.

"Isn't this a long time to mourn?" he asked.

The black-veiled head shook slowly back and forth.

"I loved my husband very much," the woman said. "I don't think a traditional mourning period is inappropriate."

The death of Rip Foster had been a major media event. Instead of the regular obituary, the Anchorage newspaper ran a big, front-page story complete with a series of photographs of Foster, many of them with beautiful women. Foster was ever older in the photographs, his grin ever more wicked.

Kane had run into Foster now and then around town. He was usually drunk and always happy. He had plenty to be happy about. He was, by the time Kane knew him, already an Alaska legend. He'd lived the kind of life Jimmy Buffett might write a song about, and many of the more colorful stories had found their way into the newspaper.

Rip Foster was born in the early 1920s in the mining town of Flat. He hadn't gone beyond the third grade, but by the time he was sixteen he was already making a name for himself in mining circles by buying up old buildings and sluice boxes, burning them, and treating the remains with mercury to extract the gold. The story was that he'd made upward of $10,000 from the floorboards of the old Flat saloon alone.

Like many rural Alaskans, Foster had also learned how to fly early. When the Second World War broke out, he entered the Army Air Corps, was made a flight instructor, rebelled, managed to get himself transferred to the Pacific Theater, and quickly became an ace flying P-38s. When the war ended, he returned to Alaska with a chest full of medals and a big, brassy, blond Aussie sheila for a wife.

She was the first of several.

Foster bought a couple of surplus DC3s, hired a second pilot, and started hauling freight around the state. He claimed he'd won the money for the aircraft in crap games across the Pacific. He was living large when the sheila caught him with a nineteen-year-old brunette who soon became the second Mrs. Rip Foster. He sold most of the airline. The rumor was that the sheila got most of the money.

The pattern repeated itself as Foster worked his way through a river-boat company, a couple of construction outfits, a multitown car deal-ership, a big hotel, and, not coincidentally, the brunette, a redhead, and another pair of blondes. He served a couple of terms in the territo-rial legislature, and traveled throughout rural Alaska, trading in furs and Native handicrafts. If you believed rumors, he also trafficked in booze and, in Fairbanks and Anchorage, gambling houses, women, and after-hours joints.

Just reading about Foster's life had made Kane dizzy. He lost count of the businesses, wives, and alleged shady dealings, but noticed that Foster always kept a piece of whatever legitimate business he sold. When he died at last at eighty-five, worn out by living, there was a big funeral in Anchorage, memorial services in Fairbanks and Juneau, and potlatches in half the villages in the state. His death was thought to have made his final young wife very rich indeed.

"I'm sorry for your loss," Kane said. "I knew your husband slightly. He was quite a man."

Kane could hear the humor in her voice when the woman said, "He was more man in his eighties than most men are in their twenties. I miss him very much."

She cleared her throat.

"But you didn't come here to hear me feel sorry for myself," she said. "Shall we get down to business?"

Kane nodded, and the woman went on.

"I want you to prove that Matthew Hope isn't a murderer," she said.

She paused as if waiting for a reaction, so Kane gave her one.

"From what I know, that might not be easy," he said.

The woman nodded.

"Perhaps you could tell me just what you do know," she said.

"Just what I've read in the newspaper," Kane said. "Matthew Hope is a Democrat who represents several thousand square miles of Interior Alaska. A couple of days ago, he was discovered in another legislator's office, standing over the body of a woman who worked there named Melinda Foxx. She wasn't wearing much and had been bludgeoned to death. The murder weapon was a crystal paperweight that had been given to the legislator by a civic group. Hope was holding it when he was discovered. He is being held for murder and should be indicted by a grand jury soon."

The woman nodded again.

"That's a good summary," she said. "What do you think?"

"Of the case?" Kane said. "I think Matthew Hope is in a lot of trouble. The evidence is circumstantial, but I've seen people convicted with less. And if there's any evidence that casts doubt on his guilt, it hasn't made it into the newspaper. And the papers have been throwing plenty of ink at this."

The woman was silent for a moment.

"I'm afraid I've let my concern for Senator Hope distract me from my duties as a hostess," she said. "Would you like something to drink?"

She made no signal Kane could see, but the Native man appeared. Kane asked for coffee, the woman for tea. The big man brought their drinks and a plate of small cookies. He looked as incongruous handling the delicate cups and saucers as an elephant crossing a tightrope, but he got everything arranged without spilling a drop. When he withdrew, the woman took up her teacup, slid the edge under the veil, and sipped from it.

Didn't show a square inch of her face, Kane thought. She must have practiced that in front of a mirror.

"I will pay you a hundred thousand dollars to prove that Senator Hope is innocent," she said. "Plus your expenses."

Kane sat back in his chair. Thoughts chased themselves through his mind.

"That's a lot of money," he said.

"Not really," the woman said. "Not anymore. Not in politics. A state representative spends that much to get elected. And I think that you will find earning it isn't easy. A lot of powerful people would be happy to see Senator Hope convicted of this crime."

"How well do you know Senator Hope?" Kane said.

"Not well," the woman said. There was something in her voice Kane couldn't quite identify. "Not well at all."

"Then what's your interest in his guilt or innocence?" Kane asked.

The woman sipped more tea.

"How much do you know about Alaska politics?" she asked.

Kane shook his head.

"Almost nothing," he said. "My attitude toward politics was best summed up by the old lady who said, 'I never vote. It only encourages the bastards.'"

The woman chuckled.

"I wish it were that simple," she said, "but it's not."

She took another sip of tea and set her cup and saucer on a small table at her elbow.

"When my late husband was young, Alaska was a progressive place," she said, "but the coming of big oil changed all that. Alaska is now one of the most reactionary states in the nation.

"It is also becoming increasingly corrupt. Senator Hope speaks out against the reactionaries and the corruption, and that has made him enemies. One of his biggest enemies is, or was, Melinda Foxx's employer, O. B. Potter. Senator Potter caters to the religious right and to the rich and powerful. The joke in Juneau is that his goal is to afflict the afflicted and comfort the comfortable."

She picked up a cookie, broke off a small piece, popped it into her mouth, chased it with tea, and continued.

"So Senator Potter and Senator Hope disagree on almost everything. And if their ideological differences weren't enough, Senator Potter also has been featured prominently in two of the more recent scandals uncovered by Senator Hope, and would like nothing better than to see him discredited.

"Be that as it may, Matthew Hope is the leading light of Alaska's progressives. Even though he is quite young—in his early forties, I believe—he has been in the state legislature for a decade and is widely rumored to be considering a run for the governorship next year. His loss would be a crippling blow for all of us."

Kane understood what Jeffords had been trying to tell him better now. If Hope was the leader of the outs, Jeffords was very much one of the ins. The chief couldn't be seen to be helping the other man. So why was he helping him, or asking Kane to help?

" 'A riddle wrapped in a mystery inside an enigma,' " Kane muttered.

"I beg your pardon?" the woman said.

"Sorry," Kane said. "Bad habit, talking to yourself. Anyway, I take it you are a supporter of this Senator Hope."

The woman nodded.

"Of progressives in general," she said. "It's something I inherited from my husband. He was very successful in business, but he never lost the political convictions of his youth."

Kane took a sip of his coffee. It was cold.

"You're willing to part with a hundred thousand dollars to support your late husband's political convictions?" Kane asked.

"My husband left me well provided for," the woman said.

Kane got up and crossed to where the woman sat. As he leaned down to set his cup on the table, he could smell the woman's perfume and feel the heat from the fireplace. He thought he could hear a faint rustling behind him, as if his movement had alerted someone who was watching. A big guy in a very nice suit, for instance. He walked back and sat once again on the sofa.

"Well, I have to say the money is attractive," Kane said, "but I can't see exactly what I can do to earn it. A high-profile case like this will be swarming with law enforcement and prosecutors with ambitions. I doubt they'd let me waltz in and start poking around. And I'm not sure what I could find that hasn't already been found by the official investigators."

The woman's laugh surprised Kane.

"The official investigators, such as they are, are controlled by our esteemed governor, Hiram Putnam," she said, "who is, in turn, controlled by others, including your friend Tom Jeffords. Their view is that Senator Hope did this foul deed, because it is politically convenient for them to see it that way, so the investigators will only be looking for evidence to find him guilty."

Kane knew that investigations weren't that simple and that most policemen didn't give a rip about what politicians wanted, but he couldn't see where debating the point would get him anything.

"If that's true," he said, "they'll be even less interested in having me stick my nose into this."

The woman nodded.

"I've thought of that," she said. "You'll be working, officially anyway, for Senator Hope's defense attorney, William Doyle. In fact, I'd prefer that no one know I am involved. My late husband liked living in the spotlight, but I prefer a quieter life."

Oh, great, Kane thought. First Jeffords, now her. How many puppet masters can one puppet have? Well, you didn't want boring.

"William Doyle," Kane said. "You mean Oil Can Doyle? This Hope must have some money if he can afford Oil Can."

The woman was silent.

"Oh, I get it," Kane said. "You're paying Oil Can."

"That's not really any of your concern," the woman said. "Do you know Mr. Doyle?"

"Not well," Kane said. "He made a monkey out of me a couple of times on the witness stand, but that's about it."

The woman was silent, and so was Kane. He thought things over. There were a lot of reasons to walk away from the case, not the least of which was the amount of intrigue and ambiguity that were already involved. Kane hated intrigue and ambiguity.

But he hated his job more. And he wanted the money. He'd gone through his entire life without thinking much about money, but now it seemed to be important to him and there was no use denying it. Plus, if he stuck around long enough, maybe this woman would take off her veil.

"Will you do it, Sergeant Kane?" the woman asked. Her voice shifted to a lower register. "Please?"

It was Kane's turn to laugh.

"Actually, it was Lieutenant Kane there for about fifteen minutes before everything went to hell," he said, "but it's just plain old Nik now."

He thought some more.

"If you know that Jeffords is a political enemy of your man, and that I've been working for Jeffords, then why hire me?" he asked. "There must be detectives who are less . . . compromised."

The woman was nodding before he finished.

"If that were all I knew about you, then I agree, I'd be foolish to hire you," she said. "But it's not."

Kane sat silently until it was clear that the woman was not going to continue. Asking her what she meant would be futile. If she wanted to tell him, she would. And trying to guess would be more futile than that. Time to decide.

"I'll take the job under these conditions," he said. "First, I'll need some money up front for expenses. We'll talk about my fee when I've earned it. Second, I'll need a list of your—and your husband's—political friends in Juneau, and some sort of letter of introduction to them. Third, you'll have to promise that you'll tell me sometime when and where we met before."

The woman laughed.

"If you could see me now as I was then, you wouldn't forget," she said. "I'll accept your conditions and impose one of my own. I want to be kept up to date on what you find—on a daily basis if at all possible."

She flowed to her feet, and Kane found himself standing as well.

"I'll turn you over to Winthrop now," she said. "He'll see to your expense money and give you a telephone number that will always reach me. If you come by in the morning, I'll have the list and the letter you want."

She moved close to him and took his right hand in both of hers.

"It's been a pleasure, Nik," she said. "I hope to see you again soon."

She left the room like water rolling downhill. When he turned to watch her, Kane was not at all surprised to see the big Native standing there.

"Winthrop?" Kane said. He couldn't help smiling.

The Native grinned and raised a forefinger.

"Choose your words carefully, *gussik*," he said. "I'm armed."

Politics, like religion, hold up the torches of
martyrdom to the reformers of error.

THOMAS JEFFERSON

This merchant in Sitka, name of George Pilz, somebody told him there should be gold here in Southeast," the cabbie said, swiveling his head over his right shoulder to look at Kane. Fat drops of wet snow splashed onto the windshield and the cars in front of them threw up huge rooster tails of slush, making visibility near zero. The old Ford's wipers clacked back and forth in a losing effort to clear the windshield. The speedometer read fifty-five, and Kane could feel the back end drifting as the cab tried to hydroplane.

"Might be a good idea to keep an eye on the road," he said to the cabbie.

"Surethingright," the cabbie said, flicking his eyes toward the front, then back to Kane.

"So he puts out the word that any Indian brings him gold will get a hundred Hudson Bay blankets," the cabbie said. "And sure enough, a chief named Kawaee shows up in Sitka with gold. Kawaee tells old George the gold is from a creek near his village."

The cabbie was in his mid-thirties, broad-shouldered and brown-skinned with greasy, shoulder-length black hair held back from his face by a beaded band that read: Tlingit Power. He started pumping his brakes. The rear end tried to slide to the right with each pump.

"The next year," the cabbie said, "old George outfits a couple of white prospectors named Richard Harris and Joe Juneau and sends them to check things out. But they ain't the most dedicated prospectors in the world. Instead of looking for gold, they spend most of the summer drinking hootch and trading parts of their outfit for sex off the village women."

The cab slowed.

"There's a goddamn stoplight up heres somewhere," the cabbie said. Kane could see the muscles stand out in his forearms as he tried to keep his hack on the road. The tattoo of a stylized bird glided down one of the forearms.

"Prison ink?" Kane asked as the cabbie brought the car to a halt just inches from the back of a Mercedes SUV.

The cabbie glanced at his arm, then at Kane.

"Yeah," he said, his voice flat. "Us Indians is all criminals."

"Us white guys, too," Kane said. "We just steal bigger."

Kane could see the driver's grin in the mirror. His even, white teeth stood out in his bronze face like a patch of snow on a parched hillside.

"My cousin did this, when we was in Job Corps together," he said. "Anyway, here's the rest of this story. The hootch runs out and it gets colder, so Harris and Juneau ask some of the Indians—Tlingits like me—to show them where the gold is. They follow the creek up into the mountains and find a gulch fulla gold-bearing quartz. They load up samples and, after deciding not to run off to Canada with the gold, take it back to Sitka and show it to old George Pilz. And when word gets out, there's a stampede."

The cabbie laughed.

"And so ends the heroic story of the founding of the city of Juneau in 1882," he said. "My professor at the university says it's Alaska history in a nutshell: greed, natural resource development, booze, sex, and Indians doing all the work."

The light changed and the cabbie leaned on his horn.

"Goddamn yuppies," he said. "She's too busy talking on her goddamn cell to watch the light."

Kane looked out the window of the cab at the falling slush and the hills beyond. The landscape and climate were different from those in Anchorage, six hundred miles to the north. The trees were bigger, the mountains more abrupt, what fell from the clouds far more likely to be rain than snow.

Juneau is about halfway down a narrow appendage called southeast Alaska. In geography and climate, Southeast has far more in common with British Columbia than mainland Alaska, which sometimes leads those who live in the rest of the state to refer to it as "occupied Canada."

Kane knew from his reading that Southeast is part of Alaska because of historical accidents. After Vitus Bering "discovered" Alaska by sea in the mid-1700s, the Russian-America Company set up the headquarters of its fur trade at Sitka. When Hudson's Bay Company traders, traveling by land, reached the area, the companies disagreed about who could do what where. Their respective governments negotiated a border that gave the southeast coast to Russia. The United States inherited the border when it bought Alaska in 1867 and, setting aside various disputes and adjustments, that's where the border remains.

For political and economic reasons, the capital of the Territory of Alaska was moved from Sitka to Juneau early in the twentieth century.

Like Sitka, Juneau could be reached only by air or water and its isolation from the majority of Alaskans led to several attempts to move the capital. But Juneau clings tenaciously to its status and the economic benefits it brings, thwarting the attempts with skillful political maneuvers.

The cabbie was hauling Kane into downtown Juneau on the Egan Expressway, a four-lane that ran along the coast connecting downtown with a glacier-carved valley that is the city's big residential area, the airport and the bays and coves beyond. The mountains ran right down to the water, so anything that didn't hang from a hillside rested on fill or glacier outwash.

The expressway had cost millions of dollars a mile to build in the mid-1970s. The official story was that it cost so much because of all the wetlands the road had to cross. The other story, which he'd been told once by Jeffords, was that it was because the state bought a lot of gravel from a well-connected wheeler-dealer.

One thing about Alaska politics, Jeffords had told him, there's always another story.

"That's the turnoff to the prison right there," the cabbie said, pointing with his left arm. "Lemon Creek. I ain't never been incarcerated, but I got a cousin in there now—the one did this tat, in fact. And a couple of uncles. And a nephew, I think. Damn place is just fulla Indians. So I can see why you mighta thought this was prison ink."

"No offense," Kane said.

"None taken," the cabbie said. "Life is what it is."

Kane didn't say anything to that. He knew from his time on the Anchorage police force, and then in prison, that Alaska Natives were vastly overrepresented in the prison population. Just like minorities everywhere.

The cab rocketed past the turnoff to the bridge to Douglas Island and began to slow down.

"Harris and Juneau had staked what they thought was the richest ground," Kane said to the cabbie. "But the joke was on them. The gold here wasn't the kind you could dig out by hand. It was hard-rock gold, and you needed a lot of money to run a hard-rock mine. They didn't have it. Neither did Pilz. So the money to do the mining came from Outside, and the profits went Outside, too. Not much different from what the oil industry is doing now."

"You some kind of professor?" the cabbie asked. "Or maybe a political junkie, like everybody else in this town?"

It was Kane's turn to laugh.

"Me?" he said. "No, I'm just a guy who had a lot of time to read. What about you?"

"I take a few courses at the Southeast campus," he said. "And I read the paper. But I don't get caught up in what the government's doing. They ain't interested in what an Indian thinks."

He eased the cab up to the front door of the Baranof Hotel and shut the meter down. Kane made no attempt to move.

"You mean, any Indian?" Kane asked. "Or just you?"

"I don't know about other Indians," the cabbie said, twisting to look at Kane, "although I never noticed anybody paying much attention to any of us."

The meter read $18.00. Kane handed over a twenty and a five.

"No Indians at all, huh?" he asked. "Not even Matthew Hope?"

The cabbie's eyes snapped up to lock with Kane's. They were flat and hard and black. He swiveled around, wrenched his door open, and climbed out into the slush falling from the sky. He grabbed Kane's bag out of the trunk and carried it quickly under the overhang that shielded the hotel entrance. Kane followed and took the bag from him.

"You got something with your name on it?" he asked. "I'm going to need some more driving around while I'm here."

The cabbie dug a card out of his shirt and handed it to Kane.

"Name's David Paul," he said, sticking out his hand. Kane shook it. "But everybody around here calls me Cocoa. Just call that number and ask for Cocoa."

He started out into the rain, then stopped.

"Matthew Hope?" he said, turning to face Kane. "It's a goddamn shame, what they're doing to that Indian, just because he won't play their game."

In our age there is no such thing as "keeping out of politics."
All issues are political issues, and politics itself is a mass
of lies, evasions, folly, hatred and schizophrenia.

GEORGE ORWELL

The bellman showed Kane into a room on the fifth floor. The place was dark and dingy, which reminded Kane of his apartment back in Anchorage.

All it needs is the smell of fish cooking and the sound of the people next door having sex and I'll be right at home, he thought.

He astonished the bellman with a $20 tip, then unpacked. There was plenty of room left in the closet and the small chest of drawers when he finished. He looked at the pieces of the automatic. He'd brought it with him to Juneau, more to avoid leaving it in his none-too-secure apartment than because he thought he'd need it. He'd broken it down, put the pieces in plastic food-storage bags to keep the gun oil off his clothes, and distributed them throughout his checked bag. If he reassembled the automatic, it would be a lethal weapon. But would he really need it tonight, to defend himself against a lawyer? He wrapped the pieces in a towel and set the towel on the shelf in the closet. Then he let himself out and took the elevator down to the lobby.

Oil Can Doyle was in the bar, sitting alone at a small, round table and staring into a tall glass filled with amber liquid. A young woman and an older man whispered in a far corner. As Kane's eyes swept over them, the man leaned over and kissed the young woman. Even in the dim light, Kane could see his tongue working. Besides the bartender, who stood behind his bar polishing glasses, and Doyle, they were the only people in the dimly lit room.

Kane walked over and stood next to Doyle's table until the lawyer looked up. He was a small, slight man with a big nose, big ears, and a toupee that looked more like a dead muskrat than human hair. A gravy stain that looked vaguely like the Aleutian Chain marred his tie, and the front of his white shirt was sprinkled with bits of snack mix. The gray suit he wore was cheap, and the expression on his face was hostile.

"I'm not giving interviews," he said. The tone in his high, squeaky voice was unfriendly. "Don't you jackals have anything else to do but hound me?"

"I'm not a reporter," Kane said, wondering how much Doyle had had to drink. "I'm Nik Kane, your investigator, the guy you're here to see. We've met a few times in court. I used to be with the Anchorage police."

Doyle didn't say anything or offer to shake hands. Kane pulled out a chair and sat. The bartender put down the glass he'd been polishing and started for the table, but stopped when Kane shook his head.

"Good to meet you, I suppose," Doyle squeaked. They said around the courthouse that he'd gotten his nickname when another lawyer heard him speak for the first time and said, "You should get an oil can for that squeak."

If you built an unsuccessful trial lawyer from scratch, you'd end up with Oil Can Doyle, Kane thought. Looks like a bum and has the personality of a wolverine, but somehow he wins cases.

"Don't get all overwhelmed," Kane said.

Doyle screwed his face up and showed his teeth.

Good God, Kane thought, he thinks that's a smile.

"I need an investigator," Doyle said. "I can't use anybody here. The case is too political. You're not my first choice, but I'm not paying the bills. If you take this job, you'll work for me—and only for me—helping prepare the defense."

Kane waited for the lawyer to continue, and when he didn't, said, "That's some sales pitch. I can't remember when I've felt so motivated."

The two men looked at each other. Doyle shrugged.

"You can take the job or not," he said. "It's all the same to me. I can always bring in somebody else."

Kane could feel himself smiling as he looked at the other man. Clearly, Doyle wanted him to turn the job down. So why was he here in the first place? Was Jeffords pulling strings? Was somebody else? Kane could feel the bottomless pit of political calculation opening under his feet, and he didn't like the feeling one bit. He could console himself with the thought of the money, but he knew he was here for more than that, although he couldn't say just what.

The two men were silent. The bartender walked to the couple in the corner, took some money from the man, and walked back behind the bar. The couple walked out of the bar. They might have been father and daughter, except that the man had his hand on the woman's ass.

"I've already decided to take the job," Kane said, watching for Doyle's reaction. The lawyer didn't even twitch. He'd be a great poker player, Kane thought.

"Well, that's just wonderful," Doyle said, twisting up his face and showing his teeth again. "But just so you don't misunderstand, I expect you to turn over everything you find out to me, and to not discuss anything with anybody else. Anybody else at all."

Kane didn't say anything to that. Silence wasn't a lie.

Doyle leaned forward again and picked up his drink.

"Here's to a mutually beneficial relationship," he said and drained it.

He held his empty glass above his head and rattled the remaining ice. The bartender came over to the table. Doyle handed him the glass.

"This is Tony," Doyle said to Kane. "He is a fine bartender, which is a treasure rarer than pearls."

The bartender, a middle-aged fellow with dark hair and a pencil mustache, nodded to Kane. Kane nodded back.

"Tony is going to bring me another," Doyle said, "and I'm sure he'd be happy to bring you whatever you'd like."

Kane shook his head.

"No, thanks," he said.

Tony took Doyle's glass back to the bar.

"Too good to drink with me?" Doyle squeaked.

"Probably, " Kane said, "but that's not the reason I turned down a drink. I'm an alcoholic."

Doyle shook his head.

"So am I," he said, "but I don't let a little thing like that stop me."

Tony returned with a full glass and a bowl of snack mix. He set them on the table and went back to his station behind the bar. Doyle popped a handful of snack mix into his mouth, chewed, drank, and said, "Tell me what you know about all this."

"What I've read in the newspaper," Kane said. "I was hoping you could tell me more."

Doyle nodded again.

"Instead of listening to me talk, why don't you look over what's on paper so far?" he said. "Although there's not much that hasn't been in print. Along with purple prose and bootless speculation."

"You don't like the press?" Kane asked. "In the cases I was involved in, you played those reporters like a violin."

Doyle snorted.

"I like the press just fine when they're reporting what I want them to," he said. "But when they're making life more difficult for me and my client, I hate the bastards."

He pulled a big briefcase up into his lap, opened it, and pulled out a set of thin manila folders that were rubber-banded together.

"Here's the discovery," he said, sliding the folders across to Kane. "It's mostly preliminary. Notes really, from the investigating officers and examining physician. Some crime-scene photos. Like that."

He took another drink.

"I've got a transcript of my preliminary interview with my client, but it's under lock and key in my office. You'll have to come by there to read it."

He took a card from an inside pocket, scribbled on the back of it, and handed it to Kane.

"That's where I'm renting office space while I'm down here," he said.

Kane slid the folders to his side of the table.

"Any reason you're being so careful?" he asked.

"I'm always careful," the lawyer said. "But with a case like this one, I'm being extra careful."

"What's so special about this case?" Kane asked.

Doyle smiled again and shook his head.

"Didn't Tom Jeffords ever explain Alaska politics to you?" he asked. When Kane just looked at him, the lawyer continued. "Yeah, I know all about you and Jeffords. I know everything about you, except maybe where you got that scar. Somebody told me, but I forgot."

He stopped as if he expected Kane to fill in the silence.

"It was an accident," Kane said.

"What kind of accident gives you a scar like that?" Doyle asked.

"The kind where a guy wants to jam a sharpened toothbrush handle into your brain, but you turn at the last second and he accidentally misses the soft spot in your temple," Kane said.

Doyle nodded.

"Yeah, prison's a bitch, ain't it," he said. "At least that's what some of my clients tell me. But if you think that was dangerous, wait until you get into this case. Politics is a full-contact sport in Alaska, and it doesn't have a lot of rules."

He drained his glass.

"You working for Jeffords makes you kind of an odd choice to try to get my client off, given their political positions," the lawyer said.

"I'm not working for Jeffords on this," Kane said. "I'm on my own. Politics doesn't mean anything to me. Either this Hope did the crime or he didn't. If he didn't, I'll find out. I'll find out if he did, for that matter. And I'll let you in on whatever I find. So if you're going to worry, worry about something besides me selling out you and your client."

Doyle looked steadily at Kane, then shrugged.

"Fair enough," he said. "Why don't you read through those files and come see me in the morning. Maybe we can work together."

He closed his briefcase, got to his feet, and put on a frayed ankle-length topcoat with a matted collar that looked for all the world like it had been made of the same stuff as his toupee. When he saw Doyle getting ready to leave, the bartender hurried over with the bill and handed it to him.

"Why, Tony," Doyle squeaked, "it's like you don't trust me." He set the bill down on the table. "My colleague will take care of it." To Kane he said, "Is there anything else I can do for you before I go?"

Kane nodded.

"You can tell me if there's a Catholic church around here," he said.

The lawyer peered at him.

"Seriously?" he said.

Kane nodded again.

"I have no idea," he said, and left, moving like a man walking on a slippery surface.

Kane looked at the bill, dug some money from his wallet, and, after making sure there was plenty for a tip, handed it to the bartender.

Tony gave him a small nod of appreciation.

"The church is three blocks up and one block over," he said, pointing. "It's called the Cathedral of the Nativity of the Blessed Virgin Mary. Big name for a wooden church."

Mary, Kane thought. Mother of Jesus. Maybe she can help me figure out how to deal with my son.

The folks you help won't remember it and
the folks you hurt won't ever forget it.

BILL CLAYTON

K ane put on his coat and stuck his nose out the lobby entrance. The
slush storm had stopped, so he decided to carry the folders with
him rather than detour to his room. The bartender's directions sent
him uphill. He walked slowly, trying to stretch each step to chase some
of the soreness from his muscles. I'm getting too old for the kind of
roughhouse that Robert Bland threw my way, he thought.

The streets were a mosaic of darkness and pools of light from the
streetlamps. Few cars, and fewer people, moved along them. Kane
walked carefully over the congealing slush. The surface would be
unwalkable if it froze overnight. The hill got steeper with each block.
Kane was grateful to reach the door of the church without having fallen.

Inside, a light burned in the tabernacle lamp. Kane walked to the front of the church, knelt, slid a folded bill into the offering slot, and lit a votive candle.

"O God, the Creator and Redeemer of all the faithful," he said softly, "grant to the souls of Your servants departed full remission of all their sins, that through our devout prayers, they may obtain the pardon, which they have always desired. Who live and reign, world without end. Amen."

As he prayed, he thought of all the dead people he knew. His father, who'd left the church to worship the bottle. His mother, so furious in her devotion. His sister Rose, killed by cancer, and his brother Kevin, killed by the Viet Cong. People he'd killed. People he'd seen dead in war. In car accidents. In crimes of passion. In the cruelties and mishaps of the criminal life. Lots of dead people. Not enough ghosts to fill this church, maybe, but enough to fill several pews. Life is tenuous and full of peril, he thought.

Kane got to his feet, walked back down the aisle, and sat in one of the pews. His mother had drilled religion into him and his brothers and sisters. Although he'd stopped practicing the faith as soon as he'd left her house, parts of it still popped into his head. Like the prayer for the dead, and the patronage of Mary for mothers and families. If his own mother were still alive, she'd tell him to pray for help in dealing with his son.

Since childhood, Kane had been attracted to the simple ask-get transaction of prayer. But all it had ever gotten him was sore knees. Lately, he'd begun to see religion as just another form of dependency, with God taking the place of booze, and the church, with all its rules about how to live your life, as not much different from prison. Still, it was one thing to recognize a dependency, another to break it. He didn't really understand the grip the religion of his youth had on him still. He didn't follow the faith's teachings or believe in its mythology. But he did, somehow, find enough comfort that he visited often.

As he sat, Kane realized that he regretted not having simple faith. Not many things scared him, but the prospect of trying to reestablish a relationship with his son did. He could use all the help he could get. But he would have to do this on his own. Laurie, who'd always been the intermediary with the children, wasn't there for him anymore, and the chances of divine intervention were pretty slim.

The first thing I'd better do, he thought, is stop kidding myself. I'm not trying to reestablish a relationship with Dylan. I'm trying to establish one. I wasn't that great a father even when I wasn't in prison.

He'd never really made a decision to have children, or even had a real discussion with Laurie about what becoming parents would mean. He'd met her, fallen in love, gotten married, and they'd started having babies: Emily, the oldest, the child most like Kane; Amy, the middle child, competitive and independent; Dylan, the youngest, the child he knew the least about. By the time Laurie was twenty-five, they had the three and then, apparently, she'd decided that was enough. They'd never talked about stopping, either, although Kane, familiar with the stresses and strains of a big family, wouldn't have objected.

It all just happened, Kane thought. One minute he'd been a guy in his early thirties with a good job, a gorgeous young wife, and plans for fun and travel. The next he'd been a father, with enough responsibilities to keep him pinned down for years and years. Could I have been more unprepared?

How could I have taken on so much responsibility with so little thought? he asked himself. In the past, he'd always explained such things away by telling himself that was just who he was. But that explanation seemed facile and useless to him now.

Things happen for reasons, he thought. You are who you are for reasons.

His parents had some responsibility for who he was, although he was still figuring out just how much. He'd been shaped by their silent lessons as much as their spoken ones, maybe more. One of the unspoken lessons was that married people had kids, and so Kane hadn't really given fatherhood much thought.

He hadn't really been very good at it, either. Because his own father had taken a powder, Kane had gotten it into his head that just sticking around made him a good father. He and Laurie had had what the religious right called a traditional family: a father who worked and dispensed discipline when called upon, a mother who stayed home and did the child-rearing, and children who, unless they were much more self-aware than Kane had been, would repeat the process. No consideration given to what any of them, as individuals, might want or need.

When he thought about his life before prison, the clearest images came from work: in uniform, tooling around in a patrol car; in plain clothes at a crime scene; just sitting around the station chewing the fat with other cops. Then came snapshots of his life with Laurie. Then the time he spent drinking. Or, maybe, considering the relationship he'd had with booze, those last two were reversed. Either way, he just didn't remember doing many things with his kids.

At the time, he thought he wanted to be a better father. He wished his job gave him more time with the kids, he told himself, but at least they weren't living on the charity of the parish.

But now? Now he could see that if he'd really wanted to be closer to his children, he would have been. He could have spent less time at work and a lot less time in bars.

And, of course, the irony of ironies was that Kane had failed just the way his father had. Oh, he could tell himself that his father had run off while he had been taken away. But the truth was they'd both been drunks and, however the specifics had sorted themselves out, their drinking had led to their absences from the lives of their children.

And he'd left Laurie to clean up the mess. Whether she admitted it or not, that had to have had something to do with her decision to get a divorce. He'd broken the unspoken deal, hadn't he? Why shouldn't she break the spoken one?

Kane sighed and shrugged his shoulders.

What's done is done, he thought. The question is, what do I do now?

As usual, the answer was silence. Kane was used to that. He'd been asking God questions since he was a kid, and this was just the latest in a long list that had brought no booming voice, or even a whisper in his head.

Kane stood, walked out of the church, and began picking his way downhill toward the hotel.

Children are plastic, Kane thought. They adapt. Maybe Dylan is still young enough to adapt to me. To find some way to forgive, forget, and move on. Maybe I haven't lost him forever.

Should I look him up first thing? he asked himself. Should I wait to run into him? Should I hope I don't run into him?

Kane's feet started to slide and he brought himself up short. The downhill slope was as slippery as the slope of his life, and if he wasn't careful he was going to take a fall. So he focused on where he put his feet and proceeded down the hill, one step at a time.

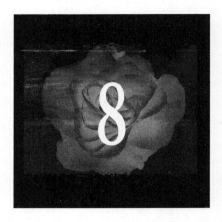

8

The art of politics consists in knowing precisely when it is
necessary to hit an opponent slightly below the belt.

KONRAD ADENAUER

Kane opened the door to his hotel room and found two men in top-
coats standing inside.

"Please come in, Mr. Kane," one of them said politely. "We need
to talk."

Kane stepped into the room and closed the door behind him.

"Who are you and what do you want?" he asked.

Both men were in their late twenties and over six feet. One was
dark-haired and the other blond, but otherwise they were as alike as
two peas in a pod: fit, short-haired, clear-eyed, and clean-shaven.

"Oh, he sounds crabby, doesn't he?" the dark-haired one said.

"Yes, he does," said the blond one. "I hope it's not contagious. I
hope we don't get crabby, too."

Kane took a few steps into the room, took off his overcoat, and dropped it on the bed. The two men's eyes followed his every move.

"I've had a long day," he said, "so you can cut the comedy and get to the point."

The dark-haired man took a case from his topcoat pocket and flashed a badge.

"I'm Sergeant Smith," he said with a smile. "This is Trooper Jones. We're with the Alaska State Troopers Criminal Investigations Bureau."

"Smith and Jones?" Kane said.

"Yeah," the other man said. "We get a lot of comments about that."

Kane said nothing. The three of them stood there looking at one another.

I really don't need this, Kane thought. I'm sore and tired. I just want to take some aspirin and go to bed.

But the two men looked content to just stand there, so he said, "Perhaps you could tell me what the state troopers are doing breaking into hotel rooms."

The two men looked at each other.

"We didn't break into this room, did we, Trooper Jones?" the dark-haired one said.

"Why, no, Sergeant Smith," the blond one said. "The door was open. Mr. Kane must have forgotten to close it."

Smith shook his head.

"That was just an invitation to crime, wasn't it?" he said. "Don't you think Mr. Kane should be more careful?"

Jones nodded.

"He certainly should be more careful," he said, "especially when he leaves something like this lying around."

He pointed to the coffee table. Kane took a couple of steps forward, as if to see better what he was pointing at. On the table was the hotel towel, unrolled to show the pieces of the .45.

"Perhaps you could tell us what you are doing with this, Mr. Kane," Smith said.

Kane shrugged.

"This is Alaska," he said. "Anyone can own a gun. Or a hundred guns."

"Not anyone," Jones said. "Not a convicted felon."

Kane gave him a grin.

"Yeah," he said, "that's right. So I guess it's a good thing I had my record wiped clean, isn't it."

The two men looked at each other again.

"Just what are you doing in Juneau, Mr. Kane?" Smith asked.

Kane thought about telling them the truth. But their vaudeville routine was getting on his last nerve.

"I'm here for the golf," he said.

"Golf?" Jones said. "There's no golf here in the winter."

"I must have been misinformed," Kane said.

The two men looked at each other again.

"It sounds to me like Mr. Kane thinks he's funny," Jones said. "Does it sound that way to you?"

"It does," Smith said. "It sounds like he thinks he's funny. Do you think you're funny, Mr. Kane?"

Kane looked at the two men and shrugged.

"Why don't the two of you just leave," he said, his voice edgy with sudden adrenaline, "before I call some real cops."

Smith took a step forward. His nose was nearly touching Kane's.

"We don't need any more comedians in Juneau right now," he said, trying to make his voice sound hard. "We have the legislature." He smiled at his own joke. "Why don't you plan to be on the next airplane out of here."

Jones moved a couple of steps to his left so he could see Kane over Smith's shoulder. Kane took a half-step back, the backs of his legs hitting the bed.

I wonder if, to someone watching from above, it looks like the three of us are doing some odd dance, he thought.

"I don't think I'll be leaving soon," he said. "Now that I'm here, I think I'll see the sights."

"Oh, that's too bad," Smith said and slapped Kane across the face. He leaned close and said, "On the airplane, tomorrow."

Kane sighed and kneed Smith in the groin. Smith squealed. Kane put his hands on Smith's shoulders and shoved. He flew backward and banged into Jones, who was trying to get something out of the pocket of his topcoat. Jones fell onto the coffee table. The coffee table collapsed and the pieces of Kane's .45 slid onto the floor. Kane pivoted and hit Smith with his elbow. Smith went down at his feet. Jones was lying on his side amid the pieces of coffee table, still trying to get something out of his pocket. Kane took a couple of quick steps and kicked him on the chin. Jones stopped trying to do anything at all. Smith was stirring, so Kane kicked him, too. He lay still.

Kane stood there taking deep breaths for a few moments, waiting for his heartbeat to slow, then went through their pockets. Smith's badge said, "Souvenir of MGM." Jones's overcoat pocket contained a .38 revolver, the hammer snagged on the pocket's lining. Jones didn't have a badge, but he did have a .32 automatic in an ankle holster. Smith wore a .38 on his belt and a matching .32 auto on his ankle. Each had a roll of bills in his pocket, but neither carried any ID whatsoever.

Kane piled all the guns on the bed. Then he dialed the Juneau police and asked the dispatcher to send somebody up. He picked up the pieces of his own gun, wrapped them in the towel, and put them back on the closet shelf.

The two men were just beginning to stir when the police arrived.

"These men broke into my hotel room and threatened me," Kane said. "They pretended to be Alaska State Troopers. The dark-haired one hit me. They don't seem to be carrying ID. Their guns and phony badge are on the bed."

"How do we know that's what happened?" one of the cops asked.

"Just that I say it," Kane said, "but you can see the guns and phony badge on the bed. And the desk clerk will confirm that this is my room. I'm telling you that I didn't let them in. That's enough for a collar right there."

There was more palaver when the two men were on their feet, but the police took the men and weapons away on Kane's promise to come down in the morning and swear out a complaint.

Kane locked the door behind them, retrieved the towel from the closet, sat, turned on a lamp, and examined the pieces of the .45. They looked okay, but he was too tired to assemble them to be sure. He left the pieces on the nightstand, got up, opened the dresser, and unrolled a pair of socks, revealing two wedges. He put the wedges in the crack under the door and tapped them into place with his foot. Maybe it's locking the barn door, he thought, but I'll sleep better.

He brushed his teeth, took a couple of aspirin, removed his clothes, and climbed into bed. He lay for a while thinking about the two men, but didn't get very far. So he thought instead about Dylan. What I need is a plan, he decided as he fell asleep.

Men who are engaged in public life must necessarily aim at reducing opposition to a minimum, and one of the most obvious means to that end is by misrepresenting, discrediting or ruining their opponents.

FREDERICK SCOTT OLIVER

The next morning, showered and dressed, Kane sat down at the little desk, poured himself a cup of watery room-service coffee, and read through Doyle's files. There wasn't much there: a brief statement from the janitor who had found Matthew Hope with the body, a statement from a security guard, the arresting officer's preliminary report, and a preliminary medical report.

The janitor's statement was straightforward enough: He'd been cleaning, saw a light, found Hope standing over the body, fled. He didn't remember seeing Senator Hope or anyone else in the hallways, but he'd been in and out of many rooms, cleaning.

The security guard heard the janitor's screams, intercepted him, and, when he'd managed to get a coherent statement, dialed 911. The guard had found Hope sitting on a coffee table with his head in his hands and kept him there until the police arrived. While they waited, Hope told the security guard he hadn't done it. The guard, who was stationed on the ground floor, had no idea who might have been on the fifth floor that night.

The arresting officer reported that, by the time the first officers responded, Hope would only say that he wanted a lawyer. Hope was taken to the police station. A lawyer named Simmons, who was also in the legislature and one of Hope's allies, arrived and said his client wouldn't be answering questions. Hope was booked on suspicion of murder.

The arresting officer's report included several photos of the crime scene. They showed the body lying very close to the desk belonging to the office's inhabitant, Senate Finance Committee Chairman O. B. Potter. There were no signs of a struggle. A white blouse and black skirt belonging to the victim were neatly folded on an armchair. A white lace bra lay at one end of the big, leather couch, a pair of white lace thong panties at the other end. The body wore white stockings and a white lace garter belt, embroidered with the now-famous white rose, that held them up.

The body had been identified by a coworker, a Letitia Potter. Ms. Potter had answered the phone when investigators called the home of Senator O. B. Potter, and volunteered to come to the crime scene.

Some relation of Senator O. B. Potter, Kane thought. Ah, nepotism.

The medical examiner said the victim had been freshly dead when the janitor discovered Hope standing over her body. The cause of death was blunt-force trauma. The killer managed to do the job with a single blow, which, the ME noted, suggested both strength and luck. The wound was consistent with the crystal paperweight Hope had been holding when discovered. The only other thing he noted was indications that the victim had recently engaged in vigorous sexual intercourse. Maybe rape, maybe not.

Kane bundled the files back together, got up from the table, and looked out the window. Juneau was spread out below him, going about its early-morning business on icy streets and sidewalks. A steady stream of automobile and foot traffic was headed toward the three big government buildings on the hillside to his right. To his left, the land and buildings sloped away to the water. Clouds obscured the tops of the mountains across the channel on Douglas Island, and a fog bank hugged the water. He could just make out the mast of a fishing boat groping its way down the channel toward open water.

The lack of information in the files didn't surprise Kane. He'd done hundreds of investigations in his years on the force, dozens involving death. He knew that the paperwork would pile up as the investigation went on: statements from people who had been in the building that night, statements from people who knew the victim and the suspect, reports on all the forensics that were popular on TV these days, the grand jury report. All of the information would make its way, as the law required, to the suspect's attorney and then to Kane. In two weeks, the files would be an inch thick. In a month, three inches.

Eventually, the files would contain Matthew Hope's life, at least as much as investigators could discover.

This attempt to capture a human being on paper always struck Kane as a bizarre form of literary endeavor. Kane had often joked about it with other cops. "The Case File as Novel," he'd say. Cops were among the most prosaic people in the world, much more comfortable in the world of physical objects than the world of ideas. When Kane talked like that—usually, he had to admit, after he'd had a few drinks—they gave him the fish eye and mumbled that he was crazy. And by their lights, Kane knew, he was.

The files wouldn't be a complete portrait of Matthew Hope. The picture would be most vivid on the day of the murder, then fade as it moved back in time. There might be half of the Matthew Hope who'd gotten off the airplane in January to begin the legislative session, only a bit of the Matthew Hope who celebrated his first election to public office, a trace of the Matthew Hope who walked across the front of the multipurpose room to take his high school diploma, nothing of the Matthew Hope who entered school for the first time clutching his mother's hand.

But by the time they were complete, the files would contain all of one part of Matthew Hope's life: his future. What was in them would dictate whether he returned to the legislature or spent the rest of his life inside concrete walls topped with ribbon wire.

Most of the prosecutors Kane had worked with had seen the detective's job as helping them write just that conclusion to the life stories in the files. Oil Can Doyle would no doubt say that it was now Kane's job to make sure Matthew Hope's story ended with him walking out of the courtroom a free man. But Kane had never seen his job the way lawyers did. The question he wanted to answer wasn't "How do I get Matthew Hope off?" It was "Who killed Melinda Foxx?"

Kane shook his head and turned from the window. He knew he'd been staring for some time without really seeing anything. "Woolgathering," Laurie always called it.

Kane was suddenly overwhelmed by an urge to call her on the telephone, to hear her voice. He missed just talking with her, about things both trivial and important. But she was making a new life for herself now, just as Kane guessed he was, and she didn't want him trying to drag her back into the old one. Maybe later, when they were both more securely the people they were becoming, he could call her and they could chat. But not now.

He took a sip of coffee and grimaced. Now it was cold as well as watery. He dumped what was left in the sink, rinsed the cup, and set it on the room-service tray. Time to get going. His first move would be to return the files to the lawyer and ask him what he'd learned from Hope. Kane sat on the bed, picked up the pieces of the automatic, and assembled them. He thought about carrying the gun with him, but in the light of day he couldn't imagine why he'd need it. Besides, it would be a problem at some of the places he planned to go.

He ejected the clip, wrapped it and the gun in a towel, and set them back on the closet shelf. He got down on his knees, wiggled the wedges loose, and put them back in his suitcase. He put on his coat and left the room.

When he got off the elevator on the ground floor, he went looking for the bellman. The day shift had taken over, so Kane gave the new man a $20 handshake.

"I've got a pile of splinters where my coffee table used to be," he said. "Can you have somebody take care of it and put it on my bill?"

"Sure thing," the bellman said. "Big party?"

"In a manner of speaking," Kane said, and asked for directions to a coffee shop and Doyle's office.

"We have a coffee shop right here in the hotel," the bellman said.

Kane gave him a look.

"I've had the hotel coffee," he said. "Try again."

The coffee shop the bellman sent him to was a bakery, too, so Kane breakfasted on a toasted bagel with cream cheese and a large coffee. One sip convinced him that he wasn't going to be drinking the hotel coffee anymore.

Fortified, Kane followed the bellman's directions to the address Doyle had given him. He'd walked to the coffee shop on nearly level ground, but Doyle's office was downhill and Kane had to creep along. Shop owners had thrown rock salt and blue or pink ice melt onto the sidewalk in front of their stores, but the footing was still treacherous and Kane found himself flailing to stay upright more than once.

Doyle's office was in a 1930s building, a narrow flight of stairs above an Italian restaurant, then along a narrow hallway that provided access to the offices of an accountant, a fish buyer, and a lobbyist, as well as a lawyer named Alan Prell. The outer office held a desk, a fax machine, a couple of mismatched chairs, some old hunting and fishing magazines, and a receptionist who appeared to be at least eighty, brick-red hair notwithstanding. The receptionist grilled Kane for minutes. Many of her questions were about whether he was a reporter, but Kane got the feeling he'd have gotten the same treatment even if there hadn't been a White Rose Murder. Finally, she ushered him into a dusty office that contained a metal desk, a metal filing cabinet, two metal chairs, and Oil Can Doyle.

Doyle wore a linty polypropylene pullover with the collar of what looked like a Hawaiian shirt sticking out of it. His toupee sat at a slightly different angle than it had the night before. The watery sunlight revealed a coating of dust on the toupee. Doyle had a spot of what appeared to be dried egg yolk on his chin.

"You were lucky to get past Helga," he said, motioning Kane to the unoccupied metal chair. "She must like you."

Kane set the file folders on the desk and shed his coat. Seeing nowhere to hang it, he dropped it on the floor against the wall and sat.

"All Helga likes is being in charge," he said. "She did everything but check my prostate." He gestured with his arms. "Swell place you got here. Sending Mrs. Foster's money straight to the Caymans?"

Doyle looked at him for a long moment before speaking.

"Oh, I get it," he said. "That's supposed to be a joke."

The lawyer arranged his mouth in his grimace of a smile. Then his face went deadpan again.

"One of the things you'll discover when we get to know each other better is that I have no sense of humor," Doyle said. "I have no friends. I have no hobbies. I have no romantic entanglements. I don't follow sports or play high-stakes Texas Hold 'Em. I don't do anything but work to keep my clients out of jail. I work hard. I have to work hard to overcome my lack of talent, my lack of charm, my lack of humor, and all the other things God forgot to give me. So don't waste my time making jokes or small talk or anything else. Just do your job and let me do mine."

Kane nodded.

"Fine by me," he said. He shifted in his seat, knowing that nothing he did would make the metal chair more comfortable.

"I read the files," he said. "Not much there. What else do you know?"

The lawyer shook his head.

"Very little," he said. "At the preliminary hearing, the DA put on the janitor, security guard, arresting officer, and medical examiner. That was enough to bind my client over. The judge also compelled a DNA swab, so there may be some forensics they won't show us until they're done testing. There's a bail hearing tomorrow morning. In a case like this, the state will want to keep Senator Hope in jail and, if he decides to let the senator out, the judge will probably want a big number. But, with Mrs. Foster's financial help, Senator Hope should be able to make bail."

Doyle looked at a yellow legal pad that lay on the desk.

"There's a grand jury meeting, but I don't expect that they'll indict for a couple of weeks. They'll want to try to nail down the corners of the case before they do."

He looked up at Kane.

"They should have detectives talking to pretty much everybody in the Capitol. I'll get copies of the statements, and of the full autopsy, but I won't be getting any of that for a while. The DA doesn't want to make this any easier for me than he has to."

He reached up and patted his toupee a couple of times like he was patting a dog.

"I think you should conduct your own interviews up there in the Capitol, if you can get people to talk to you," he said.

"Why wouldn't people want to talk to me?" Kane asked.

"Politics," the lawyer said. "It's a good thing for some people if

Senator Hope is carrying this charge around as long as possible, even if he isn't found guilty in the end. The removal of his vote, and his voice, from the process advances their political agendas."

Kane nodded. He was already thinking about how hard it would be to get a straight story out of anybody involved with the legislature. Even if they wanted to be honest, their political ambitions and animosities would color everything. It'll be like trying to grab a handful of snakes in a vat of olive oil, he thought.

"What about your client's version of events?" Kane asked.

"Our client," the lawyer said. "He's our client now. I'll let you read his statement to me, but there's nothing very revealing in it. He says he knew the victim, had dealt with her once in a while because she worked for the Senate Finance chairman. He says he'd been at a reception, returned to the Capitol to do some work, and went to Potter's office on the off chance he'd be there. Said he wanted to talk about a domestic partners bill of his that's hung up in the committee. Said he found the woman's body and the next thing he really remembered was somebody reading him his rights."

Kane let the silence gather before he spoke.

"That's it?" he said. "Nothing about who saw him at the reception. In the Capitol? Nothing about what kind of work he had to go back to the office to do? Nothing about how often he'd seen the victim? What he thought of her?"

By the time he finished, Doyle was red in the face.

"It's just his preliminary statement," the lawyer all but shouted. "I'll have plenty of time to get all that."

"Jesus," Kane all but shouted back.

The two of them were silent for a minute.

"Okay, the truth is, I can't get the guy to talk to me," Doyle said. "I've visited him every day, but that's all he'll say. That, and that he didn't kill Melinda Foxx."

"Then I suppose I'd better have a try," Kane said. "I'll need a letter of authorization from you to show to the people at the prison and, I suppose, to Hope."

Doyle slid a folded paper across the table.

"Already done," he said. "Here it is."

Kane opened the paper, read it, refolded it, and tucked it into the pocket of his suit coat next to the letter from Mrs. Foster.

"So he's hiding something, but you don't know what," Kane said.

The lawyer nodded.

"Then I'd guess we'd better let that go until later," Kane said. He thought for a moment. "What do you know about the victim?"

The lawyer shook his head.

"Not much yet," he said. "She was twenty-four. Graduated from Princeton a couple years ago, went to work for Potter. Said to be good at her job."

"Nothing about her personal life?" Kane asked after he'd finished making notes in the little notebook he always carried. "Her habits? Her ambitions?"

"So far it's all *de mortuis nil nisi bonum*," Doyle said. "But that should change soon. Gossip is the common currency of the legislature."

He looked at his watch.

"I've got to get to work," the lawyer said. "You can reach me here or where I'm staying, at the Mendenhall Apartments up the hill." He rattled off a couple of phone numbers. "Or you can try my cell." He gave Kane that number, too. "Now, what are you going to do first?"

"I'm going to read Hope's statement," Kane said. "Then I have to make a stop at the police station."

"The police station?" Doyle said. "What for?"

"Well, normally it would just be a courtesy call, to let them know I'm working on the case," Kane said, "but in this instance I have to follow up on an incident from last night."

"Incident?" Doyle said.

So Kane told the lawyer about his encounter with Smith and Jones. When he finished, Doyle said, "They were trying to scare you off? What sense does that make?"

Kane shrugged.

"You said yourself that there are people who want to see Hope stay in prison," he said. "Or maybe they're involved somehow in Melinda Foxx's death. Maybe I can pick up something from the cops on that, if they've gotten around to questioning those two. But what I'd like to know is, how did they find out so fast that I was working on the White Rose Murder?"

Doyle snorted and waved a dismissive hand.

"There's nothing faster than the political rumor mill," the lawyer said. "I had people calling me up about Matthew Hope an hour after I'd agreed to represent him. And it's even faster here in Juneau when the legislature is in session. There were probably people here who knew you were going to take the job before you did."

"Maybe so," Kane said. "However those guys found out, you should be careful. Nothing would slow down Hope's defense like his lawyer suddenly quitting. Or maybe falling down and breaking a leg."

For once, Doyle actually looked surprised.

"I'm an officer of the court," he said. "They wouldn't dare."

Kane got to his feet, picked his coat up from the floor, and put it on.

"Whatever you say," he said. "Anyway, once I'm done at the police station, I'm going to see your client, our client, in jail. He might be more likely to talk to me there than when he gets back into his comfort zone, his normal environment."

The lawyer nodded.

"I suppose you're right," he said, "although I don't think you can call the legislature a normal environment."

10

Being in politics is like being in a football game. You have to be smart enough
to know the game and stupid enough to think it important.

EUGENE MCCARTHY

I need a place to sit and read," Kane said to the receptionist.

Helga gave him a stern look.

"I have my own work to do, you know," she said, as if she hadn't
been leafing through a women's wear catalog when Kane emerged
from Doyle's office.

Kane stood there until, with a sigh, Helga got to her feet and
showed him into a small conference room. He sat at the table and read
the statement. It was every bit as unrevealing as Doyle had said. Kane
walked into the reception area, laid the file on Helga's desk, and said,
"Please see that this gets back to Mr. Doyle."

Helga looked up from her catalog. The fashions in it looked like
they were for women several decades younger than she.

"I don't work for you," she snapped.

Kane gave her his best smile.

"Of course you don't," he said pleasantly. "If you did, I'd fire you. Now, before your burst something, why don't you tell me where the police station is."

"Only if they're going to put you in a cell," Helga said. Kane kept his mouth shut and she gave him the directions.

Kane left the office and walked the half-dozen blocks from Doyle's office to the police station, following Helga's directions carefully downhill, then along the flat. He could see the ruins of the millhouse of the Alaska Juneau gold mine hanging from the hillside above the town. Most of the flat part of downtown was built on rock the miners had gouged out of the A-J in their search for gold. The fog had lifted from the water, and across the channel the homes of Douglas Island, built on the hills in patches stripped from the forest, were visible. Another mine, the Treadwell, had been located on the island. The miners there had been so enthusiastic that they'd followed the gold out under the channel's bed and finally been flooded out.

Even though it was given over mostly to government and tourism now, Juneau retained some of the hard edge of its mining past. A handful of grimy-looking bars crouched among the tourist shops like winos at a cotillion. A few of the people Kane passed on the street looked like they knew the inside of those bars better than the outside world.

Kane told the woman on the front desk at the police station his name and business there. She told him to take a seat and wait. Maybe ten minutes later, a rumpled guy came out of the back and looked around the waiting area. He was about six feet tall and nearly as wide. His suit looked like it had been slept in, or maybe dragged behind a car. He walked over to Kane.

"So it really is Nik Kane," he said. "Long time, no see."

Kane looked at the man, trying to recall his name. A dozen years fell away and they were at a conference in Anchorage. Even with the extra thirty pounds he was carrying, not all of it muscle, he looked like his nickname. Tank. Something that started with a *C*. Crawford, that was it. Harry Crawford, known as Tank.

"They still calling you Tank?" Kane said, getting to his feet and offering his hand.

Crawford eyed the hand warily. The shooting, and the drinking that had preceded it, had made Kane a problematic figure for other Alaska cops, and Kane was never sure what sort of reaction he'd get.

Crawford folded his big mitt around Kane's hand, gave it a quick shake, dropped it, and patted his stomach.

"Yeah," he said, "still Tank. Although the weight I've put on, I'm not rolling quite as fast. I don't know what happened. A few years ago everything I ate and drank started staying with me. Now I'm on South Beach and going to the gym. Nothing seems to do any good."

Kane nodded.

"You're lucky you're not eating prison food," he said. "You'd weigh six hundred pounds."

Crawford looked him up and down.

"I don't know, bubba," he said. "You don't look so bad." He pointed at Kane's scar. "From the neck down, anyway."

The two men laughed more than the witticism deserved.

"Come on back," Crawford said.

Kane followed him back into the station to a metal desk that was set facing another just like it. A young guy with an unruly head of curly red hair sat at the second desk.

"That's Hugh Malone," Crawford said, taking a seat at the desk. "He's a mick, if you can believe it. And my partner, if you can believe that, too."

Kane nodded at Malone and sat in a chair next to Crawford's desk.

"They get younger every year," Kane said.

"You got that right, bubba," Crawford said, then sat looking at Kane. Kane looked back. The silence lengthened. Finally, Kane broke it.

"I'm here to make a statement about being burglarized and assaulted last night," he said.

Crawford looked down at his desk, took a deep breath, and said, "You don't have to make a statement, Kane. The arraigning DA decided to kick those guys loose. Said she wouldn't go forward with a he said/he said, especially when it was two-to-one."

Kane sat there thinking, then said, "That won't cut it. The arraigning DA's, what, a year out of law school? She's going to decline a case of breaking and entering and impersonating police officers all by herself? With an ex-cop as the complainant? I don't think so."

"Think what you want, bubba," Crawford said, his voice harsh. "That's the way it is. Maybe the ex-cop's record had something to do with it."

Kane could feel the heat climbing up his neck.

"What the hell is going on, Crawford?" he said. He could hear the anger in his own voice.

"That's all I'm telling you about this," Crawford said, getting to his feet. "Now, you got anything else?"

Kane stayed in his seat.

"Yeah, I do," he said. "I've been hired by Matthew Hope's lawyer. I was hoping you might tell me if there's anything I should know that isn't in the files."

Crawford looked at him, then at his partner.

"There's no law against hoping," he said. "People in hell hope for ice water. But you know I couldn't discuss this case with you even if it was still mine."

Kane raised an eyebrow.

"Still yours?" he said.

Crawford gave him a disgusted look.

"Case has been taken over by the state troopers," he said.

"No kidding?" Kane said. "A murder in your jurisdiction and the troopers got it? How'd that happen?"

"How do you think it happened?" Crawford spat. "Goddamn politics, that's how."

"Now, Harry," the younger detective said.

"Don't 'Now Harry' me, bubba," Crawford said. "You know goddamn well this wasn't the chief's idea. He said it came from the mayor. And somebody's probably twisting the mayor's arm, too. Or offering him something. Christ, I hate politics."

Kane couldn't think of anything else to say to that, so he got to his feet.

"I guess I'll have to go talk to the troopers," he said. "Good to see you, Tank. Malone."

"Lots of luck with the troopers," Crawford said. "When I gave what I had to the chief, he said he'd been told to take it straight to the governor's chief of staff. Police work going to a political appointee. Go figure."

Kane turned to go.

"You watch your ass, bubba," Crawford said. "The media's all over this like white on rice, and all the politicians are looking for someone to sacrifice to the cameras and notebooks. Little guys get ground up in deals like this."

Kane found his way back to the front desk, asked the woman where the nearest coffee shop was, and walked to it. He sat over a cup of coffee, thinking for a while, then took out a card, looked at it, and punched a number into his cell phone.

"I'm looking for Cocoa," he said. He listened for a moment. "Okay, have him call me at this number." He rattled off his cell phone number, ended the call, and sat nursing his coffee. A few minutes later, his phone rang.

"Cocoa?" he said. "Nik Kane. The guy from your airport trip yesterday. I need a driver. A trip out to the valley, some waiting, and a trip back. How much? Okay, that's fine. I'm at the Heritage Coffee place on South Franklin. Twenty minutes? See you out front."

While Kane drank his coffee, he read a copy of the thin local daily someone had discarded. "Bail in White Rose Murder?" the front-page headline screamed. Below that story, which was rehashed information glued together with speculation, was a sidebar saying that reporters from several large, Outside newspapers had arrived to cover the killing, along with a couple of Seattle TV crews and people from at least two supermarket tabloids. The story even reported a rumor that a representative of the famous crime reporter Dominick Dunne was in town.

Jesus, Kane thought. The situation reminded him of the Doonesbury strip on the Patty Hearst trial: "Meanwhile, outside the courtroom, jugglers and dancing bears were seen in the streets."

He scanned the rest of the headlines. A meeting on the school budget. A house fire. Inside, a story on the attempt to raise oil taxes and, above it, a headline that read: "Domestic partners bill stalled in committee."

The story said that a bill by Senator Matthew Hope, a Democrat, to legalize domestic partnerships for gay couples was buried in the Senate Finance Committee and, according to committee chairman O. B. Potter, a Republican, would never get out.

The bill had been headed for a floor vote, the story said, when Potter asked that it be referred to his committee on the grounds that the state would have to hire more bureaucrats to process the civil unions paperwork.

"I believe in the sanctity of marriage and the family," Potter was quoted as saying. "Homosexual marriage or civil unions or whatever you want to call them are a threat to marriage."

The bill's sponsor, the article said, was unavailable for comment because he was being held for murder. A statement from his office said that the bill was about civil rights, not sexual practices.

"We shouldn't be discriminating against people based on their sexual orientation," the statement quoted Hope as saying, "just as we shouldn't discriminate against people based on their race or religion. The voters amended our constitution to ban gay marriage, and it's only fair that gays have a legal way to establish their partnerships."

The story quoted a political science professor as saying it was amazing that, in a state as conservative as Alaska, Hope had gotten the bill through two Senate committees, but that its chances of becoming law were still very poor. Now that Hope was involved in a criminal case, the story said, the fate of the bill was more uncertain than ever.

"We're still hopeful that the bill will get an up-or-down vote on the Senate floor," said a spokesman for a gay rights group. "Our legal rights deserve protection as much as anyone's."

A Jimmy Joe Carlisle, the spokesman for something called Defenders of Alaska Families, said his organization "and all God-fearing Alaskans" were grateful to Potter for his courage in blocking the bill and that they would continue to oppose any recognition of "the plague of homosexuality."

"God created Adam and Eve, not Adam and Steve," he said. "Homosexuality is a sin and we should not condone it. We should be helping the sinners to renounce their vile practices, not enshrining them in the law."

Racketa, racketa, racketa, Kane thought. Blah, blah, blah.

Situations like this were the reason he hated politics. Nobody seemed interested in fixing problems anymore. They just wanted to pose and prance for their supporters. Kane found it hard to believe that who was sleeping with whom was any of the government's business, or that gay people had any less right to enter into legal relationships than straight people. What was it the guy said? "Let gays marry. Why should straights be the only ones who suffer?"

Well, the bigots had made sure gays couldn't marry in Alaska, Kane thought. Now they were apparently going to prevent any legalization of gay relationships. Then what? Pink triangles?

Shaking his head in disgust, Kane took his coffee cup and walked out onto the sidewalk. Across the street the hillside rose sharply, the few buildings clinging there giving way quickly to trees.

Being here, Kane thought, is just more evidence of how vast Alaska is. You'd think it would be big enough to allow everyone to live in peace. But Alaskans were a contentious lot and, with the imported poisons of the American religious right, the lack of tolerance and respect grew a little every year. Sooner or later, every dispute arrived here, in the state capital, to arouse, to enrage, to bring out violent passions.

Violent enough to lead to murder? Kane thought. I guess I'll find out about that.

11

It's a very good question, very direct,
and I'm not going to answer it.

GEORGE H. W. BUSH

Kane finished his coffee, walked back into the building to use the restroom, then walked out onto the sidewalk again. A couple of guys wearing bill caps that read "M/V Pelican" walked past him and turned into a place with a sign over the door that said, "Lucky Lady." As Kane was wondering what kind of beer the dive had on tap, a horn honked and Cocoa waved at him from the driver's seat of the old Ford. He walked over and got in on the passenger's side. The heater was blasting and a voice blared from the radio.

"Rush Limbaugh?" Kane asked.

"Yeah," Cocoa said, turning the radio down. "Gotta support those recovering drug addicts."

Kane laughed.

"Lemon Creek prison," he said.

Cocoa put the Ford in gear and they threaded the streets of downtown onto the expressway and back out the way they'd driven the day before.

"Going to serve out your sentence?" Cocoa asked. "Or just visiting?"

"Just visiting," Kane said. "Matthew Hope. I'm working on his case."

Cocoa gave him a grin.

"You don't look like any lawyer I ever seen," he said.

Kane smiled back.

"I'll take that as a compliment," he said. "I'm a detective. I'm working for Hope's lawyer."

Cocoa flicked the wheel and slid the cab around an SUV that was crawling along.

"Don't know why they take them out of the garage if they don't want to drive them," he said. "So you're a detective. Got a license and everything?"

Kane shook his head.

"Don't need a license to be a detective in Alaska," he said.

Cocoa nodded.

"No surprise," he said. "Don't need a license for much of anything. You figure Hope's got a chance?"

Kane shrugged.

"Too soon to know," he said. "He's got himself a good lawyer and there's no conclusive evidence."

Cocoa snorted.

"Conclusive evidence," he said. "I like that. Since when do they need conclusive evidence to put an Indian in jail?"

Kane didn't have an answer to that, so he let the rest of the ride pass in silence. About fifteen minutes later, Cocoa wheeled the cab up to the prison entrance.

"I hate to ask you to wait," Kane said, "but I've got no idea how long this will take."

"No problemo," Cocoa said, "you're paying for it. I'm going to drive on down the road and find some coffee. When do you want me back?"

Kane thought for a moment.

"The lawyer's secretary was supposed to call and tell them I was coming," he said. "So it'll probably only take twice as long as it should. Give me your cell number and I'll call you."

Cocoa laughed.

"You're used to dealing with prisons, then?" he said.

"You don't know the half of it," Kane said.

He punched the cabbie's number into his cell phone and got out of the cab. Cocoa pulled away. Kane stood looking at the prison. This was his first visit to a prison since he'd gotten out himself.

You can do this, he thought. They can't keep you. You can leave anytime you want.

The prison was a set of low buildings surrounded by fencing on a large tract of land in the valley carved by the Mendenhall Glacier. Even though he was a couple of miles from the channel, Kane could still smell the ocean. He stood sucking fresh air into his lungs, then walked through the entrance doors and across the lobby to the desk. A short, broad-shouldered woman in uniform sat there leafing through papers. She did a good job of ignoring him.

"I'm here to see Matthew Hope," he said at last.

The woman looked up from her papers.

"Too late," she said, pointing to the clock on the wall behind her. "Morning visiting hour's pretty much over."

"Not for me," Kane said, taking Doyle's authorization letter from his pocket and waving it at her. "I'm from his lawyer."

The woman glared at him, got to her feet, and took the letter. She looked at it for a long time, her lips moving.

"I'll need to make a copy of this," she said, and went through a door behind the desk.

Kane looked around the room. Beige paint. Cheap couches. Worn carpet. The smell of cleaning fluid. An old Native man asleep in one corner, cap pulled down over his eyes. Kane walked to the front window and looked out. A vast swath of snow-covered open land and a few industrial-looking buildings in the distance. Not very pretty, but a good field of fire. He walked back to the desk and leaned on it.

She's playing stall ball, he thought. But she doesn't know who she's dealing with. One thing I learned how to do is wait. He focused his eyes on a spot a couple of feet in front of him, emptied his mind, and waited.

The woman came back about fifteen minutes later. She handed Kane the letter.

"He's at lunch," she said. "You'll have to wait."

Kane pointed to the clock. It said 10:15.

"Lunch?" he said. "The guy's a state legislator and I'm a duly authorized member of his legal team. You sure you want to jack me around? On a case the newspapers are so interested in? What do you think your boss would say about a story detailing how you tried to prevent a prisoner from getting his proper legal help?"

The woman glared at Kane, opened her mouth, closed it, picked up the telephone on her desk, muttered into it, listened, and put it down.

"Take a seat," she snarled. "They'll bring him to visiting."

By the time the second door clanged shut behind him, the hair on Kane's neck was standing straight up. The guard, a young, beefy guy with a mullet, led him down an empty hallway and opened a door.

"In here," he said.

Kane entered the small room.

"Buzz when you want out," the guard said. He couldn't have sounded less interested.

Kane took a seat in one of the chairs that faced a thick glass partition. His ears picked out the familiar sounds of prison: muffled thumps, the ringing of a bell, the scraping of an amplified voice making announcements. His nose picked up the smell of disinfectant, cooking, and human bodies. All around him, 150 or so men and women went through the motions of life without freedom.

I'm not one of them, he thought. I can leave anytime I want.

He took deep, slow breaths.

I can leave anytime I want, he thought.

A door opened on the far side of the partition. A man in a bright blue jumpsuit and handcuffs came through it, followed by a tall, sandy-haired guard. The prisoner looked to be about five feet ten and slim. His face was puffy and his dark hair lay flat on his head. Must have missed a shower, Kane thought.

Matthew Hope looked like his picture in the newspaper, but older.

Must be the lines around his eyes and mouth, Kane thought. I know how he got those.

The guard removed the cuffs and left the room. Hope sat.

"Handcuffs, huh?" Kane said. "They're giving you the full treatment, aren't they."

He took Doyle's letter out of his pocket and held it up to the window.

"Read this," he said. He held the paper up for a minute, then, at Hope's signal, replaced it in his pocket.

"So you can see that I work for your lawyer," he said. "I'd like you to answer some questions."

Hope said nothing. When that had gone on for a while, Kane said, "Okay. You can do the stoic Native thing if you want. But you're in a pile of trouble, brother, and you're not helping yourself by not talking to the people who are trying to help you."

A smile flicked across Hope's lips.

"That statement is so convoluted that it would fit right in on the floor of the Senate," he said, his voice tinny through the speaker. "Besides the fact we can both talk around a subject, what makes us brothers?"

Kane shrugged out of his suit coat, rolled up his left sleeve, and showed Hope a small tattoo. Hope leaned forward to examine it.

"Raven," he said. "Tlingit."

"Yeah," Kane said, rolling the sleeve back down and fastening the button. "Drawn by a fellow named Peter Benson, who's doing what'll probably be the rest of his life for killing a couple of guys in a bad dope deal. He inked it for me after we all did *banya* together in Wildwood."

Hope looked Kane over carefully.

"You're not Alaska Native," he said.

Kane shook his head.

"Out in the world, I'm just another *gussik*," he said. "But you've got to talk to somebody."

Hope's smile came and went again.

"Don't overestimate Native solidarity," he said. "Like everything else in politics, it's relative. For instance, did you know that the Tlingit once exercised a trade monopoly over my people?"

He smiled once more.

"Besides, why should I trust someone who's been in prison?" he asked.

Kane laughed.

"Well, you've still got a sense of humor," he said. "That's a good sign."

He cleared his throat.

"I'll bet if you ask around in here you'll find somebody I did time with who can tell you whether I'm trustworthy or not," he said. "But that's not really the point. As far as I can tell, the authorities like you for this murder. That means they might not be motivated to look too hard for evidence you didn't do it. But me? I'm motivated to help you by the best motivation there is—money. And if I'm going to help you, you're going to have to tell me a whole lot of stuff, including some things you probably really don't want to tell me."

The two men sat in silence while Hope seemed to consider what the detective had said.

"I went to a reception after work," he said at last. "City of Petersburg. They serve good shrimp. I talked to some people there, ate a mess of shrimp, left. Went back to the Capitol to finish reading up on the next day's bills. Then I went looking for Senator Potter to discuss a bill of mine that's stuck in his committee."

Hope stopped talking. Kane waited. He knew from experience that Natives spoke in a different rhythm than whites and that silence, even prolonged silence, didn't necessarily mean that Hope was finished.

"A light was on in the senator's office," he said. "Miss Foxx was lying there. There was a lot of blood. I guess I kind of blacked out then. The next thing I remember was a policeman reading me my rights. Just like on TV. *Law and Order* or one of those shows."

Hope went silent again. Kane waited. When he was convinced Hope was done talking, he said, "Had you been drinking?"

Hope looked at the detective for a long while.

"You think because I'm Native I must have been drinking?" he said.

Kane shook his head.

"No," he said, "because you say you blacked out. In my experience, blackouts and booze go hand in hand."

"Your professional experience," Hope said, "or your personal experience?"

"Both," Kane said, and waited.

"I don't drink," Hope said. "I've seen too many people fall into the bottle and not be able to climb back out. I can't explain the lost time. Shock, maybe. I haven't seen very many dead people before. And there was a lot of blood."

Kane nodded and made a note in his notebook.

"When did you get to the reception?" he asked.

"I don't know, maybe about five-thirty, six o'clock," Hope said.

"When did you leave?"

"I'm not sure."

"When did you find the body?"

"I don't know for sure."

Kane sighed.

"You went to the reception at six o'clock and discovered the body near eleven," Kane said. "That's a lot of time to account for with eating shrimp and doing paperwork."

Hope sat silently. Kane sighed again.

"You got any friends in the legislature?" he asked.

"Friends?" Hope asked. "Why do you need to know that?"

Kane slapped his notebook against an open palm.

"Because," he said, "whether you like it or not, I'm investigating this killing, and I don't know the first thing about the legislature. I'd ask you, but you don't seem very talkative. So do you have any friends there or not?"

Hope shook his head.

"Friends," he said. "You know what Harry Truman said about friends in politics, don't you? He said, 'If you want a friend in Washington, get a dog.' Same thing's true in Juneau."

It was Kane's turn to sit without saying anything. Finally, Hope went on, "But if you want to know how the legislature works, go talk to the Senate minority leader, Toby Grantham. He's been in there for thirty years or so, and he's a Democrat like me, so he might help."

Grantham's had been one of the names on Mrs. Richard Foster's list. Kane closed his notebook and tucked it into his shirt pocket. He followed it with his pen.

"Let me tell you how this is," he said. "When we're finished talking, I'll walk out of here, get in a cab, and go back downtown. I'll maybe get a coffee, then I might go up to the Capitol and talk to some people. Then I'll pick a place and have lunch. Tonight, I'll decide where to get dinner, whether to go to a movie or watch a little TV. Then I'll choose when to call it a night, turn in, get some sleep."

He paused, but Hope just sat there.

"What you'll do is very different," Kane said. "You'll do exactly what you're told to do exactly when you're told to do it. Eat, sleep, work, go to the bathroom. You'll see the same people and the same rooms and the same walls. Over and over and over again."

He paused again.

"There's going to be a bail hearing," Hope said. "I have a right to get out on bail. State law says so."

Kane looked at the other man for a long moment.

"You get out on bail," he said, "and you'll think everything will be all right. You'll lead an almost normal life, if you don't think about it too hard. But then there will be a trial, and if you stick to this sorry story you just told me, the jury will convict you and you'll spend the next twenty years or more doing exactly what you're told to do exactly when you're told to do it. And staring at the walls in between. Maybe you're tough enough to take it. Maybe you're not. Some people are. Lots aren't. And maybe your people on the outside will wait and maybe they won't. You married?"

Hope's gaze was steady, but Kane could see the pulse throbbing in his temple.

"No, I'm not," he said, "but I've got family, lots of family who would wait for me. But they won't have to. I didn't kill that woman."

Kane waited for him to continue, and when he didn't said, "That's it? That's the best you've got? I didn't do it?"

Hope remained silent.

"So are you going to tell me the truth now?" Kane said.

The two men looked at each other for a long time.

"I've told you what happened," Hope said at last.

Kane looked steadily at the other man, then shook his head.

"You know," he said, "for a politician, you're a crappy liar."

He got to his feet and pushed the buzzer. The door behind Hope opened and the sandy-haired guard came in. Hope got to his feet and the two of them left. Without the distraction of talking to Hope, Kane could feel the room start to close in on him. The door to Kane's room opened and the guard with the mullet came in.

"Ready to go?" he asked.

Kane nodded. He went through the door and down the hall, the guard behind him. The urge to start running was nearly irresistible, but he fought it down and concentrated on putting one foot in front of the other at a steady pace. He forced himself not to fidget while they waited for the guard in the booth to open one locked door, then another. When he reached the lobby, Kane continued straight across the reception area and out into the cold. He stood there for a long while, breathing in and out. Then he took out his cell phone and called Cocoa.

"You can come and get me now," he said. "I made my escape."

He stood outside, ignoring the cold, until Cocoa's cab pulled up. He got in.

"How was your visit?" the cabbie asked.

"Piece of cake," Kane said. "I could get out anytime I wanted."

There are no true friends in politics. We are all sharks circling,
and waiting, for traces of blood to appear in the water.

ALAN CLARK

Alaska's Capitol is a U-shaped concrete building faced with bricks
and slabs of limestone, a block long and half a block wide. The
main entrance is on the front of the U, framed by four marble pillars,
two stories tall, which support a small balcony of the sort that a queen
might wave from.

When it was built, before Alaska became a state, the building housed
the federal bureaucrats who ran the territory, making it the only state
capitol building in the United States that wasn't built as a Capitol.
Because it was built on the slope of a hill, the building has six stories at
the front but only five at the back. The first floor is called the ground
floor, the second floor is called the first floor, and so on.

Perfect, Kane thought, folding the brochure titled "Facts About

Alaska's Capitol" and sliding it into a coat pocket. A building that follows its own rules full of people who make their own rules.

Senator Toby Grantham's office was on the ground floor, down the hall from the print shop and the mailroom. The outer office was the size of a box of saltines. A gorgeous, dark-haired young woman sat at a desk flanked by a pair of closed doors. Her desk, a couple of chairs, and a coatrack barely left room for a visitor.

The young woman welcomed Kane with a big smile and asked if she could help him.

"I'm here to talk to Senator Grantham at the suggestion of Senator Matthew Hope," Kane said, handing her a card.

The woman switched off her smile.

"Oh, it's a terrible thing, terrible," she said. "I'm sure Senator Hope had nothing to do with that woman's death." She got to her feet. "I'll get Senator Grantham's senior staff." Still holding the card, she disappeared through one of the closed doors.

Kane took off his coat and hung it on a rack. He looked around the reception area. The walls were crowded with what he took to be class photos, but on closer examination they turned out to be photographs of the legislature through the years. He was looking at the oldest of them—the caption said "12th Alaska Legislature"—when the door behind him opened.

"That's Senator Grantham there," a woman said. She walked over and stood next to Kane, pointing at what appeared to be a college kid. "That photo was taken in 1982. Doesn't he look young?"

"He certainly does," Kane said.

The woman was a head shorter than Kane, with shoulder-length blond hair and blue eyes. She wore a dark suit and a white blouse open far enough to show the beginning of spectacular cleavage. She smelled of soap and tobacco smoke. Kane guessed her age at thirty.

"I'm Alma Atwood," she said, extending a hand. "I'm Senator

Grantham's chief of staff. Jennifer said you'd like to speak with the senator?"

Kane took her hand, which was soft and warm and dry.

"I would," he said. "I'm Nik Kane, part of Senator Matthew Hope's defense team. Senator Hope suggested I talk to your boss."

He was startled to realize that he was still holding the woman's hand, so he dropped it, dug Doyle's letter of authorization out of his coat pocket, and, since Grantham was on her list, Mrs. Foster's letter as well. He handed them to the woman. The woman opened each in turn, read them, and nodded.

"I'm sure the senator will want to speak with you," she said. "If you wouldn't mind waiting?"

She took the letters, knocked at the other closed door, and opened it. Kane could hear a booming voice saying, ". . . organized labor gets off its ass and—" The closing door cut the voice off.

Kane sat in one of the chairs and waited. The woman emerged a while later.

"The senator can give you a few minutes now," she said, "but he does have a lunch appointment."

She opened the door and passed through it in front of Kane.

"Mr. Kane, Senator," she said.

Grantham sat behind a big, tidy desk of dark wood. His office was much bigger than the outer office. RHIP, Kane thought.

The senator got up and walked around the desk, extending a hand. Kane shook it. The hand was as big and soft as a catcher's mitt. Kane had no urge to hold on to it. Grantham was big and soft, too, and no longer looked like a college kid. He had salt-and-pepper hair that hung over his shirt collar and a big belly that hung over his belt. He wore a gray, pin-striped suit and a starched white shirt that gaped above the belt to show a not-so-white undershirt beneath. Red veins were visible in his beak of a nose and he smelled of aftershave and alcohol.

"Thank you, Alma," he said in a voice as well seasoned as an oak barrel. The woman left, closing the door behind her. "Please have a seat, Mr. Kane."

Kane sat in one of the wing chairs facing the desk. Grantham leaned over the desk, picked up the letters, and handed them to Kane. He sat in the other wing chair.

"So you are here on behalf of Senator Hope," Grantham said, "and with the recommendation of Mrs. Richard Foster. That's a potent combination. What can I do to help?"

"I've been hired by the defense to investigate the murder of Melinda Foxx," Kane said. "I don't know anything about politics or how the legislature works or the defendant or the victim. So pretty much anything you can tell me will help, Senator."

Grantham laughed.

"You've got your work cut out for you, don't you?" he said. "I've been at this thirty years and I'm not sure how either politics or the legislature works."

Grantham propped his chin up with a hand and sat there.

"There's a lot I could tell you," he said at last, "so much that probably all it would do is confuse you. And unless you're trying to get a bill passed, it wouldn't help anyway. For your purposes, just think of the legislature as a nomad camp. There's maybe five hundred of us if you count legislators and staff and lobbyists and reporters. Most of us don't live in Juneau, we just camp out here when we're in session. We work together and socialize together and don't mix much with the locals. I've always thought we'd make a fascinating study for a sociologist. Or an anthropologist. Or even a psychiatrist."

Kane showed the senator a smile at the witticism.

"So you all know each other pretty well?" he asked.

"Fairly well," Grantham said. "There's a significant burnout factor, so people leave and new people take their places. And there's a tendency to socialize with your own kind—legislators with legislators, staff with staff, and so on. Except lobbyists. It's more or less their job to be on good terms with everyone."

From where he sat, Kane could look out three windows located at intervals in the wall and see people walking past, going up or down the hill. He saw heads in the first window, torsos in the second, and legs in the last. His kids had had a game like that when they were little, matching the proper heads, bodies, and legs. *Sesame Street* characters, as he recalled.

"Did you know Melinda Foxx well?" he asked Grantham.

"Only superficially," Grantham said. "I tend to spend most of my time dealing with other senators and their staffs, and, since he's the chairman of the Finance Committee, there's no getting around Senator O. B. Potter and his staff. So I had dealings with Miss Foxx and knew her well enough to say hello to."

"And to socialize with?" Lane asked.

Grantham shook his head.

"Maybe twenty years ago," he said, "but I find I don't have the energy to keep up with these young women anymore."

"So you don't know much about her personal life?" Kane asked.

Grantham shook his head again.

"I think you'd be better off talking to someone more her age," he said, "probably other members of the staff."

"And what can you tell me about Matthew Hope?" Kane asked. As he waited for an answer, the head of a pretty brunette became a robust torso, then a shapely pair of legs.

"I don't know Senator Hope all that well, really," Grantham said. "I'm not sure anyone does. Native legislators are a minority, and since most of them are Democrats, and the Republicans run things, they are a minority within a minority. So they play things close to the vest and tend to not socialize much. Plus, Hope only came over to the Senate from the House two years ago."

"You are in the same party," Kane said.

"We are," said Grantham, "but people tend to assign too much significance to that. We share the same values, but we don't agree on everything and we don't all get along."

"Does Hope have any friends here?" Kane asked.

Grantham was silent for a moment.

"None that I know of," he said. "The legislature, particularly the Senate, isn't given to friendships. We each have our own priorities and careers to worry about. You'd be better off thinking of our relationships as alliances that are constantly shifting. The alliance among members of the same party is important but not definitive. There are personal and regional considerations, electoral considerations. It's a complicated business."

Kane shook his head.

"So this is going to be worse than I thought," he said.

"Probably much worse," Grantham said with a smile.

"Did Senator Hope know Melinda Foxx?" Kane asked.

"I'm sure he did, although I have no idea how well," Grantham said. "Ms. Foxx took care of bills in the Finance Committee, so every senator knew her and dealt with her at one time or another. Many of the members of the House, too, as well as most of the staff."

"She took care of bills," Kane said. "What does that mean, exactly?"

Grantham smiled.

"Ah, Government 101," he said. "Most committees deal with bills, with laws legislators want passed. If the passage of a bill would require the government to spend more money, it is sent to the Finance Committee. In addition, the Finance Committee writes the budgets. So the committee staff works either on the bills that are sent to the committee or on the budgets. Ms. Foxx worked on bills."

Kane nodded, and the senator continued.

"Senator Hope is the prime sponsor of only one bill," he said, "to allow civil unions, and it is in the Finance Committee right now. So he probably has had conversations with Ms. Foxx about moving it out of committee. Although I can't think of a reason why he'd bother."

"Why not?' Kane asked.

Grantham smiled again.

"Gay rights isn't the most popular issue in the legislature," he said. "Senator Potter, who is very conservative and has a lot of conservative, especially conservative Christian, support, is worse than most on the subject. He grabbed the bill on the flimsiest pretext just to block it. So that bill would have trouble getting out of his committee, too, even if Senator Hope weren't on his hit list."

"Why's that?" Kane asked.

Grantham shifted in his chair.

"I wouldn't normally be retailing gossip," he said, "but I want to do everything I can to help Senator Hope. Several months ago, he released information showing that the state Department of Transportation was leasing office space from Senator Potter at three times the going rate, without a competitively bid contract. There's an investigation going on right now that's likely to be embarrassing for both Potter and the governor. And just before the session started, Potter was accused of taking illegal campaign contributions from a couple of oil field service companies. Everyone thinks Hope was the source of that information, too. So it's not very likely that Potter would do Hope any favors. And that's putting it mildly."

Kane took his notebook out of his pocket and wrote in it.

"That wasn't too smart, was it?" he asked. "Getting on the wrong side of someone as powerful as Senator Potter?"

He watched as a pair of chubby legs became a round body, then a fleshy head.

"Not if Senator Hope wants to get anything done in the Senate," Grantham said. "But everyone thinks he's got bigger plans, and he's sacrificing effectiveness inside the legislature for political points outside it."

Kane wrote some more.

"So you don't think Senator Hope is serious about his civil unions bill?" he asked.

"He may be," Grantham said. "He did manage to pry it out of a couple of committees in the Senate. But Senator Potter seems to be dug in pretty solidly against it, and I'm not sure what inducements Senator Hope could offer to change his position."

"Inducements?" Kane said.

"Between senators, an inducement is usually a vote," Grantham said, "as in 'I'll vote for your bill if you'll vote for mine.' A less kind term for that is logrolling. But Potter doesn't have many logs to roll, and those he does have aren't the sort of logs Senator Hope is likely to help him roll."

"I can feel the water closing over my head," Kane said.

Grantham saw the confused look on Kane's face and chuckled.

"Just think of it as a big swap meet," Grantham said, "with votes as the currency."

"If you say so," Kane said. "I suppose this makes sense, in its own way. Do you support the civil unions bill?"

Grantham smiled.

"I do," he said. "I think it's a matter of human rights."

"I just read that in the newspaper, coming from Hope," Kane said.

Grantham chuckled again.

"We all tend to use the same talking points," he said. "But why so many questions about the legislation? Do you think it's involved somehow in what happened to Miss Foxx?"

"God knows," Kane said. "Could Senator Hope's interest in Melinda Foxx have been personal? Social?"

Grantham shrugged.

"As I said, I know very little of their social lives," he said. "Either of their social lives. But Senator Hope is single and so was Ms. Foxx."

Kane nodded.

"I've been told that even married men aren't always immune to the temptations of a legislative session," he said.

"That's true," Grantham said. "Spending four months in Juneau every year is more than some spouses can take. So some legislators are here alone, under constant pressure and surrounded by young women and men. Under these circumstances, it's no surprise that some stray. But if Ms. Foxx was involved with any legislator, married or single, I hadn't heard about it."

"Does your wife come with you?" Kane asked, nodding toward a large photo of Grantham and a woman his age that was turned half toward him on the senator's desk.

Grantham shook his head.

"Unfortunately, no," he said. "She's back in Anchorage, tending to our children and grandchildren."

That line of questioning seems to be petering out, Kane thought.

"How important is the civil unions bill?" Kane asked.

Grantham considered his answer.

"I suppose it is important to certain interest groups," he said, "and it could have some repercussions at election time. But it is far from the session's most important issue."

"Which is?" Kane asked.

"Oil taxes," Grantham said without hesitation.

"Why are they important?" Kane asked.

Grantham greeted the question with a smile.

"You're not very political, are you?" he asked. When Kane shook his head, the senator continued. "Oil income accounts for about eighty to eighty-five percent of the state's general revenue. Our current tax structure is outdated. With the value of oil as high as it is, we're letting a lot of money get away. There's a bill to change the tax system. The oil companies oppose it. Hundreds of millions of dollars are at stake."

"Is Senator Hope involved in the tax issue?" Kane asked.

"We're all involved in it," Grantham said. "One thing people don't understand is that we have hundreds of issues, big and small, to deal with every session. This session, no issue is bigger than oil taxes. The House has sent us a bill, so the ball is in our court. The Senate is sharply divided and every vote counts. So, yes, Matthew Hope is involved in the oil tax issue. As are we all."

There was a knock at the door and Alma stuck her head in.

"Your lunch appointment is here, Senator," she said.

Grantham got to his feet. Kane did, too.

"I'm sorry I can't be more help," the senator said. "And I'd appreciate it if you didn't tell the press we've talked. They're so hungry for a story about this murder, they don't care who they hurt in the process."

He ushered Kane out of his office. One of the whitest men Kane had ever seen stood in the reception area. He was probably six inches over six feet, and so broad he looked square. His hair was the color of straw and his eyes were a blue so pale they were nearly white. His skin was the color of copy paper.

"Hello, George," Grantham said. "Mr. Kane, this is George Bezhdetny. George is a lobbyist. Mr. Kane here is a detective, working for Matthew Hope's defense."

The man took Kane's hand gently, as if he was afraid he'd break it. Looking at him, Kane was afraid of the same thing.

"Pleased to meet you, Mr. Kane," the man said. His voice was a low rumble shot through with an accent Kane couldn't identify.

"You, too, Mr. Bezhdetny," Kane said. "Senator, if you don't mind, I'd like to talk to Ms. Atwood for a while."

Grantham took an expensive-looking overcoat from the rack. Kane and the big man had to step back to give him room to maneuver himself into it.

"If she's willing to talk to you, I have no objection," he said. "Shall we go, George?"

The two men left the office.

"That guy's not very big, is he?" Kane said.

The dark-haired young woman laughed. Alma made a face. Neither of them said anything.

"Do you get to eat lunch?" Kane asked Alma. "I'm buying." He turned to the dark-haired woman. "That invitation includes you, too."

The two women exchanged a look.

"I'm afraid Jennifer will have to stay here to answer the phones," Alma said, "but I'd be happy to join you. Just let me get my coat."

She went into her office. Kane had his coat on by the time she returned, wearing a bright ski jacket. When he held the office door for her, Alma gave him a big smile.

"Oh, a gentleman," she said. "I like that."

Kane smiled back.

"You must have a lot of those here," he said, as they walked down the hall.

"Not as many as you might think," she said.

13

If you are sure you understand everything that is
going on, you are hopelessly confused.

WALTER F. MONDALE

When they reached the lobby, Kane and the woman had to navigate around a knot of people surrounding a well-dressed, dark-haired young woman. They waved notebooks and shouted questions and, every time the woman tried to take a step they shifted to block her way. In the glaring light from the TV cameras, the woman looked dazed.

"Oh, that's Mary David, Senator Hope's staff," Alma said. "She looks like she's in trouble."

"How well did your boss know the White Rose?" somebody shouted. "Were they having an affair?"

"How about you?" another called. "Are you sleeping with him?"

"Wait here," Kane said.

He forced his way through the circle of reporters, earning himself some startled looks and angry mutters. When he was next to the young woman, he said softly, "Hello, Miss David. I'm working for your boss's lawyer. Would you like to get out of here?"

The woman nodded her head.

"Please," she said, a note of panic in her voice.

Kane took her arm and started forward. A man in a three-piece suit and carrying a tape recorder blocked their way. Kane put his hand in the middle of the man's chest and pushed. The man stumbled backward.

"Hey," he said. "You can't do that. I'm a member of the press. Who do you think you are?"

"I'm the guy who is going to tie your nose in a knot if you don't stop impeding this woman's lawful progress," Kane said in a loud voice. "That goes for the rest of you, too. Miss David has nothing to say and wants you to leave her alone. So get out of the way."

"The public has a right to know," the man in the three-piece suit said.

Kane laughed, put his hand on the man's chest, and shoved again, harder. The man banged into a TV cameraman behind him. The camera slipped off the man's shoulder and clipped the man on the side of the head.

"Ow," he said. "You all saw that—he assaulted me."

"Last chance," Kane said, taking another step forward. The man shrank to the side. Kane led the woman to the door, then turned and stood in the doorway while she made her escape. When one of the reporters tried to get through another of the entryway doors, Kane reached out and grabbed his shoulder.

"You really don't want to do that," he said.

Deprived of their prey, the pack of reporters broke up. Kane stood there watching until Alma walked up to him.

"That was bold," she said.

"I hate bullies," Kane said.

Alma put her hand on Kane's arm.

"Around here, we treat reporters with kid gloves," she said.

"I guess that's because you care what they write about you," Kane said. "The ladies and gentlemen of the fourth estate. What a laugh. Shall we go?"

Kane and Alma became part of a steady stream of people leaving the Capitol, the court building across the street, and the state office building a half-block away.

"Pretty much everything you can see from here is state government," Alma said. "It's what keeps Juneau going."

Kane let her pick the lunch spot, so they walked carefully downhill, avoiding the biggest patches of ice. Alma took a cigarette from her purse and gestured with it.

"I hope you don't mind," she said.

"I don't," Kane said, "but I thought smoking was not politically correct anymore."

"It's not," Alma said. She stopped, turned her back, and cupped the cigarette to light it. Turning, she sucked in a lungful of smoke and let it trickle out her nostrils. "I guess I'm just an addictive personality. You don't smoke?"

"I did," Kane said with a wry smile, "but I had the opportunity to break the habit."

As they chatted their way downhill, they passed several men chipping ice off the sidewalks. That and all the ice melt spread around made the footing better, but both Kane and the woman placed their feet carefully. During the walk, Kane learned that Alma was thirty-two, originally from Minnesota and working her tenth legislative session, all of them for Grantham. She also said that she was thinking about giving up legislative work to go to law school.

"It's just not as much fun as it used to be," she said.

They reached the narrow strip of flat land that rimmed the water. Across the street was a big, blue, shedlike building built out over the channel on pilings.

"This was once the hangar for the airline that flew seaplanes out of Juneau," Alma said. "They'd take off and land in the channel right there. A man who'd ridden in them said that the first time he took off in one, there was so much water splashing over the little porthole window he thought they were sinking."

The building held a number of places to eat and a few tourist shops. Their restaurant was built along the channel side of the building, big windows giving a view of the water and Douglas Island beyond. Both the bar and the restaurant were packed.

"Do you live in Juneau?" Kane asked as they waited for a table.

"Year-round, you mean?" Alma said. "No. I spend the interim, the time between sessions, in Anchorage. Here I rent a place across the channel. In fact, you can just see it from here, a little brown place down by the water."

She took his arm, pulled him close, and pointed. Kane looked along her arm and pretended to see her place.

"You come back to the same place every year?" he asked.

She smiled.

"One of the perquisites of being a longtime staffer," she said. "I've got the moving back and forth thing down pretty well."

One of the waitstaff led them to a table well away from the windows.

"This is what comes of not being anybody," Alma said. "The window tables are full of lobbyists and legislators and important staffers."

Kane picked up the menu, scanned it, and set it down again.

"Was Melinda Foxx an important staffer?" he asked.

Alma set her menu on top of his.

"I suppose I can talk to you about this," she said, "or else the senator would have said something. But even though I don't really know much, I'd appreciate it if you didn't tell anyone we discussed this subject. As you just saw, the media pressure on this is tremendous, and that means the political pressure is, too. I don't want the press hounding me, or anything I say to cause problems for my boss."

Kane nodded.

"Fair enough," he said. "I suppose everyone I talk to about this is going to be a little wary. So I won't tell anyone we've talked about this. Now, was Melinda Foxx an important staffer?"

Alma looked at him for a time.

"I suppose I'll just have to trust you," she said. "Was Melinda important? Yes. Many of the most important bills have to go through the Finance Committee, and she was in a position to affect what happened to them. So she was important."

The waitress brought them water and bread and said she'd be right back.

"Tell me about the civil unions bill," Kane said.

"There's not much to tell, really," Alma said. "When Senator Hope introduced the bill last session, everyone thought it was just for show. Something to energize his support among progressives. Alaska is such a conservative place, no one thought the bill had a chance. But the bill actually moved through a couple of committees. Nobody knows how. Then it got sent to the Finance Committee, and now it's stuck there."

"I read an article about it," Kane said. "Senator Potter and his allies have some pretty old-fashioned views about homosexuality."

Alma laughed.

"Old-fashioned," she said. "I like that. They're a bunch of bigots, is what they are."

"So you think civil unions are a good idea?" Kane asked.

Alma gave him a look.

"I'm a woman who likes men," she said with some heat. "Does that mean I should have more legal protections than a woman who likes women?"

Kane raised a hand in defense.

"Hey, I've got nothing against gay people," he said, "and I don't know enough about civil unions to know whether they're a good idea.

Marriage isn't working out so well for a lot of straight people these days."

Like me, he thought.

"I'm sorry to bite your head off," she said. "It's just that the system stacks the deck against getting anything progressive done because it gives power to Cro-Magnons like O. B. Potter. The civil unions bill isn't the only piece of legislation stuck in his committee."

"Did Melinda Foxx have strong feelings about the bill?" Kane asked.

"If she did, she kept them to herself," Alma said.

She gave an embarrassed smile.

"Like I should be doing," she said. "It isn't really smart for staffers to express opinions on policy issues."

The smile left her face and she knit her brows.

I'm paying an awful lot of attention to the way she looks, Kane thought. Danger, Will Robinson. Danger.

"Why are you asking so much about that bill?" Alma asked.

Kane shrugged.

"I'm not sure," he said, "except that legislative politics are Matthew Hope's business and were Melinda Foxx's business, and understanding what people do for a living helps me to understand them."

"Is that what you try to do?" Alma asked. "Understand people? I thought detectives looked for evidence and clues and stuff."

The waitress returned. Alma ordered a salad. So did Kane, along with a cup of coffee. When Alma raised an eyebrow at him, he said, "Fighting my weight. I've finally got it down to where I want it, but keeping it there isn't easy."

"Tell me about it," Alma said "That's why there's something called the Juneau Twenty. It's the twenty pounds most everyone gains every session from all the free eating and drinking down here."

The waitress left.

"You asked about evidence and clues and stuff?" Kane said. "People love to think of detecting as a scientific enterprise these days, particularly with all these CSI shows on TV. But I've never put much stock in that. I'm certain that something in Melinda Foxx's life caused someone to kill her, and if I can figure out what that was I'll find the murderer. So I'm trying to find out as much as I can about her whole life. So you don't know what she thought about the civil unions bill?"

It was Alma's turn to shrug.

"I haven't got a clue," she said. "Like I said, it's a bad idea for staffers to express their personal views on legislation. Particularly if they have a boss with ambitions for higher office."

"Senator Potter has ambitions?" Kane said "What ambitions are those?"

"The story is that he's thinking of running for governor, like practically everyone else," Alma said. "Governor Hiram Putnam is so low in the polls that this table would have a good chance against him. And the rumor going around is that the price to get even the mildest bill out of that committee is financial support for Senator Potter's run for governor."

Kane took out his notebook and made a note.

"That's not legal, is it?" he asked.

Alma shook her head.

"No," she said, "but quite a few legislators don't seem to care much about legalities. Including Senator Potter."

Kane wrote for a minute, then asked, "Was Melinda Foxx important to you and your boss? Did—does Senator Grantham have a bill he wants to get through the Finance Committee?"

Alma shook her head.

"When you've been in the legislature as long as he has, and in the minority as long as he has, you know that you're not going to get any bills passed, so you don't bother," she said. "You introduce the bills, so you have something to show the voters, but you know that someone in the majority will steal the idea if they think it's any good, and otherwise your bills are going to just sit there."

"That must be frustrating," Kane said.

Alma nodded.

"It is," she said, then added quickly, "but it's the way things are. It's not a reason to kill somebody, if that's what you're thinking."

Kane looked out over the room full of people. The ones at the window tables were talking loudest and gesturing most broadly. Like they're on stage, Kane thought. And I guess in a way they are.

Alma shifted in her seat so she could take in the whole crowd.

"I know someone at every one of these tables," she said. "I've been here too long."

The waitress brought Kane's coffee. It wasn't as watery as the hotel coffee, but it wasn't great.

"What about other legislation?" he asked. "Like the oil tax bill?"

"I see," Alma said. "My senator was giving you his 'importance of oil taxes' speech. Well, he's right. Before the White Rose Murder, the press was focused on the domestic partners bill, but the legislature—the governor's office, too, for that matter—was focused on oil taxes. Now the press is focused on the murder and the legislature is still focused on oil taxes."

She paused.

"Although I suppose the two are related in a way," she said.

"The murder and oil taxes?" Kane said. "How?"

"Everyone thinks that if the oil tax bill gets to the floor, the vote will be very close," she said, "so close that if Matthew Hope—or any other senator likely to vote for it—isn't there, or changes their vote, the bill will fail."

"And lots of people would like it to fail?" Kane said.

Alma nodded.

"There's the oil companies, the lobbyists they employ, their political allies," she said, "and, of course, the governor."

"Why would the governor want it to fail?" Kane asked.

"Because if it passes," Alma said, "the governor will have to either veto a bill that the polls show Alaskans support, or sign a bill his main political financers, the oil companies, oppose. So he'd much rather it just died in the Senate."

Kane sat quietly for a moment.

"This is complicated, isn't it?" he said. "And cold-blooded."

Alma laughed.

"Complicated and cold-blooded," she said. "That's a pretty good description of Alaska politics."

Kane thought some more.

"Your boss said the oil tax bill is worth hundreds of millions of dollars," he said. "I can understand that as a motive for political action. Even for murder."

Alma shook her head.

"That's just politics," she said. "Nobody gets killed because of politics."

Kane thought about his time in Vietnam but didn't say anything. The waitress set their salads in front of them. Kane and Alma ate for a while, then he said, "I'm not sure I understand the reason for all this political maneuvering. If it's just a question of Alaska getting fair value for its oil, why not just raise the taxes and be done with it?"

Alma opened her mouth to speak, but Kane raised a hand.

"Don't bother answering that," he said. "I'm sure it is hopelessly naive and completely unrealistic. Tell me instead about what you know about Melinda Foxx as a staffer."

Alma ate for a while longer, then drank some water.

"I know that this is, was, her second session," she said. "I know that she was very smart and picked things up quickly. I know that the bill part of the committee ran very smoothly, and that it wouldn't have been long before she was running Senator Potter's entire office. If she could get around Ms. Senator Potter, that is."

Kane raised an eyebrow.

"Senator Potter's daughter, Letitia," Alma said. "She spends a lot of time in his office. Some people say it's so he can keep an eye on her. Others say it's so she can keep an eye on him." Her voice dropped to a whisper. "He might be old, but he's got fast hands, that man." She raised her voice again. "Whatever the reason, she's there a lot and acts like the chief of staff. So Melinda would have had to reach some sort of accommodation with her."

She forked up some salad.

"Did you know Miss Foxx personally?" Kane asked.

Alma nodded, swallowed, and said, "A little. Staffers usually hang out with other staffers from their own party. But my senator loves information about what the majority is up to, so it's sort of part of my job to keep an eye on their staff. I talk with them some, hang out with them some, drink with them some. So I knew Melinda Foxx better than I otherwise might."

She ate more salad and seemed to be marshaling her thoughts.

"Melinda was very ambitious," Alma said, "but in some ways very naive, too. Like you were saying, she thought that good public policy was more important than politics. Everybody comes in here like that. Most of us get over it, but Melinda hadn't. At least she said she hadn't."

"Do you have some reason to doubt her?" Kane asked.

"Not really," Alma said. "But around here you quickly learn not to take things at face value. Anyway, she seemed, I don't know, satisfied enough with her job. And then, maybe six months ago, she started acting differently. Happier, I guess. Like something was working out well for her."

"Got any idea what?" Kane asked.

"I don't," Alma said. "If it was something in her office, I'd be the last to hear about it. And as far as I know, Melinda had put her private life on hold. At least I never heard about her dating anybody."

Kane found that his plate was empty. He was still hungry.

That's the problem with salad, he thought. It doesn't really fill you up.

"So you don't know why she changed?" he asked.

"I don't," she said. "Maybe one of her coworkers could tell you. But I suppose you'll find it difficult to get any of them to talk to you."

Alma finished her salad, set her fork neatly on the plate, and pushed it away from her. Kane caught the waitress's attention and made a writing motion in the air.

"I don't know," he said to Alma, "I can be surprisingly charming."

That earned him a grin. The waitress handed him the bill. Alma reached for her purse, but Kane waved her away.

"My treat," he said, and laid some cash on the bill. He helped her into her coat and they left the restaurant.

"I'll bet half the people in that room are wondering who you are," she said.

"Only half?" Kane said. "I'm disappointed."

Alma laughed.

"I don't know what we'd do for entertainment here without gossip," she said.

They stepped out the door and Alma quickly lit a cigarette. As they walked up the hill, Kane said, "And what about Senator Hope? What do you know about him?"

Alma blew smoke.

"His politics are great," she said. "He really seems to believe in good government and helping people. Some people say that's just show, because he wants to be governor, but that's not what I think. Politically, he's very attractive."

"And personally?" Kane said.

"Personally, he's very attractive, too," Alma said. "He and I came to the legislature the same year, and I know a lot of the women wanted to serve under him, if you know what I mean. More than one of them did, according to rumor. The women he's dated say he is very nice and considerate, but he never dated the same woman for very long and none of them succeeded in snaring him."

"Were you one of the women he dated?" Kane asked.

Alma shook her head.

"No," she said in a tone Kane couldn't quite identify, "I was busy with other things."

They walked the rest of the way in silence, Alma smoking and Kane lost in thought. A large crowd had gathered in front of the Capitol, carrying signs that said things like: "Support Public Education" and "Children Are Our Future." A tall, bald man in a suit stood on the landing. He seemed to be just wrapping up a speech over a portable sound system.

"What's that about?" Kane asked.

"Teachers' fly-in," Alma said. When Kane gave her a questioning look, she went on, "People come to Juneau to put pressure on the legislature all session. There are probably two or three demonstrations like this a week, plus people visiting offices and packing the galleries and so on. Today, it's teachers."

"What do they want?" Kane asked.

"What most everybody wants," Alma said. "More money. That's why the oil tax bill is so important to the legislature. They can use the extra money to make everybody happy."

Alma dropped her cigarette on the sidewalk and ground it out with her toe, then picked up the butt.

"Don't want to litter," she said. "It's not environmentally friendly."

Kane and Alma wound their way through the departing crowd, then climbed the steps. When they reached the entrance, Alma dropped her cigarette butt into an ashtray.

"Can you think of any reason Matthew Hope would have for murdering Melinda Foxx?" he asked.

Alma shook her head.

"I can't," she said, "but I can't think of any reason anyone else would, either."

They shook hands, and Kane found himself, as before, holding on to hers.

"Thanks for talking with me," he said.

"Oh," she said, "we'll have to see each other again."

"Why's that?" Kane asked.

"Well, because my boss will want to know all about you, and I'll only be able to find out so much by doing research," she said, smiling. "Besides, you'll soon learn that the best chance you have of getting anybody to tell you the truth here is to get them drunk."

Kane released her hand and held the door for her as they walked into the foyer.

"Maybe I could buy you dinner tonight, then," he said.

Alma smiled and put her hand on Kane's arm.

"That sounds perfect," she said. "I don't usually get off until seven or so, so maybe we could meet. Are you at the Baranof?"

Kane nodded.

"Let's meet in the bar and see what happens from there," Alma said.

"I should warn you, I don't drink," Kane said as she moved away.

"I should warn you," she called over her shoulder, "I do."

Democracy is a device that insures we shall be
governed no better than we deserve.

GEORGE BERNARD SHAW

Kane's cell phone rang as he was waiting for the elevator.

"Mr. Kane," a woman's voice said. "This is Mrs. Richard Foster. I was calling to see that you'd gotten settled in okay."

"If you mean, am I at work on the case, Mrs. Foster," Kane replied, walking away from the elevator, through the foyer, and out onto the steps, "I am."

The woman's laugh came through the telephone.

"I guess that is what I meant," she said. "I understand Mr. Doyle can be difficult, and I understand you don't suffer fools gladly."

Kane smiled.

"Oil Can may be as strange as a snake's suspenders," he said, "but he's not a fool. We'll get along fine, and if we don't I'll take his toupee hostage and threaten to starve it to death."

That brought an even bigger laugh.

"That toupee is something, isn't it?" she said. "The first time he saw it, my late husband said he'd trapped one just like it over by Lake Minchumina."

Kane's smile turned into a grin.

"I believe that," he said.

"Have you discovered anything yet?" the woman asked.

Kane watched people climb the hill, then enter one of the government buildings. Lunchtime here is like the tide, he thought. First it goes out, then it comes back in again.

"Only that Senator Hope might be a difficult client," Kane said. "He doesn't seem to want to cooperate with me or his attorney. Perhaps you could talk to him about that."

There was silence on the other end of the line.

"Perhaps I can," she said. "Well, I'm sure you're busy, so I'll let you go. Keep in touch. Good-bye."

Kane stood there for a moment, looking at the cell phone in his hand. Just what is going on there? he asked himself. Shaking his head, he put the cell phone away, went into the building, and rode the elevator to the fifth floor.

A couple of women were laying papers on the big table in the Senate Finance Committee room, and a couple of men sat talking quietly on one of the pewlike benches. Kane walked through the room, looking at nameplates next to the doors that opened off it. Senator O. B. Potter's office was at the far end. The reception area was dominated by a short flight of stairs that led to a fire door. The reception desk was empty. The door to Kane's right was closed, but the one to his left was open to a room stuffed with two big, metal cabinets, several metal bookshelves overflowing with paper, and two desks, one of which was occupied by a fit-looking man in his thirties reading a thick document and eating an egg-salad sandwich. He had tightly curled blond hair and a bulb beach tan. He wore a dark, chalk-stripe suit and a pink shirt, set off by an even pinker tie festooned with Looney Tunes characters. A black band circled his left biceps.

"Excuse me," Kane said. "I'm looking for Senator O. B. Potter."

"Take a number," the man said without looking up from his reading. "Everybody wants to see the Finance chairman."

I wonder how snotty he'd be if I cinched that tie up some more, Kane thought.

"I'm here to see Senator Potter on a matter not related to the Finance Committee," he said.

The edge in his voice drew the man's eyes from the document.

"No kidding?" he said. "Something like a murder? You're only the three-hundredth reporter to try to interview the senator. Or me. Or even the poor pages, who don't know a thing."

He shrugged.

"Not that I care. I don't do appointments," he said. "I should be writing a five-billion-dollar operating budget, but because Melinda managed to get herself killed, I'm reading some really long and boring backup on a bill to reauthorize the board of hairdressers. Can you believe it?"

"That sounds like a real tragedy," Kane said. "Can you tell me how to make an appointment with the senator?"

The man shook his head, took another bite of sandwich, and went back to his reading. Kane walked over and stood above him.

"I'm being polite, but I can be less polite," he said. "You may be a very important guy in this crowd, but I'm not part of this crowd. I'm not a reporter, either. I have a legitimate reason to see your boss, so if you continue to be so puffed up over how important you are, I might just decide to dribble you around the room to see how you bounce."

The man looked up at Kane and smiled.

"That's very butch," he said. "With a personality like yours, I can understand how you got that scar. I don't normally work in this little nest of offices, but I think that if you take a seat out in the committee room and wait, a mousy-looking, middle-aged woman named Anita will return from lunch and sit at the reception desk and you can ask her."

He popped the rest of the sandwich into his mouth, made a shooing gesture with his hand, and went back to his reading.

I guess I can beat the crap out of this guy, Kane thought, or sit and wait.

He walked out and sat in one of the chairs that lined the wall. People came and went, more coming than going, so the benches began to fill. The crowd seemed to be more women than men, overwhelmingly white and tending toward middle age. Most were wearing business clothes and carrying briefcases or armloads of files. A bearded kid in jeans and a polo shirt rolled a TV camera in and positioned it at the back of the room. A small woman hustled past Kane into Potter's office, hung up a coat, took a seat behind the reception desk, and put on a telephone headset. Kane went and stood in front of the desk.

The woman had generic brown hair of standard length and regular features. She wore a blouse, vest, and skirt of muted colors.

If she were any more ordinary, she'd disappear, Kane thought.

The woman seemed to be listening to something in her headset while writing on a message pad.

"My name is Nik Kane," he said. "I'd like to see Senator O. B. Potter."

She stopped writing, raised a hand, punched a button on the phone, listened, wrote some more, punched the button again, listened, wrote, punched, listened, wrote, punched. When she finished, she removed the headset.

"I'm sorry," she said, "but Senator Potter is very particular about getting his phone messages."

"You mean, Ms. Senator Potter is very particular," the man called from the adjoining office, stretching the "Ms." out until it sounded like a big bee buzzing.

"Oh, Ralph," the woman said. Then, to Kane: "He's such a scamp. How may I help you?"

Kane repeated what he'd said, which seemed to fluster the woman.

"I'm afraid the senator is very busy," she said. "Could you tell me what you'd like to see him about?"

"The murder of Melinda Foxx," Kane said.

That seemed to fluster the woman even more. She touched the black cloth circle on her arm and said, "Oh, what a terrible thing. Poor Melinda. Poor, poor Melinda." She seemed to gather herself. "But the senator has left strict instructions. No reporters. The reporters have been very brazen since the . . . since the tragedy."

"Can't blame him for that," Kane said. "But I'm not a reporter. I'm a detective."

"Are you with the authorities?" the woman asked.

"You mean, the investigators haven't been here?" Kane replied.

The woman must have heard the surprise in his voice.

"Well, not here in the office," she said. "Are you one of them?"

"I'm working for the defense, for Senator Matthew Hope," he said.

The name set the woman blinking very rapidly.

"Oh," she said. "I'm not sure what to do about that. Let me go ask."

She got to her feet, walked around Kane, knocked on the closed door, and let herself through.

"Good luck," the curly-haired man called, laughing.

After the woman had been gone several minutes, Kane stuck his head into the adjoining office.

"Is there a back way out of there?" he asked.

The man laughed.

"Nope," he said. "There's the way you came in and the fire escape. That's it."

He got to his feet, put on an overcoat, and climbed the stairs to the fire door.

"Smoke break," he said and went through the door, kicking a brick into the opening to keep the door from closing fully. Through the crack, Kane could see him light a cigarette, lean against the railing, and blow smoke into the air.

The door to the other office opened and the mousy woman came out, followed by another woman. The other woman was half Kane's age, nearly his height, and probably a significant fraction of his weight, but her shape would have made the Venus de Milo weep with envy. Her dark hair was cut short, and she wore understated makeup and a suit that was both conservatively cut and bright red. Her features, particularly her nose, were too strong to meet conventional ideas about beauty, but all in all she looked like a junior high school boy's wildest fantasy.

"Mr. Kane?" she said in a voice that sounded like angels singing, "I'm Letitia Potter. The senator is my father. May I help you?"

She held out a hand. Her nails were short and polished in the same color as her suit. Kane took the hand. It felt as cool and hard as marble.

"Pleased to meet you, Ms. Potter," he said. "As I told this lady here, I'm working for Matthew Hope's defense team and would like to speak to your father about Melinda Foxx. You, too. In fact, everyone who works in this office."

The woman nodded as Kane spoke, and when he was finished, said, "I'm not sure what my father could tell you. He and I were at home together the night poor Melinda died. They made me come in and identify the body. It was horrible."

Kane thought for a moment about the lack of emotion in her voice, then said, "Well, Ms. Potter, since Ms. Foxx worked for the senator, I was hoping there were some things he might tell me about her. Or perhaps you might. Or her coworkers."

The woman nodded again.

"Please, call me Letitia," she said. "Ms. Potter is so formal. And you are . . . Nik? Is that short for something?"

Kane nodded.

"For Nikiski," he said. "My father hoped to homestead there but never managed it."

"Nikiski. How Alaskan," the woman said, then paused. "I'm not sure what my father might be able to tell you, Nik. He can't see you now, because he's got a committee meeting in"—she looked at her watch—"three minutes. The other senators get so cranky if they're kept waiting. And I really think he, and I, and everyone else in the office should speak to the authorities before we discuss poor Melinda with anyone else. So perhaps you could leave a card, and we'll call you when it's an appropriate time to talk."

Kane tried to remember the last time he'd been told to kiss off so nicely, but couldn't bring anything to mind. So he handed the woman his card and walked out into the now-crowded committee room. At the door to the hall he stopped, turned around, and stood. The curly-haired man came back in from the fire escape, went into his office, and reappeared carrying a bunch of folders. He took a seat near the head of the committee table and spread the folders out in front of him.

A minute later, a short, solid-looking old man came out of Potter's office and took a chair at the head of the table. Letitia Potter followed him, moving like she was on ball bearings. She took a seat behind the old man. When they were seated, Kane could see a strong family resemblance in their hairlines and eyes and the jut of their jaws.

Senator O. B. Potter looked around, banged a gavel on the table, and said, "The committee will now come to order."

The small clumps of people who had been talking together broke up. Some took seats at the table. Others returned to the benches.

"Today's agenda is," Potter said, then paused as the curly-haired man crept forward to whisper in his ear. Potter picked up a piece of paper and read the names and titles of several bills in a strong, clear voice tinged with a southern accent. When he was finished he ran his fingers through his thick white hair and said, "Carrie, are you here to testify for the administration on the bill to extend the board of hairdressers and cosmetologists?"

A woman got up from the front bench and walked to a small table that faced the committee. She set several folders on the table, adjusted the microphone, and said, "Carrie Lawson for the Division of Occupational Licensing in the Department of Commerce, Community, and Economic Development, Mr. Chairman."

Potter nodded to her and said, "Please proceed."

The woman opened the top folder, picked up a piece of paper, and began reading.

If anyone at the committee table listened to the woman, he or she did a good job of concealing it. Potter leaned back to have a whispered conversation with the curly-haired man. A couple of the committee members read documents and made notes on legal pads. Another seemed to be reading through her mail. A young, thin, black-haired man got up from the table and walked past Kane, through the doorway, and out into the hall. As he passed, he jerked his head at an older man with a mustache, who got to his feet and followed him out. Members of the audience whispered to one another. People came and went.

The woman finished reading. Potter asked if anyone had any questions, thanked her, and asked if there were any other witnesses. A woman in a big, blond, beehive hairdo took the seat at the witness table, introduced herself as the director of the state's hairdressers association, and began reading a statement.

The other people in the room paid her every bit as much attention as they had her predecessor. The only person who seemed to be paying attention was Letitia Potter, and she seemed to be watching every activity in the room except the testimony. She sat with her elbows on the arms of her chair, her hands steepled in front of her face, and her lips pursed. Except for her darting eyes, she looked like a statue, a great statue by some long-dead Greek.

The committee did something with the bill, and Potter read off the next. Kane tore his eyes from Letitia Potter and left the room.

15

I tell you folks, all politics is applesauce.

WILL ROGERS

All Kane got from two more hours in the Capitol were the coffee jitters.

Mary David served him coffee and cookies, and thanked him for rescuing her from the press.

"I'm afraid I wasn't prepared for so much . . . intensity," she said. "We're not so in-your-face in the Native world."

Then she told him with a show of great reluctance that she wouldn't feel right talking to him without clearing it with her senator first.

The minority leader in the House of Representatives ground his own coffee and served Kane a brew thick enough to walk across. He said Matthew Hope had been an important member of the minority during his time in the House. He said Hope would make a fine governor. He said Hope was an unlikely murderer. He said he was happy to see an independent investigator involved in the case. He said all that very fast, interspersed with a barrage of bad puns.

The rest of the legislators seemed to be in committee meetings of some sort. Kane stuck his head into a couple of the meetings, but they looked as random and pointless as Potter's committee.

The hallways were thick with people. Staffers walked rapidly from place to place with folders under their arms, looking important. Small groups of men sat on chairs and benches in the hallways, chatting or talking on cell phones. On one floor, a dark-haired man in a suit interviewed somebody who looked a lot like V. I. Lenin in front of a TV camera. They had collected a crowd, either because people were interested in what the Lenin look-alike was saying, or because the interview all but blocked the hallway.

Kane tried stopping some of the staffers to talk, but they waved him off or met his questions with blank stares or noncommittal comments. He thought he might run into Dylan somewhere in the building, but didn't. He gave up for the day and left the Capitol.

As he picked his way down the icy sidewalk to Doyle's office, Kane felt jumpy and frustrated.

I have a client who won't talk, he thought, a lawyer who doesn't want me around, and a tribe or cult or whatever the hell you'd call the legislature that doesn't seem to want to talk to strangers.

His feet went out from under him as he crossed the last street before Doyle's office. He landed flat on his back. His head bounced on the ice. Stars danced in his eyes. The fall pounded the air from his lungs and left him gasping. A man and woman rushed over to help him to his feet.

"Are you all right?" the male half of the pair asked. It took a moment for Kane to recognize his son.

"Hello, Dylan," Kane said, taking his son's hand and practically pulling him down, too. He released the hand, rolled over on his hands and knees, and got carefully to his feet.

"Dad," Dylan said. "What are you doing here?"

Kane wanted to snarl like an injured animal, but he forced himself to stay calm and breathe.

"I'm here working on a case," Kane said, "when I'm not falling down and making a damn fool of myself."

"Oh, lots of people fall," the woman with Dylan said. She was small and pretty, maybe forty. Wisps of red and black hair stuck out from under her patchwork cap. "The sidewalks suck now. But a couple of warm days and it'll all be clear pavement again."

Kane looked at Dylan, then at the woman.

"I'm Nik Kane," he said, offering his hand. "Dylan's father."

The woman put her mittened hand into it and they shook.

"Samantha," she said. Then, to Dylan: "You didn't say your father would be in town."

"I didn't know," Dylan said to her. "But we have to get going or I'll be late for our staff meeting." Then, to Kane: "As long as you're going to be all right."

"I think I'll be fine," he said. The truth was that his back hurt and something that felt a lot like blood was creeping through his hair. But he was afraid that if he said anything about any of that, they would try to rush him to the hospital.

Dylan turned to walk off.

"Aren't you going to make arrangements to see your father?" Samantha asked.

Dylan turned, dug into a coat pocket, and handed Kane a card.

"I'm working for Representative Duckett," he said. "Give me a call and we'll get together."

Kane took the card.

"Thanks for the hand," he said.

Dylan and Samantha continued up the hill. Kane limped the remaining distance to Doyle's office, thinking: Now, that was a heart-warming reunion.

He did snarl when Helga tried to head him off. He blew by her into Doyle's office, sat down and ran through his day. When he got to Letitia Potter's implication that she hadn't talked to investigators yet, Doyle held up a forefinger.

"That's interesting," he said.

He picked up the telephone, punched in a series of numbers, and waited.

"Sean?" he said. "Francis Doyle. You want something on the White Rose investigation that didn't come from me?" He listened for a minute. "No, I'm not willing to talk to you on the record. I'm doing your goddamn legwork as it is. Do you want it or not?" He listened some more. "Okay, I'll give the story to somebody else. There's plenty of press in town." As he started to put the telephone down, Kane could hear a voice calling, "Wait. Wait." Doyle gave him one of his frightening smiles and put the receiver back to his ear. "You're going to have to check it out anyway, so you'll have more than one source. Anyway, here's the deal: The governor's office has taken over the Melinda Foxx investigation, and no one has talked to O. B. Potter or his staff yet." He waited. "Well, gee, Sean, I don't know. Does it sound political to you?" He waited some more. "Sure, sure. You know me. I'll be happy to share anything else that might help my client's case. Uh-huh. 'Bye." He put the phone down.

"That oughtta goose those bastards," he said.

"Not to mention calling the entire investigation into question," Kane said.

Doyle's face contorted again.

"I want you to stop doing that," Kane said.

"Stop doing what?" Doyle asked.

"Smiling," Kane said. "It creeps me out."

The lawyer looked at Kane and nodded.

"Other people have said the same thing," he said. "What are you going to do next?"

Kane put a hand to the back of his head and felt the big lump that was forming.

"I'm going back to the hotel to rest my old bones," he said, "then I'm having dinner and a barhop with Alma Atwood. Maybe if everybody but me gets liquored up, I'll actually learn something. What time is the bail hearing?"

"Ten a.m.," Doyle said, and gave him a room number.

"I'll see you there," Kane said. He got to his feet and left the office. Helga glared at him as he passed her desk.

"You have blood on your collar," she said in a voice ripe with satisfaction.

Kane stopped and turned to look at her.

"For just one minute in my whole life," he said, "I'd like to be as tough as you."

He took it slow going to the hotel. Every step jarred his aching head, and his back was stiff.

I'm probably doddering like an old man, he thought, but I don't care.

No messages awaited him at the hotel. Kane rode the elevator to his floor wondering if he had a concussion. But when he looked in the mirror in his bathroom, his pupils seemed to be the same size. He got ice at the machine down the hall, wrapped some in a washcloth, and held it to the lump on the back of his head.

This is exactly the sort of situation that's helped by three fingers of whiskey, he thought.

When frigid water from the melting ice began running down his hand and under his sleeve, Kane got to his feet, put the ice in the sink, and patted the back of his head dry. He shook out a couple of aspirin and swallowed them. He stripped off his clothes, set the alarm clock, and climbed into bed. He could hear voices and cars passing on the street, but he ignored them. He lay there wondering if, somehow, he'd pissed Alaska off and the damage it had just doled out was the place's way of telling him to beat it. The thought didn't make him smile. He was feeling his age and more, and the hand of depression rested on his shoulder as it often did during the winter. More often every year, he thought. Maybe I should leave.

Then he thought for a while about his son, wondering what he could do to bridge the gulf that had opened between them.

He fell asleep on that thought and dreamed he was being tried for un-Alaskan thoughts by the entire state legislature. Letitia Potter, wearing a very small bikini, was the prosecutor. Doyle was his lawyer, but all he did was play with his toupee, which scampered around the defense table knocking files to the floor. The jury was twelve Dylans. The verdict was unanimous and, as they put the noose around his neck, he woke up thrashing and sweating.

16

My final warning to you is always pay for your own drinks.
All the scandals in the world of politics today have their cause
in the despicable habit of swallowing free drinks.

Y. YAKIGAWA

Kane got out of bed feeling every second of his age. His head hurt and his back was as stiff as the price of a ticket to a Rolling Stones concert. He examined himself in the bathroom mirror and found that the bruises from his fall were forming nicely. He turned on the shower as hot as he could stand it, letting the warmth loosen his back muscles. He washed gingerly around his head wound, toweled off carefully, and dressed in slacks and a black turtleneck. Bending over to tie his shoelaces was no fun, but Kane managed it with a minimum of cursing. He slipped on a gray Harris tweed sport coat and examined the result in the mirror on the back of the closet door.

Not bad, he thought. You look like your grandfather going on a date.

Actually, Kane thought he looked pretty good with his clothes on.

He was down near his weight when he'd joined the police force, and his trips to the gym were paying off.

Take away the prison food and the booze, he thought, and losing weight's not so hard.

He stepped off the elevator into the spillover from some sort of party in what was normally the coffee shop. A banner over the door read: "Defenders of Alaska Families Welcomes the Legislature." People were drinking, chatting, and eating finger food. O. B. Potter and his daughter were talking to a cadaverous man with a bad haircut. Kane thought about going in and bracing them about Melinda Foxx, but decided against it. As an excuse to get another close look at Letitia Potter, that would work fine. As a method of actually getting information, he had his doubts.

All the tables in the bar were full, so he took the last empty stool and ordered a club soda. Tony set the glass down in front of him, slid a bowl of snack mix next to it, and nodded. Kane nodded back, turned, and surveyed the room. His time as a cop and a prisoner had given him an ability to read crowds for trouble, and he didn't see any here. Some forced joviality perhaps, but no trouble.

Alma Atwood moved through the bar, nodding and smiling to people like she knew them all. She was wearing a tight pair of jeans tucked into knee-length leather boots and what looked to Kane like a piece of underwear beneath a little sweater with one button. Her coat was over her arm. She stopped to talk to people at a couple of tables, then caught Kane's eye and walked over. When she got close enough, he let out a low whistle. Alma laughed.

"Guys don't do that anymore," she said. "It's sexist. Nice, but sexist."

"I guess I'm just trapped in the Dark Ages," he said.

Kane got off the stool and stood back so Alma could wiggle onto it.

"That's an operation worth watching," he said, sliding in to stand next to her.

Alma laughed again. Kane raised a finger. Tony looked over and nodded.

"I read up on you today," Alma said. "When I was done, I wasn't sure it was safe to come here."

"Why not?" Kane asked.

"The newspaper stories make you sound dangerous," she said.

Tony came over and stood in front of them. Alma ordered a Cosmopolitan. When Tony left to make her drink, Kane said, "Well, you can't believe everything you read in the newspapers."

Alma nodded.

"That's true," she said. "Some of the things they write about the legislature are so totally bogus. But, well, you have killed someone. And you've been in prison."

Kane thought about whether to correct her body count and decided not to. Instead, he said, "Yes, I have. I'm not proud of it."

Tony came back and set a pink drink in front of Alma. She picked it up and took a sip.

"Oh, that's so good," she said. She drank some more. "Are you bitter about prison? You were acquitted, after all."

"Exonerated," Kane said. "There's a difference."

He drank some club soda. He could tell by the way Alma sat and looked at him that she wanted an answer.

"I wasn't legally wrong to shoot that kid," he said. "I had the right to defend myself. But I was morally wrong. I was drunk. If I hadn't been drunk, I might have been able to handle the situation better, probably without shooting anyone. So I deserved what I got, no matter what the law says."

He drank some more club soda.

"Don't get me wrong," he said. "I hated prison. All 3,679,200 minutes of it. I hated not being free, being told what to do, living with a bunch of damaged men, knowing that my kids were growing up without me. I hated it all, but I can't say I didn't deserve it."

Alma reached over and laid her hand on his cheek.

"I'm so sorry," she said softly. Then: "You have children?"

"I have children nearly as old as you are," Kane said. "Two girls and a boy. The boy works here, in the legislature. His boss is someone named Representative Duckett."

Alma smiled.

"Is he dark-haired and thin?" she asked. "Named Dylan?"

"That's him," Kane said.

"Oh, he's very appealing, in a needs-mothering kind of way," she said. "And now that you mention it, I can see a family resemblance."

Her tone changed.

"Do you have a wife, too?"

Kane nodded.

"She's my ex-wife now," he said. "That's something else prison cost me. My marriage. I think. Maybe we wouldn't have made it to the finish line even if I hadn't spent time in prison. Who knows?"

Alma ran her hand along his cheek.

"And the scar?" she asked. "Is that prison, too?"

"It is," Kane said. "Some people get T-shirts to remind them of where they've been. I got this."

He laughed. It wasn't a pretty laugh.

"What do you say we talk about something that's not so depressing," he said. "Something that makes sense. Like politics. I still feel like I'm wandering in a strange country without a map."

Alma laughed, too, and took her hand away.

"Okay," she said. "Let's try to orient you. We'll begin with this room. Starting in the left corner, that's a table of people from the governor's office. The next two tables are oil company employees on a fly-in visit, lobbying against the oil tax. Then there's a lobbyist, his wife, and two members of the House and their wives. On our right are staffers from the Senate President's office, a lobbyist with some clients, and a table of—how odd, I don't know those people. Here at the bar are three researchers on the nonpartisan legislative staff, a lobbyist, us and a couple of reporters."

"Do people always sit only with their own kind?" Kane asked.

Alma finished her drink.

"This early in the evening, yes," she said, "but later on we might see anything."

Kane signaled the bartender.

"That was an impressive display," Kane said, "but you left out the two women at that end of the bar."

Alma dropped her eyes and smiled.

"Those are two of my girlfriends," she said. "They wanted to see what you looked like."

Kane laughed.

"Hope I pass muster," he said.

"I'm sure you do," Alma said. "Now, why don't you tell me about your adventures in the legislature today."

Kane recounted his doings in the Capitol and Alma explained what he'd seen. The bills in the Finance Committee were foregone conclusions, so nobody had to pay much attention. The men sitting in the hallway were lobbyists; they couldn't have offices in the building, so they hung out waiting to buttonhole whoever they were after. Staffers were always trying to impress people with their importance, so they couldn't talk to just anybody in the hall. And so on.

This topic took them through the second drink and into the hotel dining room. It was packed, but a harried-looking maître d' managed to find them a corner table. Kane held Alma's chair, then sat and looked around the room in silence.

"Penny," she said.

"I was just wondering," Kane said, "if we got this table because the bellmen said I was a good tipper, or because you look like a three-alarm fire."

Alma dropped her eyes again and, if Kane wasn't mistaken, blushed. That's a good sign, he thought. She can still blush.

A waiter came over and put a Cosmopolitan in front of Alma and a club soda in front of Kane.

"Compliments of Mr. Bezhdetny," he said and left.

"Mr. Bezhdetny?" Kane said.

"Over there," Alma said, nodding toward a table. "George Bezhdetny, the lobbyist who took my senator to lunch today."

Kane could see the big, white man looking at them, so he raised his glass and inclined his head. Alma did the same.

"He's an odd-looking guy," Kane said. "Who does he work for?"

"Most lobbyists have more than one client," Alma said. "I can't keep track of who hires whom. Besides, George is kind of a lightweight."

"Lightweight?" Kane said. "A guy that size?"

"Political lightweight," Alma said. "There are something like two hundred and fifty people who lobby the legislature professionally every year. Maybe twenty percent of them have important clients and make what you or I would think is big money. The rest have clients that aren't so important and just make a living, or even part of a living, from lobbying. George has always been in that second group. Although, now that I think of it, he does seem to be spending a lot more money recently. Maybe he's got some new clients, with money."

They looked at the menus for a while, then made small talk. The waiter came over to take their orders.

"I'm not sure what I want," Alma said, picking up her menu again.

"You can have it all, sweetie," the waiter said. "Mr. Bezhdetny is buying."

"No, he's not," Kane said.

Alma laid a hand on his arm.

"Let him," Alma said. "It's what they do."

"It may be what he does," Kane said, "but it's not what I do."

He laid his napkin on his plate, got to his feet, and walked to the lobbyists' table. There were a dozen people arranged around it. Everyone looked up at him.

"Mr. Bezhdetny," he said, "I want to thank you for the drink and your kind offer of dinner, but I must decline."

"It's George," Bezhdetny said. "May I ask why not?"

"Well," Kane said, "if you know why I'm here . . ."

"Everybody in town knows why you're here by now," said a woman who had obviously had plenty to drink.

"Anyway," Kane said, "my job requires me to act on behalf of my client. I can't have any conflicts about that."

"Good God," one of the male diners said scornfully, "it's only dinner."

Kane recognized him as one of the senators who hadn't been paying attention during the Finance Committee meeting.

"I know," Kane said to him with a smile, "that's how it starts, isn't it, Senator?"

He nodded to Bezhdetny, whose face had turned red. Embarrassed? Pissed off? Kane didn't really care.

"Thanks anyway, George," he said and returned to his table.

"Well, you're a snappy one, aren't you?" the waiter said.

"What I am is a good tipper," Kane said levelly, "if I like the service."

"Point taken," the waiter said. He took their orders, then left.

"People will be talking about that," Alma said. "I don't think anyone's turned down a free meal in this town since the glaciers receded."

"Yeah, well, maybe they should," Kane said. "But let's talk about something else. Where in Minnesota are you from?"

So Kane learned that Alma had been born in Bob Dylan's hometown, Hibbing, and that she'd come up one summer in college to work as a seasonal park volunteer, liked it, and come back after graduation.

"My degree is actually in resource management," she said. "I just sort of fell into political work."

The talk went on like that through dinner, Alma asking questions about Kane and answering questions about herself. She had a glass of wine with dinner, then another. Kane thought about saying something, but decided that it wasn't his business to monitor her alcohol intake. The room was warm and pleasantly noisy, the food adequate, and the company interesting. The dining room was nearly empty when Kane signaled for the check.

Buttoned into their coats, they left the hotel and walked downhill. Alma put her arm through his and her hip bumped him with every other step.

"This is really fun," she said, "but the place we're going might take some getting used to."

The place was a small, dark bar shaped like a triangle, full of smoke and noise and people. Several shouted greetings to Alma as they entered. The bar ran along two sides of the room, then bulged out in a U. The area in between was jammed with people standing, drinking, and trying to converse over the din. Much of the bar was lined three deep with people waiting to order. Alma led Kane through the crowd to a couple of empty stools at the far end of the U. She draped her coat over the stool and sat down on it. Kane sat next to her.

"Damn, just finding a seat makes you thirsty," she said.

Kane waved at the bartender.

"In a minute, honey," she called to him.

A guy turned away from the bar balancing a tray.

"Shots, shots, shots," the crowd chanted.

The guy lowered the tray and hands snatched shot glasses from it.

"Shots, shots, shots," the crowd chanted.

The green liquid in the shot glasses looked like mouthwash or dish soap. The guy plucked the last shot glass from the tray, lowered the tray, and held the glass up high.

"Shots, shots, shots," the crowd chanted.

"Three, two, one, down the hatch," the guy yelled and sank his shot. Everyone else with a glass did the same. The guy gave an exaggerated shiver, then held up the tray. Hands put the empty glasses on it and he turned toward the bar again.

Most of the people in the room were Alma's age or younger.

"These all staffers?" Kane asked, raising his voice to be heard over the crowd.

"Most," Alma replied. "The guy buying the drinks is a lobbyist. There are a couple more of them in here, two legislators I can see, and a couple of reporters."

The bartender reached them.

"Hi, Alma," she said. "Mad in here tonight. What can I get you?"

"I want a Cosmo," Alma said. "And he wants . . . What do you want?"

"Club soda," Kane said, "with a twist."

"Club soda?" Alma said. "Why're you drinking club soda?"

"Because if I drank anything stronger," Kane said, "I might shoot somebody else."

Alma giggled.

"Reeeally?" she said. "Are you carrying a gun?"

Kane shook his head. The bartender brought their drinks and Alma took a gulp of hers. Kane took a $50 bill from his wallet and put it on the bar. The bartender whisked it away and brought back a pile of smaller bills. Kane left them on the bar.

"Alma-Alma-Alma," a voice called from across the room. Kane could see a young man waving her over.

"That's the Senate President's aide," Alma said. "I gotta go—I gotta go talk to him. Don't go away. I'll be back."

She picked up her drink, kissed Kane on the cheek, and set off through the crowd. Kane sat and watched the scene. People talked earnestly in twos or threes, the groups breaking up to re-form with new members. In a corner, a long-haired young woman dressed in office clothes cried in earnest. A small woman with short, streaked hair stood with her back to Kane, trying to comfort her. The bartender roused a guy who had been sleeping with his head on the bar, and he lurched to his feet and stumbled toward the door.

The crowd opened up to Kane's right and he could see several people sitting at what appeared to be the bar's only table. The people were all young women except for one older, dark-haired guy with glasses. As Kane watched, he took off his glasses and stretched something over his head to cover his nose. He took deep breaths through his mouth and blew through his nose. The thing on his head grew. The curly-haired guy from Potter's office detached himself from one of the groups, walked over, and sat down on Alma's stool.

"Christ, what a day," he said and waved an empty glass at the bartender.

The thing on the guy's head was still growing. The women at the table were giggling. The curly-haired guy looked over at the table.

"Sam," he yelled, "Sam, Sam, Sam."

Other people picked up the call, and soon everyone was chanting, "Sam, Sam, Sam."

"What's that thing on his head?" Kane asked.

"Condom," the curly-haired guy said. "That's his trick. He blows up a condom until it pops. Says it impresses the women."

The condom had reached ridiculous proportions.

"Sam," the crowd chanted, "Sam, Sam, Sam."

The crowd was rewarded with the sharp crack of the condom exploding. Everyone cheered, then went back to what they were doing.

"Some trick," Kane said.

"Everybody wants to stand out around here," the curly-haired guy said.

The bartender put a full glass in front of the curly-haired guy.

"There you are, Ralph," she said.

"I'll get that one," Kane said. The bartender plucked some bills from his and went off.

"Thanks," the curly-haired guy said. "I'm Ralph Stansfield."

"Nik Kane," Kane said.

They shook hands. Stansfield took a good pull on his drink and said, "So what did you think of Ms. Senator Potter?"

"She's really something," Kane said.

"She is that," Stansfield said. "She really keeps the office humping. I mean, humming."

It was only when he giggled that Kane realized he'd had a lot to drink.

"You work there long?" he asked.

"Long enough," Stansfield said. "I'm like the furniture. I go with the office. I know budgets, so whoever gets the chairmanship, I work for them. Until now."

"Trouble?" Kane asked.

"Not really," Stansfield said. "Ms. Senator Potter thinks maybe they need somebody who is a little more ideo . . . ideologically pure. But I think I can convince her they don't. Yes, I can do that."

He giggled again and took another drink.

"What was Melinda Foxx like to work with?" Kane asked.

"Didn't really work with her," Stansfield said. "She did bills and, like I said, I do budgets. But she seemed okay. Ambitious, though, and a little naive. I'm sur . . . sur . . . surprised she lasted so long in that office, with Ms. Senator Potter there. The office was too small to hold all that ambition. Thank God I don't have any. Just want to be left alone to do my job."

He finished his drink and held up the empty glass.

"Look at this place," he said. "Nothing but power and greed and sex. Everybody's getting some. Like that woman you're with, Alma, Alma, what's her name, Miss Thing there, she's been doing old Grantham for years. But I hear he's just replaced her with the younger item who answers his phone. Lucky for you, not so lucky for her. This is no place to get old if you're a woman staffer. But until you do, you can always get some. Like those two."

He nodded to the woman who'd been crying and the woman who had been trying to comfort her. They were kissing passionately.

"How about Melinda Foxx?" Kane said. "Was she getting any?"

The bartender put another drink in front of Stansfield, looked at Kane, and, when he nodded, took some more bills.

"Oh, yes," Stansfield said. "Oh, yes, she was getting her monkey petted, all right."

"Who by?" Kane asked.

Stansfield giggled.

"Oh, I'll never tell," he said, shaking his head. "No, no I won't."

"Was it you?" Kane asked.

That set off a giggling fit. When Stansfield had himself under control, he said, "Nope. Wasn't me. Not my type."

"Not your type?" Kane said. "Why not?"

"She didn't have a penis," Stansfield said, then giggled some more.

"Oh," Kane said, hoping he didn't sound as embarrassed as he felt.

"We don't all flounce, you know," Stansfield said. "Particularly those of us who work for Christian right senators with harpy daughters."

"I suppose not," Kane said. "So it wasn't you. Who was it?"

"Won't say," Stansfield said, "won't say. Unless maybe it's pillow talk."

Kane shook his head.

"Thanks for asking," he said, "but I'm afraid you're not my type, either."

"Is it the penis?" Stansfield asked.

"It's the penis," Kane said.

"I figured," Stansfield said, "but if you don't ask, you don't know."

He slid off the bar stool and grabbed his glass.

"Thanks for the drink," he said and walked off, moving like a man crossing a tightrope.

Time passed. People came and went. Kane got cruised by a couple of young women who went back, giggling, to their groups of friends. In between their visits, he spent a long time listening to a man tell him why it was important to change the rules governing the catching of various types of salmon. The man spoke earnestly and in great detail, apparently mistaking Kane for someone worth talking to.

From time to time, the crowd chanted, "Shots, shots, shots." Kane noticed that Alma's was among the hands plucking full shot glasses from the tray and putting empty ones back. He was about ready to leave the bar when she returned and threw her arms around his neck.

"I want to go," she said. "I want you to take . . . to take me home and—and fork me 'til I can't stand up."

She hiccuped, giggled, and belched booze into Kane's face. Then she let go of his neck and stepped to the side like somebody trying to compensate for the rolling of a ship. Kane put an arm around her waist to steady her and slid off his stool.

She leaned into him and said, "Did I say fork? I meant . . ."

Kane put his finger on her lips.

"I know what you meant," he said, "but you already can't stand up. Let's get you home."

He looked at his change on the bar, plucked a $20 bill from it, and left the rest for a tip. Still balancing Alma, he managed to get into his coat and maneuver her into hers. He steered her through the crowd and out into the cold.

"Where's your car?" he asked.

"My carsh," Alma said, wobbling. "My carsh. I don't know."

Kane pulled her closer to steady her. She giggled and nuzzled his neck. He took his cell phone from his pocket and, one-handed, flipped it open and called Cocoa.

"You working?" he asked. "Thank God. I'm in front of the Triangle. Come get me."

He put the phone away.

"Ooh, I need to lay down," Alma said. "I need you to lay down with me."

"I know," Kane said. "We're going to your place now."

Cocoa's cab came around the corner and stopped. He rolled his window down.

"Need help?" he asked, grinning.

Together, they eased Alma into the backseat and belted her in.

"She pukes in my cab, you're paying to have it cleaned," Cocoa said, as they both climbed into the front.

"Sit with me, sit with me," Alma called.

"Better sit with her," Cocoa said. "They're very unpredictable when they're like this. I know. I'm a cabbie."

Kane got out and into the backseat.

"Where are we going?" Cocoa asked.

"Good question," Kane said. "Alma—where do you live, Alma?"

"Good luck," Cocoa said.

Alma giggled.

"I live at home," she said.

Kane sighed and put his hand into one of her coat pockets, then the other. He found keys and a hairbrush and some tissues. He patted her jeans and her sweater but found nothing.

"Hmm, I like that," Alma said. "Pat me s'more."

"Crap," Kane said.

"Try the coat again," Cocoa said. "Inside pocket, maybe."

Cocoa was right. There was an inside breast pocket and buttoned inside it was a wallet. All the ID bore an Anchorage address, but folded up and shoved into the change purse was a receipt for a security deposit. Kane read the address off.

"Good detective work," Cocoa said. "Of course, I already knew where she lived. I've driven Alma home many times, haven't I, Alma? Her and pretty much everybody else who works in the legislature."

"You're a scream," Kane said.

"Yeah, ain't I," Cocoa said. He put the cab in gear. Kane put the paper back in the wallet and the wallet back in the pocket.

"Kiss me," Alma said and passed out against him. He arranged himself on the seat and held her as Cocoa drove.

"Where'd you find her?" Cocoa asked.

"Won her in a raffle," Kane said.

Cocoa laughed.

"What was she, third prize?" he asked.

"Just drive," Kane said.

They went over the long bridge between Juneau and Douglas Island and bore to the left along a two-lane lined with condos and apartments. Kane thought about the scene in the bar and the fact that most of those people had to be at work the next day.

Ah, to be young and stupid again, he thought.

Cocoa slowed and turned left. He drove downhill, then turned right into the driveway in front of a small, square, brown house.

"This is it," he said. "Hers is the downstairs."

"What downstairs?" Kane said.

"There's actual beach on the island," Cocoa said. "These places are built on a slope down to it. Gives everybody a water view. Her door is down the sidewalk there."

"You know an awful lot about this," Kane said.

"Like I said, I been driving Alma home for years," Cocoa said, "more often than not from a bar."

Kane took the keys from Alma's pocket, got out of the cab, and walked quietly down the sidewalk. He found a door and tried the most likely-looking key. The door opened. He closed it and walked back to the cab.

"Help me get her inside," he said.

Cocoa got out and the two of them extracted Alma from the cab and half walked, half carried her into the apartment. They sat her on the couch. She fell over on her side.

Kane thought about all the times he'd been in Alma's condition.

"I can't leave her like this," Kane said.

"You do what you need to do," Cocoa said. "I'm going back to the cab. Want me to wait?"

Kane looked at him.

"You abandon me here," he said, "and I'll hunt you down and kill you like the dog you are."

Cocoa laughed and left the apartment. Kane picked Alma up, carried her to the bedroom, and laid her on the bed. He took off her boots and sweater and loosened her jeans. Her breathing was shallow and her color wasn't good.

"You've had too much," Kane said.

He went out to the kitchen, found a big, pink plastic glass, and poured salt into it. He filled it with lukewarm water and carried it into the bathroom. He found a big towel and took it into the bedroom. He got Alma more or less on her feet, wrapped the towel around her neck, and shuffled her into the bathroom. He positioned her in front of the toilet, picked up the glass, and put it to her lips.

"Drink this," he said.

She drank, then started to struggle. He kept the glass against her lips and poured the contents slowly into her. She fought and gasped and choked. When the glass was empty, he set it down. She stood quietly for a moment, then her eyes snapped open.

"What have you done to me?" she asked, and vomited. Kane tried to keep her head aimed at the toilet as all the booze she'd drunk and every morsel she'd eaten came back up.

It took a long time. She groaned and slumped against him when she was finished. He wet a washcloth and wiped vomit off her mouth and neck and the tops of her breasts, then walked with her back into the bedroom. Her breathing was stronger and her color was better. He laid her on the bed again, put a blanket over her, and propped a pillow against her back so that she couldn't roll onto it and drown if she vomited again.

Kane rummaged in the kitchen, found rubber gloves, paper towels, and 409, and cleaned the bathroom as best he could. He knotted everything inside a plastic grocery bag and put it in the garbage. Then he washed his hands, checked on Alma once more, and walked into the living room. He took the $20 bill from his pocket, laid it on the counter, and found some little sticky notes with hearts on them and a pen. He wrote "cab fare" on one of them and stuck it to the bill. He set her keys on top of the note, left the apartment, making sure the door locked behind him, and joined Cocoa in the cab. Cocoa was reading a thick book called *Guns, Germs and Steel.*

"So," he said, leering at Kane over the book, "what happened in there?"

"What do you think happened in there?" Kane said. "I poured salt water into her until she barfed."

"Sweet," Cocoa said. "I always say, you don't really know a woman until you've seen her puke. Back to the hotel?"

Kane nodded and closed his eyes. Cocoa marked his page, set the book down, and put the cab into gear. They drove off. Neither man said anything as the cab made its way back downtown.

It was nearly 1 a.m. when Kane walked into the hotel.

"Oh, Mr. Kane," the night desk clerk called. He held up a big, bulky brown shipping envelope. "Someone left this for you."

Kane walked over, took the envelope, and got into the elevator.

Probably something from Doyle, he thought as the elevator lifted him to his floor. God, do I need some sleep.

In his room, he tore open the envelope and dumped the contents on his bed. It was a large plastic bag. Sealed in the bag was a dead cat, its head attached to its body by only a flap of skin. A note pinned to the plastic bag read, "Leave or it's you next."

Kane looked at the cat and the note. It seemed needlessly cruel to kill a cat just to scare him, particularly when it didn't work. He thought about calling the cops, then thought about the time it would take for them to get there, take his statement, and ask questions. He was just too tired for all that. He put the cat back into the shipping envelope, put the envelope in the closet, and shut the door. Then he got ready for bed. He was asleep the moment his head hit the pillow, and he didn't dream of dead cats or live women or anything at all.

Men are moved by only two things: fear and self-interest.

NAPOLEON BONAPARTE

The beeping of Kane's travel alarm sounded as loud as the backup warning of a truck about to run over him. He groped around and managed to knock the alarm off the bedside table. It lay on the floor, still beeping. He said a bad word loudly, but that didn't make him feel any better. He felt around, found the alarm and silenced it, then lay back. Tension locked his neck muscles, his ears rang from all the bar noise, and the secondhand tobacco smoke left the inside of his mouth feeling like something foul had crawled into it and died.

Great, he thought. I didn't have a drop to drink and I've got a hangover anyway.

Kane groaned his way out of bed and stood under the hot shower for a long time, then turned the handle all the way to cold and capered around under the icy blast for as long as he could stand it. As he toweled himself off, he looked in the mirror and inventoried the damage of aging and a life lived hard.

Just a collection of scars, wrinkles, and bags, he thought. It's a good thing that poor woman passed out and didn't have to see this.

He put on his suit and looked around the room. He walked to the closet, opened it, and picked the envelope up off the floor. Then he looked at the automatic. No sense carrying it to the police station, he thought. Or trying to get it through security at the court building.

He left his room, stopped at the bellman's station, and asked, "What do you people use to keep your feet around here?"

"Cat-quick reflexes," the bellman said. "But those Yak things, the ones that go over your shoes, they help. You can buy some at the outdoor store across the street."

Kane did, and, walking out of the store, found that he was much steadier on his feet. The minute he stepped on the linoleum floor of the coffee shop, though, his foot tried to slide out from under him.

"That's the downside of those things," the guy behind the counter said. "If they can't dig in, they're like ice skates."

Kane sat on a chair and pulled them off. He got the biggest cup of coffee the place sold and a bagel with egg and cheese and sat at a table eating and watching people come and go. Most everyone else seemed to know one another, and from their conversation he gathered that many worked for the legislature. They were, for the most part, young and healthy looking, and watching them made Kane feel older and more used up.

Letitia Potter entered the coffee shop and got in line. In a few minutes she turned to go, a bag of bagels in one hand and a cardboard carrier studded with paper cups of coffee in the other. When she got to the door, Kane got to his feet and opened it for her.

"Thank you," she said, then seemed to realize she'd seen Kane before.

"Hello," she said. "You're the man from Nikiski, aren't you?"

"Close enough," Kane said. "Do you have a moment to talk?"

She shook her head.

"Not really," she said, paused, and went on, "Oh, why not."

Kane moved the envelope off the table. Letitia set her purchases on it and sat down. She worked one of the cups loose from the carrier, took a sip, and opened the bag.

"Bagel?" she asked.

Kane pointed at the crumbs of his breakfast and shook his head. Letitia removed a bagel. As Kane watched, she sawed the bagel in half with a plastic knife, spread cream cheese on it, and ate it with ferocious concentration, washing each bite down with a sip of coffee, not pausing until she was finished.

"I was hungry," she said.

"I can see that," Kane said. "Ms. Potter, I was hoping you could answer a few questions about Melinda Foxx."

Letitia looked at Kane. He could read nothing in her eyes.

"I'm afraid I didn't know her very well," she said. "We just worked together. Or, rather, she worked. I'm a volunteer. The stupid rules won't let me work for pay in my daddy's office."

"That's too bad," Kane said. "What can you tell me about Melinda?"

Letitia shrugged.

"She was a good worker," she said. "That's all."

She paused, then smiled.

"She had very good penmanship."

That seemed to exhaust the subject for Letitia. She reached out to touch Kane's scar, then pulled her hand back.

"Did that hurt a lot?" she asked. "It must have hurt a lot."

She gave a little shiver. Revulsion? Excitement? Kane found he couldn't read her at all.

"Did you know anything about her personal life?" Kane asked. "Was she involved with anyone?"

"We aren't a family, Mr. Nikiski," she said. "I mean, my daddy and I are, but the others just work there. We aren't involved in their personal lives, and they aren't involved in ours."

She gave a little nod and got to her feet.

"I have to get this up to my daddy and his friends," she said. She picked up the bag and the coffees and turned to go.

"Ralph Stansfield says she was involved with someone," Kane said.

Letitia turned back so fast one of the coffees toppled from the holder and burst open on the floor.

"Oh, no," Letitia said, her voice sounding like a little girl's. "Daddy will be angry."

"Let me get another one," Kane said. "What was it?"

She told Kane, and he went to the counter and ordered.

Kane tried again to draw her out, but Letitia stood silently until the coffee was handed over the counter. She put it into the carrier. Kane handed her the bag of bagels and their hands brushed and he felt . . . nothing. No warmth, no spark. Nothing.

I know your libido diminishes with age, he thought, but this is ridiculous.

He picked up his envelope and put it back on the table, then swung the door open for Letitia.

"What's in the envelope?" she asked, her voice a woman's again.

"A dead cat," Kane said.

Letitia looked at him without expression, turned, and walked toward the Capitol.

Kane looked at his watch. If he moved fast, he had time to report his "gift" to the police and still make Hope's bail hearing. He put his ice grippers back on, crept across the linoleum and back out onto the ice.

He explained his errand to the same woman at the front desk of the police station, sat, and waited. Crawford came out and led Kane to his desk. Malone sat, as before, facing them.

"Now what?" Crawford said.

"This," Kane said, setting the envelope on Crawford's desk. "Somebody left it for me at the hotel last night."

Crawford prodded the envelope with a pen.

"What is it?" he asked.

"It's open," Kane said. "See for yourself."

Crawford picked up the envelope, tilted it and shook. The plastic bag containing the dead cat slid onto his desk. He leaped to his feet, sending his chair shooting backward.

"Jesus Christ, bubba," he yelled, "is this your idea of a joke?"

Kane shook his head.

"No joke, Tank," Kane said. "Somebody's trying to scare me. Read the note."

Crawford flipped the plastic bag over with his pen and read the note.

"Somebody doesn't like you," he said.

"Yeah, and we both know who it is," he said. "Or, rather, you do. I know what the two of them look like, but you know who they are."

"Can you prove it was them?" Crawford said.

"You're the cop," Kane said. "There's the evidence. You prove it."

"Hey," Malone said. "Hey, you two."

Crawford walked to a coatrack, removed an overcoat from a hanger, and shrugged his way into it.

"Let's walk," he said to Kane.

Kane followed him out onto the sidewalk. Crawford led him across a street and onto the wharf. Crawford moved across the icy ground like he was skating. They walked along until the cop turned and leaned on the railing. Kane followed suit.

"I don't know who those guys are, Kane," Crawford said. "I could probably find out, but why would I bother? Nobody's going to prosecute them for killing a cat, even if we could prove they did it."

"What about the threat?" Kane asked.

"You want them on something sure to get kicked down to a misde-meanor?" Crawford asked.

"No," Kane said, "I want to know who they are and who they're working for."

"Well, I can't tell you that and I ain't finding out," Crawford said, his voice harsh.

"What the hell is going on, Crawford?" he said. He could hear the anger in his own voice.

"That's all I'm telling you about this," Crawford said. "But I will tell you, you've got some powerful people taking an interest in you, and not in a good way. So like I said yesterday, watch your ass."

Kane realized that his hands were knotted into fists. He relaxed them slowly. Taking his irritation out on Crawford wouldn't help any-thing. Besides, Tank might kick his ass.

"Why'd you bring me out here, Tank?" he asked. "You could have told me this at the station."

Crawford swept a hand across the scene in front of them.

"I like looking at the water," he said. "It calms me down. I like to think about doing something simpler, like being out in a boat, fishing. There are king salmon that swim through here even in winter, feeding, getting ready to run up the rivers to British Columbia in the spring to spawn. They're good fighters and great eating, really moist from the fat that insulates them against the cold water. There are days I like my job and days I'd rather be fishing. Lately, there are more days I'd rather be fishing. This is one of them."

Crawford straightened up.

"Like I said, bubba, watch yourself," he said and walked back toward the police station.

18

A judge is a lawyer who knows a politician.

ANONYMOUS

Kane walked thoughtfully up the hill to the court building. He cleared security, sat, removed his ice grippers, and put them into his pocket.

All this putting them on and taking them off, he thought. I guess this isn't a very practical solution to the ice problem.

He looked at the directory and found the courtroom. It was small, with only three rows of wooden benches for spectators. The benches were nearly full, and almost everyone on them looked like a reporter of some sort. The man Kane had shoved around the day before gave him a hard look. Kane responded with a big smile and took a seat in the back, squeezing between a pair of old-timers who looked like regulars. One of them was sitting on a padded seat she'd brought along, and the other had a yellow pad balanced on one knee and a pen in his hand.

Every courthouse Kane had ever been in had its regulars, older people who used up their days watching the real-life dramas that played out in courtrooms.

"Courtroom always this full?" he asked the woman.

The woman shook her head.

"Nope," she said. "Most days it's just me and Herman there, maybe some family members or friends. But this is a big case. Murder, and it's political, too."

Doyle was sitting at a table inside the low railing that separated the spectators from the actors. A tall, dark-haired man and a short, stout woman with flyaway hair sat at the other table. The jury box was empty. A woman sat at a desk next to the judge's dais, fiddling with paperwork. She looked up at the clock on the wall, then at the lawyers.

"Are we ready for the defendant?" she asked.

The lawyers nodded, and she pushed a button on her desk. Matthew Hope came through a side door, wearing handcuffs and an orange jumpsuit. The orange suit would make him stand out better if he made a break for it. He was accompanied by a state trooper wearing a flak vest. Camera shutters clicked. The trooper herded him into the seat next to Doyle. He leaned over and removed Hope's handcuffs, then walked back to the door he'd come through and leaned against the wall.

The woman at the desk looked around, nodded to the lawyers, and pushed another button. The door behind her opened and a short, frizzy-headed guy in a black robe walked into the room. The woman and the lawyers and the spectators got to their feet.

"Superior court in and for the state of Alaska is now in session, the Honorable Gerald Sellers presiding," the woman said.

"That's funny," the woman next to Kane whispered. "This is supposed to be old Judge Ritter's courtroom."

The judge mounted some steps and sat down on the dais.

"Please be seated," he said, looking around the room.

"He's a good one," the woman whispered to Kane, "not one of these political hacks."

The man on the other side of Kane was writing furiously on the legal pad in what looked like pictographs. He muttered quietly to himself as he wrote.

"The first case is *State of Alaska v. Hope,* a charge of murder in the second degree, petition for bail," the clerk said.

"Mr. Doyle," the judge said, looking at Oil Can, "how would the defense like to proceed?"

Doyle got to his feet.

"Your Honor," he said, "my client is a member of the Alaska State Senate, a man without a criminal record, and the state has not seen fit to bring its case to a grand jury. We request release on his own recognizance."

Doyle sat down.

The dark-haired man and the woman had been whispering furiously during Doyle's remarks.

"Mr. Davies?" the judge said.

The pair continued whispering.

"Who are the other lawyers?" Kane asked the woman.

"The guy is Bob Davies," she said. "He's an assistant district attorney who tries lots of cases here. But I don't know the woman."

"Mr. Davies?" the judge said sharply.

The dark-haired man got slowly to his feet.

"Sorry, Your Honor," he said. "We were expecting Judge Ritter."

The judge nodded.

"Judge Ritter is ill and I've been assigned to take his cases today," he said.

"Old sot's probably got the brown bottle flu," the woman whispered.

The dark-haired man shuffled some papers on the table in front of him.

"Your Honor," he said, "the state has substantial evidence linking the defendant to this crime and expects DNA evidence that is being processed now to provide more. We anticipate going to the grand jury soon, and ask that he be held in custody until then."

Doyle was on his feet like he'd been shot from a cannon. The judge held up his hand.

"I'll hear from you in a moment, Mr. Doyle," the judge said. "Now, then, did I hear you correctly, Mr. Davies? The state wants to keep Senator Hope here in jail because it might have more evidence that might result in an indictment?"

The dark-haired man shifted from one foot to the other and looked at the woman sitting next to him.

"Well, Your Honor, it's more than that," he said. "The defendant was found with the body and—"

The judge cut him off.

"I've read the file, Mr. Davies," he said. You could have used the tone in his voice to cut diamonds. "Is that all you've got?"

The dark-haired man looked at the woman again.

"Mr. Davies," the judge said, "are you in charge of this case or not?"

The dark-haired man looked at the judge.

"Well," he said hesitantly, "yes, Your Honor, I am."

"Then," the judge said, "who is this woman who is so clearly giving you orders?"

"Your Honor," the dark-haired man said.

"Don't 'Your Honor' me," the judge said. "Kindly identify your associate. I don't like strangers in my court."

The dark-haired man said, "This is Miss Talia Dufresne, Your Honor."

"See?" the judge said. "That wasn't so hard. Does Ms. Dufresne work for the district attorney's office?"

The dark-haired man seemed to be squirming now.

"No, Your Honor," he said.

There was a moment of silence.

"Well," the judge said, "what's she doing here, then?"

More silence.

"Mr. Davies," the judge said, his voice heavy with warning.

"Ms. Dufresne works for the governor's office," the dark-haired man said. "She's here observing."

That set the spectators buzzing. Photographers tried to get a better angle on the woman, and the clicking of their cameras joined the hubbub.

"Your Honor," Oil Can squeaked.

The judge held up his hand again.

"Not yet, Mr. Doyle," he said, "I think I can handle this one. You spectators, please be quiet."

The noise stopped.

"Is Ms. Dufresne a part of the prosecution team, then, Mr. Davies?" the judge asked.

The dark-haired man squirmed some more.

"Well, not exactly, Your Honor," he said. "She's more of an advisor."

The judge nodded.

"If your presentation here is based on her advice, Mr. Davies, I'd tell you to get a new advisor," the judge said. "You and I and everyone else in this courtroom know that Senator Hope is entitled to bail as a matter of settled constitutional law in Alaska, unless you can show the most unusual and exigent circumstances. Can you do that?"

The dark-haired man shook his head.

"No, Your Honor," he said.

"Then sit down," the judge snapped.

The dark-haired man sat. The judge turned to look at Oil Can.

"Mr. Doyle," he said, "I am releasing your client on his own recognizance—"

The dark-haired jumped to his feet.

"Your Honor—" he began.

"One. More. Word. Mr. Davies," the judge rapped, "and you will be taking Senator Hope's place in jail on a contempt charge. You had your chance, and you blew it. Now. Sit. Down."

The dark-haired man sank into his chair.

"As I was saying, Mr. Doyle," the judge said, "I'm releasing your client OR, with the understanding that you will produce him for all pertinent court proceedings."

"Thank you, Your Honor," Oil Can squeaked.

"The bailiff will take the defendant to be processed for release," the judge said. "Now, I want to see opposing council in my chambers. Mr. Davies, be sure to bring your advisor with you. Court is in recess for fifteen minutes."

The judge dropped the gavel, got to his feet, and went through the door behind the bench. Oil Can, Davies, and the woman followed. The trooper came and took Hope out the side door.

"I've been watching the courts for a dozen years now," the woman said, "and I've never seen nothing like that. I wouldn't want to be Davies right now. I'll bet the judge is chewing him a new one."

"Got that right," the man said, lowering his pencil. "When they say fifteen minutes, they mean at least a half hour. Let's go get coffee, Emma."

The three of them filed out of the courtroom behind the other spectators. The two court-watchers went off together, talking. Kane took a seat in the lobby. The reporters formed up near the door, the better to ambush the lawyers when they came out. After a few minutes, a young guy with wild hair detached himself from the group of reporters and walked over to sit next to him. He had a notebook and pen in his hands.

"I'm with the Anchorage paper," he said, "and I understand that you're working for the defense. Any comment on what happened in there?"

Kane shook his head.

"Nope," he said. "You'll have to wait for Oil Can."

"How about your investigation?" the reporter said. "Found out anything new?"

Kane shook his head.

"Really," he said, "you're going to have to talk to either the senator or his lawyer. I'm not authorized to comment."

The reporter nodded.

"Fair enough," he said. "Here's my card, in case you do want to talk to me."

He got to his feet and started back, stopped, turned, and said, "I'm not some tabloid guy. I didn't just parachute in. I cover the legislature full-time. If you ever have anything for me, I'll play it straight."

With that he returned to the group of reporters. Kane slid his card into a pocket and watched the reporter walk away. When he got back to the group, he shook his head.

Time passed. Doyle, the prosecutor, Davies, and the woman from the governor's office came out of the courtroom in a clump. Davies and the woman brushed past the reporters, the prosecutor heading for the elevator and the woman going out the door and across the street to the Capitol. Oil Can stopped and said, "Here's what I've got for you."

The reporters gathered around.

"In nearly thirty years of practicing law in this state," Oil Can said, the squeak somehow absent from his voice, "I have never seen such a blatantly political attempt to interfere in the criminal justice system. Governor Hiram Putnam has made a grave error, and I hope you make him answer for it. I'm sure you've all seen Sean here's story in this morning's Anchorage paper about the governor taking over the investigation and not questioning certain political allies. That and today's charade raise serious questions about the state's reasons for prosecuting Senator Hope, and I'm confident that he will be found innocent on all charges, because he is innocent. Thank you."

The reporters spouted questions, but Oil Can walked away from them. Kane got up and followed him, catching up with the lawyer on the sidewalk when he stopped to button his topcoat.

"Well?" Kane said.

Doyle's face was split by what looked like a genuine grin.

"Talk about your gifts from God," the lawyer said, hopping from foot to foot with glee. "Ritter is half asleep most of the time, and the time he's awake he's a member of the old boys' club who will put up with practically anything from the prosecution. So drawing Sellers instead was a great piece of luck.

"And I can't imagine what the governor was thinking, although he's such a dunce maybe he doesn't think. But our client gets out of jail free, and the prosecution looks like it's politically motivated. On top of the story about the investigation in this morning's paper, the prosecution is looking very suspect. And I think Davies is going to need first aid for the tongue-lashing the judge gave him. All in all, a good day."

"What about Hope?" Kane asked.

"What about him?" Doyle said.

"What's he going to do now?" Kane asked.

"My understanding is that he'll process out and go back to his job in the state Senate," Doyle said, "although he'll have to have the guts of a burglar to walk back into that place and try to get anything done."

He looked at his watch.

"I'm scheduled to fly back to Anchorage this afternoon," he said. "Nothing much happens here on the weekends, and I've got some matters that might keep me there until Tuesday or Wednesday. Why don't we get together after lunch and talk about how we want to proceed?"

"Fine with me," Kane said. "I've got one or two things to talk to you about anyway."

The lawyer walked away. Kane stood on the sidewalk looking up at the mountainside above the town. It was steep and heavily wooded, the next thing to wilderness a short climb away. His "hangover" was mostly gone, but he felt logy and out of sorts. He walked back to the hotel and got directions to a gym from the doorman. Taking some workout gear from his room, he walked to the gym, paid a fee, changed clothes, and went into the exercise room. At midmorning most of the people using it were women in spandex.

I don't have any real objections to that, Kane thought as he found a place to stretch.

After he stretched the kinks out, he found an empty treadmill and worked up a sweat, thinking all the while of the situation surrounding Matthew Hope. Was the governor actually as stupid as Doyle seemed to think? Just how did politics affect the case? Could Hope get a fair trial if the governor was in there playing politics?

Kane thought about calling Jeffords and asking him what was going on. But the chief clearly wanted to keep his distance. He probably wouldn't talk, and even if he did, Kane would have no way of being sure he was telling the truth. More politics.

He got off the treadmill, found the free weights, and started sliding them onto a bar. When he had 150 pounds on, he slid beneath the bar, inhaled, exhaled, and lifted. Moving slowly and carefully, he brought the bar down, raised it, brought it down, raised it, establishing a rhythm that allowed him to work all the muscles of his upper body. He could have pressed a lot more, but his form would have broken down.

No use speculating in the absence of evidence, he thought. So, instead, he thought about how he was going to treat Alma Atwood when he saw her again.

That, he thought, is a political question I've actually got some interest in.

19

In politics, stupidity is not a handicap.

Napoleon Bonaparte

Kane arrived at Doyle's office feeling as fit as a regiment of marines. He had a hard time keeping a straight face when Helga greeted him with a glare and stony silence.

"Looks like I'm winning," he said as he breezed past her into Doyle's office. He found the lawyer stuffing files into his bulky briefcase.

"Glad you could make it," Doyle squeaked. "Got anything for me?"

Kane relayed the events of the night before, leaving out Alma Atwood's spectacular meltdown.

"A dead cat?" Doyle squeaked. "Someone sent you a dead cat?"

"Actually," Kane said, "it looked like someone killed the cat and then sent it to me. It's a message."

"So what are you going to do?" Doyle asked.

"About the cat?" Kane asked. "That's Tank Crawford's problem. About the message? I'm going to ignore it, but keep my guard up. You should do the same. Anybody who would kill a cat would kill a lower life-form, like a lawyer."

Doyle took a last look around the room, snapped his briefcase shut, and looked at Kane.

"Very funny," he said. "But nobody's going to bother me. I've represented some dangerous people in my time and nobody's ever done anything worse than call me names."

Tough little devil, Kane thought. But he's a lot like all these politicians. They all think that the rules of their game—politics, law, whatever—will protect them in the real world. Unfortunately for them, they're wrong.

"What about this aide, what's his name?" Doyle asked "Do you think he actually knows anything?"

"Got me," Kane said. "He did work with the victim, so he's more likely to know something than a lot of people. But he was pretty drunk when I talked to him."

"So you don't buy the *in vino veritas* theory?" the lawyer asked.

Kane shrugged again.

"Sometimes alcohol makes people spill their darkest secrets," he said, "and sometimes it makes them lie just for the hell of it. But mostly it makes them drunk and unpredictable."

Kane watched as the lawyer struggled his way into his coat. It was like watching a pig wrestle with a python.

"Maybe you'd better go talk with him again," Doyle said when he'd finished subduing the coat. He straightened his toupee and looked at his watch. "I've got to get going. All this homeland security nonsense means I've got to get to the airport early and then waste time waiting. Talk about locking the barn door after the horse got out. Anyway, call me if you get anything useful. I'm booked back here on the Tuesday-morning plane."

Kane followed the lawyer out of the office, giving Helga his best leer as he passed. The look she returned would have stopped a grizzly bear in midcharge. Down on the street, he watched as Doyle got into a cab and drove off. It was almost one o'clock. Kane took the card Dylan had given him out of his wallet. He dialed the number listed there on his cell phone.

"Dylan Kane, please," he said and waited. "Dylan? This is your dad. You had lunch yet?" He listened. "Then how about dinner?" He listened some more. "Dylan, I'm going to be here long enough that you're likely to run out of excuses. So why don't you just skip all that and get this over with?" He listened some more. "Yeah, tonight is good. Where?" He paused. "Yeah, I can find it. When?" He paused again. "Fine, see you then."

Kane put the cell phone back into his pocket, shaking his head. Dealing with his son was going to be as tough as keeping his feet on the ice. He thought about going up to the Capitol and seeing if Alma had had lunch, but decided against it. Kane knew from experience that she'd need time to come to grips with what she'd done the night before, and he thought it was best to give her that time. So he went back into the building, sat on the stairs, put his ice grippers on, and took a walk.

His route took him onto the flat, past the police station, and along a street that followed the shoreline. The sky was covered from horizon to horizon in a film of high, white overcast. The water in the channel was gray-green and smooth as a politician's evasion. The hillside above him was a mass of dark green spruce, barren white birches, and gray willows. Only the occasional brightly painted house broke up nature's drab winter palette.

Despite the lack of sun, the day was warm and drops of snowmelt fell from building gutters and the tips of tree branches. Kane unzipped his coat as he walked, wondering if spring was finally here.

No lights showed in any of the buildings he passed. According to the signs in their windows, you could buy opals here and fudge there and T-shirts everywhere, but only when the cruise ships arrived with summer. Downtown Juneau was like the downtown of any Alaska tourist town, like the downtown of Anchorage for that matter, with year-round businesses overwhelmed by the shops of people dedicated to squeezing their livings out of the four-month tourist season. In mid-September they locked the doors and left the downtowns cold and dark until the next May.

The state has changed so much since I was born, Kane thought as he walked. Oil has made it richer and tourism has made it tackier and every economic benefit has been matched—some would say over-matched—by a social cost. We have more people and less community, more money and less sharing, more roads and fewer places to be alone. Jeez, I sound like an old-timer, a sourdough. The thought made him laugh. Maybe he did match the cynical definition Alaskans sometimes used: Sour on Alaska but not enough dough to leave.

The sidewalk petered out at the last tourist building. Kane thought about continuing along the side of the road, but there wasn't enough shoulder to make walking safe. So he turned and headed back to town. He'd gotten about a block when his cell phone rang.

"Mr. Kane?" a man's voice said. "My name is Matthew Blair. I'm chief of staff to Governor Hiram Putnam. The governor would like you to be in his office at three o'clock."

"What for?" Kane asked, irritated by the man's casual assumption that he could be ordered up like a pepperoni pizza.

"The governor has some matters he'd like to discuss privately," Blair said.

Kane felt like telling the guy where to go, but he wanted to know more about what Putnam was up to. So he said, "Three o'clock? His office? Where is that?"

In the pause that followed, Kane watched a dirty brown gull land on a railing lined with other gulls. The new arrival set off a chain reaction of squawking and flapping that ran down the railing and sent the gull on the far end skyward.

"Seriously?" Blair said, his voice full of surprise. "You don't know where the governor's office is?"

"No," Kane said, "but I am a detective, so I can find out if you don't knock off the what-a-rube stuff and tell me."

"Third floor of the Capitol," Blair said. "Just give your name to the receptionist."

He broke the connection. Kane closed his cell phone, put it into his pocket, and resumed his walk. Water from melting snow formed rivulets on the mountainside back of town. Higher up still, an eagle soared, a dark speck against the milky sky.

Tourists would ooh and aah over that, Kane thought. Outsiders— people who didn't live in Alaska—had such extreme ideas about the place. For a long time the national image was a frozen wasteland. Now it was a storehouse of nature for an overcivilized nation. For Kane and other Alaskans, though, Alaska was what it had always been, the backdrop against which they lived their lives. More spectacular than some backdrops, but a backdrop nonetheless.

John Muir can go to hell, Kane thought. We're more important than the mountains and the glaciers.

Kane stopped in a sandwich shop to eat a late lunch. Like most places he'd been in Juneau, it was crowded with people talking about government affairs. To some, anyway, those affairs included the White Rose Murder. In the course of eating a pastrami sandwich, he overheard that Matthew Hope had been exonerated, that some TV loudmouth named O'Reilly had said the murder was more proof of the evils of liberalism, and that Governor Hiram Putnam was putting pressure on the district attorney's office to get Hope's bail revoked. Among the younger people, there was a lot of speculation about who would play Hope in the TV movie.

When he finished eating and eavesdropping, Kane walked up the hill to the Capitol and rode the elevator to the third floor. A pleasant young woman took his name, whispered into her headset, and asked him to wait. He took a seat in one of the brocade chairs set in the hallway. The other was overfull of a dark-haired man talking into a cell phone.

"Who gives a fuck what that pinhead thinks?" the man was saying. "I've got the votes."

Kane listened to the man crow into the telephone for a few minutes, admiring the carrying capacity of the chair. The guy weighed well over three hundred pounds, and Kane wouldn't have been at all surprised to see the chair explode into wooden shrapnel and drop the guy onto the floor. They'd need a crane to put him on his feet.

A bulky, gray man with a face like a map of Ireland came through the office doors and walked over to where Kane and the fat man sat. His collar was open and his tie askew, and his hair looked like it had been combed with high explosives.

"Hey, Matt," the fat man said to him, "I've been waiting for a half hour to see the governor."

"Well, if it isn't Alaska's largest lobbyist," the man said. "Don't worry, we'll get to you." To Kane, he said, "You Kane? I'm Blair. Follow me."

Kane followed him through the doors, through another reception area, and into a large office. The man at the big desk didn't look up from his writing when they entered. Blair motioned Kane to one of the chairs facing the desk and sat down in the other. Kane sat and waited, studying the man behind the desk.

Governor Hiram Putnam looked like a civic monument in a suit. His shoulders were broad and his hair was abundant and his face bore the pleasant emptiness of your favorite uncle—if your favorite uncle had a room-temperature IQ. A newspaper columnist had called Putnam "the four S man: stupid, saccharine, self-important, and sleazy," and as far as

Kane knew the governor had never said or done anything to contradict that.

Putnam apparently decided that he'd taken long enough to show Kane how busy and important he was. He set his pen down and fixed the detective with a glare.

"Just what the fuck are you guys doing," he barked, "telling the newspaper that we're not investigating this murder properly?"

Kane opened his mouth to reply, but Putnam plowed on.

"We're going to find out who killed Melinda Foxx, don't you worry," he said, "and we're going to prosecute him to the fullest extent of the law. I have my best people on it, and I'm getting daily briefings on their investigation. Daily. But people have got to realize that there is other state business to be done, important business, and we can't let the one interfere with the other. My administration is committed . . ."

And Putnam was off on what even someone as apolitical as Kane recognized as a well-rehearsed stump speech. As the governor droned on, Kane looked around the room. With its wood paneling and shelves lined with plaques, certificates, and bric-a-brac, it could have been the rec room of a particularly successful aluminum siding salesman.

Putnam finished abruptly and got to his feet.

"I don't know what the fuck Tom Jeffords is doing, sending you here," he said, "but you'd better keep out of the way of the official investigation or you'll find yourself back behind bars."

With that, the governor picked up a sheaf of papers and marched out of the room. As he reached the door, he turned and said, "And you tell Jeffords that if he tries to dump me and put his pet mayor into this office, I'll run him right out of Alaska."

With that, he left.

Kane sat in the gathering silence and waited for the governor's right-hand man to get down to business.

"Who hired you?" Blair asked.

"I work for Matthew Hope's attorney, William Doyle," Kane said.

"Yeah, but who's paying you?" Blair asked. "Or him, for that matter?" Kane smiled and said nothing.

"Is Tom Jeffords involved?" Blair asked.

"I'm not working for Jeffords," Kane said.

"That's not what I asked," Blair said. "I asked if he is involved."

Kane smiled again.

"I'm not answering any more questions," he said. "I know you people think you're important, but you're not important to me."

Kane got to his feet.

"Now, unless you have something a little more interesting than speeches, threats, and questions," he said, "I'll get back to work."

He turned to go.

"Wait a minute, Kane," Blair said, standing. "You have to realize our position. This murder was a terrible crime, but like everything else that happens in this building, it's all balled up in politics, too. We want to find the killer. In fact, our people seem to think that's Matthew Hope. But we need to tend to the politics, too."

Kane turned to face the other man.

"I've got no interest in politics," he said, "so why are you trying to push me around?"

Blair shrugged.

"That's just the governor," he said. "He tends to treat every problem like it's a nail to be hammered. But I can tell you that we're interested in whatever political information you can pick up. In fact, I think I can safely say that some of the problems you're having with your investigation might disappear if you are prepared to cooperate with us."

If Kane hadn't been associated with Jeffords for so many years, he might not have been able to parse that sentence.

"You mean, you'll quit trying to cause me trouble if I play ball?" he said. "Like, for instance, a couple of guys with guns might not call on me again?"

Blair shook his head.

"I have no idea what you're talking about," he said. "I was simply referring to the level of cooperation you might expect from the official investigation."

Kane laughed.

"What official investigation?" he asked. "If you've got people investigating this crime, they must be using the cloak of invisibility. Nobody's seen them."

"Look—" Blair began, but Kane held up a hand.

"No, you look," he said. "You people don't seem to have anything to offer me and you don't really have anything to threaten me with, so you're just wasting my time."

He turned and started walking. Blair let him get to the door before he said, "Did you know that Melinda Foxx's mouth was full of cleaning fluid?"

That stopped Kane. He turned and retraced his steps.

"Cleaning fluid?" he said "What kind of cleaning fluid?"

"Some sort of industrial cleaner," Blair said. "The kind used to clean bathrooms. At least, that's what the autopsy says."

"What else did they find?" Kane asked.

Blair shook his head.

"Uh-uh," he said. "Tit for tat. Who's paying you?"

Kane thought about not telling him. He supposed he had some sort of ethical obligation not to out his employer. But he was being paid to solve a crime, and Blair might have more to tell him.

"Mrs. Richard Foster," he said.

Blair nodded at the name.

"I'm not surprised," he said. "The Fosters have been a thorn in our side forever. And I imagine she's got special reason to help Matthew Hope."

"Such as?" Kane said.

Blair shook his head.

"I'm not going into that," he said. "Is Tom Jeffords involved in your investigation?"

Kane shook his head.

"Now, now," he said, "if I was that easy you wouldn't respect me. I want a copy of the autopsy report."

"I can't give you that," Blair said. "It would be compromising the investigation."

"Don't be silly," Kane said. "The law requires the prosecution to give a copy to the defense. So I'll see it eventually. All you'd be doing is shortcutting the process."

Blair seemed to think about that.

"All right," he said. "I'll see that you get a copy of the pages detailing what they found on the body. That's all I can do. If I give you more, I'll have investigators and prosecutors screaming and throwing fits. Now, what about Jeffords?"

"Nope," Kane said. "I want that information. In my hand. Now."

Blair looked at Kane steadily.

"Ask anybody in the building," he said. "My word is good."

Kane shook his head.

"This is a murder investigation," he said, "not some political deal. The sooner you guys figure that out, the better. For all I know, you killed Melinda Foxx. So I'm not taking your word for anything."

Blair started to say something but stopped. He got to his feet, walked around the governor's desk, and picked up a folder. He walked back around the desk, and handed it to Kane.

"This is the information," he said. "But if you tell anyone I gave it to you, I'll call you a liar."

"Fair enough," Kane said, taking the folder and turning to walk away.

"What about Jeffords?" Blair asked.

"As far as I know, Tom Jeffords isn't involved in this investigation in any way," he lied, and left the room.

20

I always wanted to get into politics, but I was
never light enough to make the team.

ART BUCHWALD

Kane walked up a couple of flights, took a seat in the hallway, and
leafed through the pages Blair had given him. They looked like the
beginning of the autopsy and the test results that went with it. An
examination of the body prior to dissection found evidence, lubricant
and a few bruises, consistent with sexual intercourse and sodomy, but
no "sexual materials" other than a few pubic hairs. Lab examination
found no follicles attached to the hairs, making DNA matching difficult. The liquid found in the victim's mouth was identified as an industrial cleaner of the sort commonly used by janitors. Its presence in the
mouth had made other evidentiary inquiries in that area impossible.

And that was it. Nothing about what they'd found when they
opened her up. Well, either he'd have to find something more to trade
or count on Doyle to pry the rest out of the prosecutors.

He tucked the folder under his arm and walked down the hall to the Senate Finance Committee room. He was more anxious than ever to talk to Ralph Stansfield about Melinda Foxx, particularly about her sexual habits, but the committee was still in session. Stansfield sat at Senator Potter's right hand, almost invisible behind a pile of files. Letitia Potter sat on her father's left, her eyes watching everything at once. A man in a bad suit sat at the witness table, droning on about "methods and measures" and "full-time equivalents." The senators read their mail or stared into space or held tête-à-têtes at the side of the room.

Prying Stansfield out of the meeting would be difficult, maybe impossible, so Kane stood at the back of the room until Letitia Potter's gaze swept over him. She gave no sign of recognition.

I guess the old Nik Kane charm is working full-time, Kane thought as he left the room.

He walked down the hall to Hope's office, where a very polite receptionist told him that the senator was in a committee meeting on the second floor. On his way down the stairs, Kane was passed by energetic young staffers carrying files hurrying up and down. Every landing held people holding whispered conversations.

Hope's committee meeting was more orderly and every bit as boring. He and four other senators sat behind a raised, V-shaped desk at the front of the room, paying elaborate attention to a woman talking about mineral leasing fees. The rows of chairs behind her were filled with people. Several appeared to be asleep.

If you added up all the government salaries, lobbyists' fees, and other money being paid to people just sitting there, Kane thought, I wonder how much one of these meetings costs?

He stood in the doorway until Hope noticed him, then nodded toward the hallway. Hope nodded back and stayed put.

Maybe I need to change my deodorant, Kane thought.

He took a seat in the hallway. People came and went. He thought about his upcoming dinner with Dylan and just what he wanted to get out of it.

Do I want to do something for him? Kane thought. Do I want him to do something for me? Do I suppose that, at this late date, we're suddenly going to become a father and son like you used to see on TV? Like Ozzie and Ricky, maybe? Or Andy and Opie?

I'm not sure, he thought. Maybe with Laurie pushing me out of her life, I just wish I was special to someone. Of course, if I'd been a better father, I wouldn't have to wish.

He'd tried, or at least he'd thought so at the time. But something would come up at work and he'd miss Emily's ballet performance. He'd stay too long at a bar and not show up for Amy's basketball game. And Dylan? He'd made it to maybe one of his Little League games. No wonder the kid stopped playing sports. And then Dylan was just reaching puberty and—wham!—his father was off to prison and out of his life.

I wonder who explained the birds and bees to him? Kane thought.

The committee room began spewing people, some walking fast, others ambling out talking in twos and threes. Hope came out talking to the wild-haired reporter.

"I'm afraid I have nothing to say about the murder, Sean," he was saying. "All I did was discover the body."

The reporter started to say something, but Kane intervened.

"Hello, Senator," he said, stepping between the two men. "We need to talk."

"Hey," the reporter said, but Kane ignored him and, taking Hope by the arm, steered him down the hall toward the stairs.

"Thanks," Hope said as they reached the stairwell. "These reporters are all over me and I'm not really sure what to tell them."

"You were doing fine," Kane said. "Innocent and ignorant is just the way to play it."

People were pouring down the stairway, leaving little room for people headed up, so Kane followed Hope to the fourth floor single file, catching up to him again at his office door.

"I wasn't just trying to save you from tough questions down there," he said. "I really do have some things to talk about."

Hope went into the office. Kane followed. His outer office was just as small as Grantham's, and it contained a couple of guys in suits who perked up when Hope entered like retrievers hearing gunshots.

"Your four o'clock is here, Senator," his receptionist said.

"Be right with you," Hope said, nodding. He picked up a sheaf of telephone messages and walked into his private office. Kane followed, closing the door behind him. Hope sat behind his desk and began leafing though the messages.

"If it's about what happened that night," he said, "I've already told you everything I know."

"That's bullshit," Kane said cheerfully, "but we'll let that pass for a moment. I want to know why a couple of guys with guns are trying to scare me off your case."

"Guys with guns?" Hope said. "You'd better sit down."

Kane did, and told Hope about his encounter with the two men and the gift of the dead cat. When he finished, Hope shrugged.

"I don't have any idea who those men might be or who they might be working for," he said. "I have my share of political enemies, but none of them have ever used guns. Or sent me dead animals."

"Do you think it could be this domestic partners bill?" Kane asked. "An issue like homosexual rights can bring out some weird people."

"Gay rights," Hope said. "We don't say homosexual. We say gay. Although why we expect that group to be any gayer than the rest of us is beyond me."

He shook his head.

"Sorry," he said, "I can't help you with this. I have no idea who might be behind those threats. And I do have an appointment."

Kane got to his feet.

"Okay," he said, "but you should be careful. Guns can shoot senators, too."

He went through the outer office, up a flight of stairs and down the hall. The Finance Committee room was empty except for a couple of women putting files in some of the cabinets along one wall. A hand-lettered sign that read "Staff Meeting" was taped to Potter's office door. Kane tried the door handle. Locked. He walked back through the room, down the hall, and into the stairwell, where he was nearly bowled over by Alma Atwood.

"Oh," she said, taking a step back. "It's you. Hi."

"Hi yourself," Kane said. "How are you feeling?"

"After disgracing myself, you mean?" she said with an embarrassed smile. "I've been in a fog all day, I haven't been able to eat anything, and my head's just stopped hurting. Other than that, I'm swell."

Kane laughed.

"I hope you're drinking lots of water," he said.

"I am," Alma said, putting a hand on his arm. "I was going to try to find you later, to apologize for being such a problem. I didn't say or do anything . . . irretrievable . . . did I?"

Kane shook his head.

"Not by my standards," he said. "After all, I've done much worse."

Alma sighed with relief.

"I'm so glad," she said. "I don't know what got into me. Can I make it up to you? Are you busy tonight?"

"I regret to say I am," Kane said. "I'm having dinner with my son."

"Oh," Alma said, "that will be nice."

"How about you?" Kane asked. "What are you up to?"

"Tonight?" Alma said. "Well, Thursday night is usually when I stay home and do my laundry." She paused. "You know, maybe after dinner you could come by?"

"I don't know what I'll be doing," Kane said.

"No biggie," Alma said. "I've got a lot of laundry to do, so I'll be up until at least ten. You know where I live. And here's my number."

She wrote something on a small yellow pad, tore off the sheet, and handed it to Kane. He folded it and put it into his pocket.

"I'll make it if I can," he said. "Can I bring anything?"

"Anything but alcohol," Alma said with a laugh, and went on her way.

Kane was stopped on the fourth-floor landing by the House minority leader.

"Hey there," he said. "It's Nik Kane, right? Still trying to find out about Melinda Foxx? Come with me. I've got someone you should talk to."

He led Kane through an outer office and into an inner office about the size of a cruise ship cabin. A tall man was behind the desk, mixing drinks. Two men sat on a couch and a third leaned against the windowsill. All had martini glasses in their hands.

The minority leader made introductions.

"What's your pleasure?" the man behind the desk asked. "We have vodka martinis or vodka martinis."

"Nothing for me, thanks," Kane said.

"Ah, no drinking on the job, eh?" the man said. "A sound policy. One we follow ourselves, which is why you'd never find anyone in this office drinking before five o'clock."

"Except in months with vowels in them," one of the men on the couch said.

Everyone laughed at what was clearly a well-worn joke.

"I didn't bring you in here just to rub elbows with these reprobates," the minority leader said. "But Silversmith there, in addition to being a fine human being, is a Republican . . ."

"Boo, hiss," the man behind the desk said. "Hiss, boo."

"And," the minority leader went on, "his House district is part of O. B. Potter's Senate district."

"And you'll never get me to say an unkind word about my senator," Silversmith said from his seat on the couch. "At least not that I'll admit to later."

"We don't quote anything said in the presence of the great god vodka," the man behind the desk said. "Who needs a refill?"

"Amen," said the man leaning against the windowsill. He held out his glass and the other man filled it.

"I'm not finished," the minority leader said. "Silversmith is also a rarity amongst us, a bachelor. Which means he can actually admit to having tried to get into Melinda Foxx's pants. Unlike some people I could name."

The man leaning against the window raised his glass in a mock toast.

"Is there anything you can tell me about that, Representative Silversmith?" Kane said.

Silversmith shook his head.

"Only that it was as futile as a minority floor amendment to the budget," he said, holding out his glass.

The man behind the desk handed the martini shaker to Kane, who filled the glass and handed the shaker back. Silversmith took a sip.

"Ahhh," he said. "Smooth. Don't need a chaser, nothing can catch it. Where was I? Oh, yes, the bootylicious Miss Foxx."

"You can tell he's a Republican," the other man on the couch said. "He said 'Miss' instead of 'Ms.' "

"Miss. Ms. It's all the same to me," Silversmith said.

"Mrs., too," the man behind the desk said, "if the rumors are true."

That ignited another round of laughter.

"A slur," Silversmith said. "A canard. My seconds will call on you, sir."

If I let these guys get any more booze on board, Kane thought, they'll be plotting a panty raid.

"So what can you tell me about Miss or Ms. Foxx?" he asked.

"I can tell you she was a very desirable young woman," Silversmith said, "and seemed totally immune to my not-inconsiderable charms."

"Hard to believe," the man behind the desk said.

"Would you mind telling me about that?" Kane asked.

Silversmith laughed.

"A politician mind talking about himself?" he said. "Not likely."

He took another sip of martini.

"As you may have noticed," he said, "this is a target-rich environment for a single man."

"Don't have to be single," the man leaning on the windowsill said.

"Don't interrupt," Silversmith said. "People will think you're drunk."

"They'll be right," the man behind the desk said.

"Anyway," Silversmith said loudly. And into the silence that followed, he said, "So I didn't actually get around to Ms. Foxx until the beginning of this session. I asked around, was told she was unattached, bided my time, swooped in, and asked her out. And she said . . . no."

The man behind the desk and the one leaning against the windowsill pounded on the desktop. They and the other men said, "Woof, woof, woof."

"Children," Silversmith said, shaking his head. "I'm surrounded by children. Anyway, I pursued the lass with some diligence, but she met my every sally with polite refusal."

"So eventually he got bored and went looking elsewhere," the minority leader said.

"'Tis true, 'tis true," Silversmith said. "I had other fish to plow, greener pastures to fry."

"So what did you make of the experience?" Kane asked.

"That the woman had good taste," the other man on the couch said.

Silversmith sat straight up and looked down his nose at the man, then turned to Kane.

"As you can see," he said, "I am a man of dashing good looks and considerable charm. And I am a powerful member of the House of Representatives, the chairman, in fact, of the ultra-important State Affairs Committee. So when she turned this package down, I assumed she was a lesbo."

That brought a roar of laughter from his listeners.

"Lesbo?" the minority leader said. "You said 'lesbo' in the twenty-first century? If your constituents could only hear you now."

"Besides," the man behind the desk gasped between guffaws, "that—that's what you said about that babe in the governor's office, what's her name, right up until the night she was caught giving Senator Bodkins a blow job in that hospitality suite."

When the laughter had subsided, Silversmith said, "All right, I retract 'lesbo.' But she was gay—gay, I tell you. Or perhaps she'd already secretly hooked up. Maybe both. Who knows? I need another drink."

Kane took his leave then. The minority leader followed him out.

"Don't know if that does you any good," he said. "But Silversmith cuts a pretty wide swath through here, so if Melinda Foxx turned him down flat she must have had some reason."

"Thanks," Kane said. "I'll keep that in mind."

He looked at his watch.

"Got to go," he said. "Dinner plans."

He went down the stairs, sat on a bench in the entryway, and put on his ice grippers. Then he walked down the hill to his hotel to change clothes.

Maybe Melinda Foxx was gay, he thought. Maybe she had good taste. Or maybe, just maybe, she was at twenty-four more mature than that crew. It wouldn't be hard.

21

The future will be better tomorrow.

J. DANFORTH QUAYLE

Dylan had picked a sushi place several blocks away from Kane's hotel. Kane thought about calling Cocoa, but the night was warm enough and the exercise would do him good. The ice had melted off most of the sidewalks, so he stuck his ice grippers in a coat pocket and followed the bellman's directions uphill, across a couple of streets, past the Capitol and the state office building, then down the longest flight of steps he'd ever seen. The steps were metal grates set in a frame of four-by-fours that zigzagged down a steep hillside. Kane counted 109 of them before he set foot on solid ground again at the base of the hill.

The rest of his walk was fairly flat, and Kane spent it thinking again about Dylan. A close relationship with the boy, young man now, might not be possible, he decided. He'd just have to take things a step at a time and see where they went.

Seong's was a brightly lit, nondescript rectangle on a corner. The multistory federal building loomed over it like Godzilla over a toy Toyota. The restaurant was packed. Kane was glad to see Dylan seated at a table when he entered.

"Got here early," Dylan said as Kane hung his coat on the back of his chair and sat down. "A table can be tough to find here."

Dylan was wearing a black T-shirt with the name of some rock band entwined in a semi-obscene drawing. He was a good-looking kid, thanks to Laurie's genes, but seemed thin and drawn. He had a bottle of Sapporo in front of him. Since Dylan was still underage, Kane recognized the beer for what it was, a challenge. He ignored it.

"Is the food that good?" he asked. "To draw a big crowd?"

Dylan laughed.

"This is Juneau," he said. "You don't ask if a restaurant is good. You ask if it's open."

"That bad, huh?" Kane said.

"Actually, the sushi here is pretty good," Dylan said. "Not as good as you'd find in Boston, or even Anchorage, but edible."

Kane picked up the menu and scanned it.

"Sushi and Chinese food," he said. "Not the most common combination."

Dylan drank some beer.

"This isn't all that unusual," he said. "We've got a Mexican-Italian place downtown."

Kane recognized the small talk for what it was, a mutual defense mechanism. It continued as they ordered, then Kane cut it off by asking, "How's school?"

Dylan shrugged.

"School seems pretty far away at the moment," he said.

"You are going back to finish, aren't you?" Kane asked, wincing at something he heard in his own voice.

Dylan didn't reply.

That's right, Kane thought, drive him back into his shell. He let a couple of minutes pass in silence before asking, "How's the job?"

"Job's good," Dylan said. "My politics aren't exactly the same as my boss's, but the work is interesting and the people are nice. When they're not trying to stick a knife in your back, that is."

"Literally?" Kane asked.

Dylan gave Kane a crooked grin.

"No, not literally. At least, not yet," he said. "It's just that the legislature is pretty top-down, and the staffers whose bosses have a lot of power think they're special. And they'll mess with you just to prove it."

"That's funny," Kane said. "I would have thought the legislature was pretty democratic because every member has one vote."

Dylan picked up his menu.

"You'd think that," he said, as he read the menu, "but actual small-*d* democracy is pretty rare. Human beings are uncomfortable in unstructured groups. They like structures where they know their place. Especially Republicans. They can't seem to live without a pecking order. And once a structure is established, an individual's most important goal is maintaining his or her place in the structure. Their second most important goal is moving up in the structure, gaining more status."

He set the menu down and smiled apologetically.

"Sorry," he said. "I took a course in organizational dynamics last semester."

A waitress came over.

"Why don't you order?" Kane said. "You know the food."

Dylan rattled off the names of several sushi rolls, Kane asked for green tea, and the waitress departed.

"So your boss isn't very high up?" Kane asked.

"He is a Republican, so he's in the majority," Dylan said, "but he's just a freshman. The allocation of power in the legislature is dictated by an odd mix of partisan allegiance, seniority, geographical distribution, personal relationships, and skill."

"With skill last?" Kane asked.

"With skill last," Dylan said.

The waitress brought Kane's tea. He poured some into a small porcelain cup and sipped. The tea was watery and tasted the way a new-mown lawn smells.

"You don't sound like you think this is going to be your career," he said.

Dylan nodded.

"It's not," he said. "We've got this real-world learning requirement at school, and Chief Jeffords helped me get this job. I'm learning a lot, but politics just doesn't interest me that much. But what about you? Are you okay after that fall? You hit the street hard."

"I'm fine," Kane said, "take away a few bruises. I thought it was nice you and that woman came to help me. I could have been anybody."

"That's more Samantha than me," Dylan said. "She wants to save every living thing."

"Nothing wrong with that," Kane said. "Are you two an item?"

He watched wariness fill his son's eyes.

"Like, is she my girlfriend, is that what you mean?" Dylan said. He shook his head. "She's too old for that. Or I'm too young. But we do have fun together. And she's great in bed."

Kane opened his mouth to say something, paused, then said, "Well, she seems nice enough."

Dylan nodded and drank more beer. Kane was happy to see that he drank like his mother. Laurie could make a bottle of beer last a week.

"How is your investigation going?" Dylan asked.

"It's not really going at all," Kane said, pouring himself more tea. "Nobody seems to have known the victim very well, and those who might have don't want to talk. Did you know her?"

"Melinda?" Dylan said, nodding. "I knew her to talk to. But she was an important Senate staffer and I'm a nothing House staffer, so I didn't know her that well."

"Did Samantha know her?" Kane asked.

Dylan looked at him like he was a complex puzzle that needed solving.

"I'm not sure," he said. "She's a lobbyist, so I'd guess she did. But I don't know that for a fact."

Kane opened his mouth and shut it again.

"Well," he said at last, "I guess I can ask her."

The waitress arrived and started taking small plates from a big tray and setting them on the table. When she finished, Kane said to Dylan, "What is it I'm eating?"

"Better not to think about it," Dylan said with a grin. He picked up a pair of chopsticks and began mixing things in a small bowl. When he was finished, he plucked a ball of rice topped with something brown from a plate, dipped it, and popped it into his mouth. He was reaching for something wrapped in seaweed when he noticed Kane was just sitting there.

"Don't see anything you like?" he asked.

"Don't know what to do," Kane said. "They didn't serve sushi in prison. And my diet before that didn't run to raw fish."

Dylan shook his head slowly.

"Nik Kane, the socially retarded detective," he said. He took another little bowl, poured in soy sauce, and picked up a glob of green paste.

"This is wasabi," he said. "Do you want it hot or mild?"

"Mild," Kane said, and watched as Dylan put most of the paste back, mixing in just a bit.

"Now," he said, "all you have to do is pick up those chopsticks and eat."

Kane picked up the chopsticks, arranged them the way Dylan held his, and reached for a piece of sushi. After several stabs, he managed to grab it with the sticks, dip it in the sauce, and drop it into his lap.

"Way to go," Dylan said. "At this rate, you'll starve before you get a mouthful. Want a fork?"

Kane shook his head.

"I'm not going to let this beat me," he said.

He maneuvered a second piece of sushi toward the sauce, but it squirted out from between the chopsticks, skittered across the table, and vaulted over the side of the table into Dylan's lap. Both of them began laughing.

"That was—that was way smooooth," Dylan said with difficulty.

They both laughed some more. Then, suddenly, Dylan wasn't laughing.

"What are you doing here?" he said, his voice rough with emotion. "What the fuck are you doing? Do you think you can leave me like you did and then just come back into my life like nothing happened?"

His voice rose as he continued, and other dinners began shooting glances at the two of them.

"I needed a father once," Dylan said, "but you weren't around. I don't need you now. So why don't you just go back to wherever the fuck you came from and leave me alone?"

Dylan leaped to his feet, snatched his coat from the back of his chair, and ran out of the restaurant. Kane sat for a moment, stunned by the suddenness and ferocity of his son's attack. When he came back to himself, he could see the other diners staring at him.

"Just another successful family dinner," he said in a loud voice.

The other diners quickly looked away and began talking to one another. Kane took some money from his wallet, put it on the table, and got to his feet.

"Lotsa food left," the waitress said from behind him. "You want box?"

"No, thanks," Kane said. "I've lost my appetite."

He put on his coat and left the restaurant, retracing his steps toward the hotel.

Laurie was right, he thought. The kid hates me. And when you think about it, can you blame him? He needed a father and I wasn't there. What does he care about the reason?

His thoughts chased one another through his mind, guilt mixing with anger mixing with despair. When he reached the bottom of the stairs, he gave his head a vigorous shake.

There's no use wallowing in it, he thought. What's done is done. I reached out. He slapped my hand away. It's time to move on.

He mounted the stairs steadily, forcing himself to think about how to get people, including his own client, to talk to him. The water on the stair treads had turned to ice, so he stopped at a landing that had a bench on it and put on his ice grippers. Then, keeping a hand on the railing, he climbed. He was breathing hard when he reached the top and the big muscles in his thighs burned.

Live here and you'd have legs like Lance Armstrong, he thought.

His mind slipped back to the incident with his son.

It's like he's forcing himself to hate me, he thought. He knew what that was like; he'd done the same with his own father. If only I could tell him how useless that all is, he thought.

He was so absorbed in his thoughts that he almost missed the scene behind the Capitol. But the flicker of emergency lights brought him back, and he climbed the sidewalk beside the building to see what was going on.

The lights belonged to an emergency van and a police car, which were parked cattywhompus in the parking lot behind the building. A third, unmarked car was parked there, too, motor running and door open. A pair of EMTs and a uniformed policeman stood in a tight circle, talking with a red-haired man in plain clothes. A couple of bystanders watched as another man in civilian clothes looked at something beneath a sheet.

"Hey, Tank," Kane called. "Tank Crawford."

Crawford dropped the edge of the sheet and walked over to where Kane stood outside the railing that divided the parking lot from the sidewalk.

"Evening, bubba," Crawford said. "What are you doing here?"

"On my way back to the hotel from dinner," Kane said. "What you got?"

Crawford shrugged.

"A male Caucasian, hit the asphalt from a considerable height," he said.

"Defenestrated?" Kane asked.

Crawford gave him a grin.

"Yeah, I love that word, too," he said. "But who knows? Fell, jumped, or was pushed at this point."

"Know who it is?" Kane asked.

"Landed on his head," Crawford said, "so official ID will take a while. But his wallet says he's a guy named Ralph Stansfield."

The Juneau detective must have seen something in Kane's face, because he said, "You know this guy?"

"If it's Stansfield, I've talked to him," Kane said. "He worked for Senator Potter."

"Aw, Christ, bubba," Crawford said. "This was going to be political enough if it was somebody connected with the legislature. But this. Crap. What did you talk to him about?"

Kane thought about telling Crawford the whole story but decided against it. He didn't know what the detective, or his bosses, might do with the information.

"I was just trying to find out what it's like working in Potter's office," he said, "to try to understand Melinda Foxx better. And maybe get some inside dope about her, too."

Crawford looked at him for a long time.

"Well," he said at last, "I can't see where talking to him gets you into this, bubba. Unless he told you something?"

"No," Kane said, "he didn't."

Crawford was silent for a minute or two.

"Why don't you stick around anyway?" he said. "I've got a few things to do, and then maybe you can tell me what you know about this guy."

Kane thought about Alma Atwood waiting for him. Business before pleasure. God damn it.

"Okay," he said. "I'll wait."

Crawford walked back to where the other men were talking. Kane took his cell phone from his pocket and dialed.

"Hi, Alma," he said. "It's Nik. I'm calling to say I can't make it."

He listened.

"No, it's work," he said. "Ralph Stansfield. You know, the aide to Senator Potter? He's dead. He took a dive off the Capitol fire escape."

He listened again.

"Yes, yes, it is terrible," he said. "Anyway, I talked to him the other night, and the cops want me to tell them what was said."

He listened some more.

"No, I don't know anything," he said. "But if I hang around, maybe I can learn something. Two staffers in the same office dying in a week's time is a hell of a coincidence."

He listened, nodding.

"Yeah, I'm disappointed, too," he said. "But it's work, so I don't have much choice. Can I have a rain check?"

He smiled, nodding some more.

"Yes, I know it rains all the time in Juneau," he said. "'Bye."

He closed the cell phone, put it into his pocket, and leaned against the fence. He didn't know how long Crawford would be, but he had plenty to think about in the meantime.

22

If you want to succeed in politics you must keep
your conscience firmly under control.

<small>DAVID LLOYD GEORGE</small>

The cell phone chirped loudly on the bedside table. Kane groped
around, snared it on his third pass, and put it to his ear. It chirped
again. Sighing, he opened the phone and mumbled. No one answered.
He peered at the phone. He was holding it upside down. He righted it
and barked a hello.

"Rough night, Sergeant Kane?" Mrs. Richard Foster asked cheerfully.

"Lemme callya back," he said. "Twenny minutes."

He closed the phone, set it back on the table, and surged to an
upright position, legs over the side of the mattress, feet on the floor.
He peered at the clock. Seven A.M. He hadn't gotten loose from Crawford until after eleven, and then, for some reason, hadn't been able to
get to sleep. He'd tossed and turned and thought about the case, his

life, and how much he wanted a beer. Just one beer. Several times he'd been about to jump out of bed and head to the bar, but managed to convince himself to stay put. But with all that, it had been about 2 A.M. before he fell into a fitful sleep full of bizarre, awful, sexually charged dreams. He was grateful that he couldn't remember any of the details. But the memory of the feelings the dreams had fathered lingered on as an ache beneath his ribs, imprinted on his heart like the aftermath of a charley horse burned into a muscle.

Kane walked into the bathroom, turned the cold water on full blast, flipped the selector, and stuck his head under the torrent that raced from the shower. The frigid water snapped him awake. He held his head under the water for as long as he could stand it and emerged blowing and shaking like a seal hauling out. He adjusted the temperature, showered, and sat on the bed in his underwear. He wanted to dress and find a cup of coffee, several cups in fact, but didn't have the time. He arranged his pillows, lay down, picked up his cell phone, and dialed his employer.

"What can I do for you, Mrs. Foster?" he asked.

"You didn't call yesterday," she said.

"You're right," he said. "Sorry. Things got a little complicated."

"They got a little complicated here, too," she said. Anger crackled in her voice. "I got a call from Governor Hiram Putnam last night. An abusive, threatening call, about my involvement with Senator Hope's defense."

Ah, crud, Kane thought.

"I told his guy, Blair, that you'd hired me," Kane said. "I guess I should have warned you about that. He had information I needed, and the only way to get it was to trade."

"Trade?" she said, her voice rising. "You traded my privacy, even after I specifically told you I don't want anyone to know about my involvement?"

Kane let the silence string out, then said in a mild voice, "I'm sorry if you've been inconvenienced. But you hired me to help Senator Hope, and that's what I'm doing, the best way I know how."

"I don't see how telling—" the woman began, but Kane overrode her.

"You don't have to see," he said. "You hired me, you didn't buy me. You can fire me, and all you'll be out is some expenses. But you don't get to tell me how to do my job, and you certainly don't get to second-guess me. Those are the terms. You decide."

This time Kane let the silence lie there until the woman said, "All right, we'll do this your way. For now. Do you object to telling me what's been going on?"

"Not at all," Kane said, and recounted the previous day's events, leaving out his disastrous dinner with Dylan and ending with his session with Crawford after the body had been removed from the Capitol parking lot.

"Men with guns?" she said when he'd finished. "A dead cat? Who would kill a cat to make a point? That's so childish."

Kane said nothing and, after a few moments, she continued, "The cleaner thing is interesting. Icky, but interesting. Any ideas about it?"

They discussed the question for a few minutes without really getting anywhere. Then the woman said, "Did you learn anything from the Juneau detective about the second death?"

"Nope," Kane said, "except that he's sure it will be taken out of his hands, too, and given to the troopers, on the grounds that it might be related to the Melinda Foxx murder."

"Do you think it is?" she asked.

"Two deaths in the same office in a week?" Kane said. "I think there's a good chance they're related somehow."

"But couldn't this latest death be an accident?" she said.

"It could," Kane said. "It was Stansfield's habit to go out onto the fire escape to smoke, and I know firsthand that metal stairs were slippery last night. But until there's conclusive evidence his fall was an accident, I'm going to proceed as if it weren't, and that it's related to the first murder, and I expect the authorities are, too."

The woman started to speak, but Kane went on, "If I'm going to get anywhere on any of this, the first thing I need is cooperation from Matthew Hope. Have you spoken to him?"

"I haven't," the woman said, "but I will. I'm not sure that I can convince him to talk to you. But I'll try."

"Please try soon," Kane said. "Right now would be good."

"All right," she said. "The moment we hang up, I'll call Senator Hope." She hesitated, then continued, "I'm sorry if I lost my temper. It's just that . . . tomorrow is the anniversary of my husband's death, and I miss him so. And it's so wrong that a good man like Matthew Hope is in trouble. And listening to that sleazeball Putnam threatening me, I got angry, really angry. I felt like sending Winthrop down there to see him."

"If you do, let me know," Kane said. "I'd like to watch." He paused, then resumed, "I'll make a real effort to keep in better touch."

"Please do," the woman said and hung up.

Kane spent a moment speculating about his employer's motives. She seemed far more concerned about Matthew Hope than an interest in politics might justify. But then, politics were a lot more compelling for some people than for others.

Maybe if I understood the attraction, I'd be doing better on this case, he thought. As it is, I'm just stumbling around, as uncertain in the investigation as I am on the ice.

He closed his eyes for a moment and, when he bolted upright in the bed again, the clock read 11:30 A.M.

Aw, crap, he thought. He dressed and hurried to what he now thought of as his coffee shop for breakfast.

He was just swallowing his last bite of bagel when his cell phone rang again.

"Mr. Kane?" a man said. "This is Matthew Hope. I'm at my office in the Capitol. How would you like to go for a walk?"

"That'd be fine with me," Kane said. "Are we walking far?"

"Just around a trail they call the Flume," Hope said, "but dress warm."

"In that case," Kane said, "I'll have to go back to my hotel and put on more clothes. Say, half an hour?"

"Fine," Hope said. "Just come up to my office when you get here."

Kane got another cup of coffee to go and walked back to the hotel. In his room, he stripped off his clothes and put on lightweight polypropylene long underwear. He put jeans and a flannel shirt on top of that, then covered his feet in a pair of polypropylene hiking socks. He really needed better shoes, but with the ice grippers they'd probably do. He put a wool hat in one coat pocket and gloves in another. He was halfway out the door when he stopped, went back into the room, and removed his coat. He threaded the holster onto his belt so that it rode on his left hip. He retrieved the automatic from the towel and clipped it into the holster. Then he put his coat back on and left the room.

The steps of the Capitol were crowded again, and another man was giving another speech. Kane recognized him as the cadaverous-looking man who had been talking with the Potters at the Defenders of Alaska Families reception. His speech was full of derogatory comments about gays and "the servants of the devil who helped them in the legislature."

One part of his audience was carrying antigay signs and applauded every time he stopped to take a breath. Another, smaller group held signs supporting equal rights and greeted the speaker's rhetorical sallies with boos and catcalls. A half-dozen Juneau police officers stood between the two groups. Dylan, Samantha, and Alma Atwood stood a little apart from the second group, watching the proceedings. They were talking to one another and laughing. A big band of reporters was off to one side, filming and taking notes.

Hoping for a riot, Kane thought. Make a better story.

The whole assemblage had the entry to the Capitol thoroughly plugged, so Kane waited until the speaker had finished. A man carrying a Bible came forward to lead the protesters in a long prayer full of references to the Old Testament. The counterprotesters tried to drown him out by singing "We Shall Overcome," but they didn't have a sound system and didn't seem to know the words very well.

The prayer ended and the crowd began to break up. There were isolated scuffles, but the police dealt with them swiftly. Kane mounted the stairs to the Capitol. As he reached the entryway, the cadaverous man reached out and put a hand on his shoulder.

"Friend," he intoned, "why are you encouraging evil?"

The reporters who had pressed close to interview the man shifted their attention to Kane.

"Friend," he said, his voice hard, "take your hand off my shoulder."

"You threaten me?" the cadaverous man said. "As the Sodomites threatened Lot and his visitors? I warn you, they were struck blind for their evil."

Kane reached over, grabbed the man's wrist, and pulled his hand away.

"A guy who is trying to incite ill feeling toward gay people really shouldn't be pawing another man in public," he said, and started into the building.

Somebody in the clutch of reporters tittered. The cadaverous man started screaming, "We know who you are. We know that violence is your way. Be careful lest righteous violence overwhelm you."

Kane stopped and walked back to the cadaverous man.

"Who are you?" he asked.

The cadaverous man didn't reply.

"He's Jimmy Joe Carlisle," one of the reporters said, "the executive director of Defenders of Alaska Families."

"Well, Mr. Carlisle," Kane said, "perhaps if you were more comfortable with your sexuality, you wouldn't be trying to make trouble for your fellow citizens."

Carlisle started ranting again. Ignoring him, Kane walked into the building, past an excited-looking security guard, and into the elevator. He punched the button for the fourth floor.

I guess they never search anybody, he thought as the elevator made its slow way upward. You could bring a machine gun in here easy. Might do the state some good with it, too.

Hope's receptionist looked upset.

"Senator Hope is expecting me," Kane told her.

"He's in there now with somebody," she replied softly. "The troopers."

Kane thought for a moment and said, "I'm sure he won't mind if I join them."

He opened the door to Hope's inner office and walked through.

A couple of men got to their feet as he entered. They were big men, Kane's size, and not young.

"What the . . ." one of the men said.

"Why, if it isn't my favorite state troopers," Kane said. "Hello, Sam. What's it been? A year? A little more. And you, Harry. Still on the job? The shooflies must be asleep at the switch."

"Look, Kane," the one he'd called Harry said, taking a step toward him, "get your ass out of here or I'll throw you out."

Kane laughed.

"What is it the tough guys say, Harry?" he said. "Don't let your mouth write any checks your ass can't cash?"

The other trooper, Sam, stepped between Kane and his partner.

"There'll be none of that," he said. "Nik, you know better than to interfere in an investigation."

"Investigation?" Kane said. "You guys are investigating something? That'd be news to everybody in this building."

"Hey," Harry began, but his partner cut him off.

"What's happened so far means nothing to us," Sam said. "As of today, we're investigating the Melinda Foxx murder, and the mysterious death of Ralph Stansfield. We just started this morning."

"Great," Kane said. "You don't mind if I watch, do you? I might pick up a few pointers."

He started toward an unoccupied chair. Harry stepped into his path.

"Take one more step and I'll arrest you for obstructing an officer in the performance of his duty," he said.

Kane gave him a big grin.

"That's a good one, Harry," he said. "I'll have to remember that one." To Sam, he said, "I don't see any cuffs on the senator, so you haven't arrested him. We're in his office, and he invited me here. I'm certain he won't talk to you without his lawyer present, anyway. Will you, Senator?"

Hope had been silent, watching the other three men like they were putting on a play.

"No," Hope said, "I'd just explained that to these gentlemen, and was listening to that one," he nodded toward Harry, "threaten me with all sorts of awful things if I didn't answer his questions."

Kane took another step to put himself nose-to-nose with Harry.

"Harry here was always impetuous," he said. "And it's probably getting to be a long time between drinks for him, which would make him jumpy."

Kane saw the punch coming but made no move to block it. Instead, he hunched his shoulder, tucked his chin, and leaned in. Harry's fist bounced off the shoulder, then glanced off the side of his head. Stars danced briefly before his eyes. Before either man could move, Sam jumped behind his partner and threw his arms around him.

"That's enough," he said, dragging Harry backward. He unlocked his arms, put a hand on Harry's elbow, and steered him toward the door. "Since the senator here isn't feeling talkative, we'll leave."

"Go get your story straight," Kane said. "I'll be filing an assault charge against Harry with your internal affairs office."

Harry whirled and started toward Kane again but found Sam in his way.

"I'll kick your ass, Kane," Harry bellowed. "I'll mop the floor with you."

"Aw, Nik," Sam said over his shoulder as he kept himself between the two men, "there's no need to be filing charges."

"Sam," Kane said, "he hit me without reason. I've got you and the senator as witnesses. I figure that Harry gets one more black mark on his jacket and they'll put him out to pasture, maybe without a pension. That'd suit me just fine. He's big, dumb, lazy, and mean. He's everything that's wrong with the troopers. And he's a drunk in the bargain."

Harry made another try to get around his partner. Sam put his hand on Harry's chest and shoved.

"We're leaving now," Sam said, shoving Harry again. "You should think hard about filing that complaint, Nik."

The two men struggled through the door and were gone. When Kane was sure they wouldn't be back, he walked over and sat in one of the chairs they vacated.

"What was that all about?" the senator asked him.

"I know those guys," Kane said. "Known them for years. I solved a case for them, a mine robbery, last year. Sam is a good investigator, probably the best the troopers have got, so they get sent all over the state. But he's been carrying his partner for years—Harry isn't a good anything anymore. He's a disgrace to his badge."

The senator nodded.

"Why did you provoke him?" he asked.

"Provoke?" Kane said. "Me?"

Hope smiled.

"If you want me to tell you the truth," he said, "you should tell me the truth."

"Okay," Kane said. "I provoked him so that he'd do something stupid. Now that he has, I can use it as leverage in case I need something from those guys. In fact, I've already got something in mind."

"You'd let someone hit you for that?" Hope asked.

"Harry hits like a girl," Kane said. Then: "You still want to take that walk? It's too hot in here for the way I'm dressed, especially after doing the mambo with Harry."

"I do," Hope said and got to his feet. He pulled a pair of white wind pants over his wool pants, exchanged his slip-on shoes for a pair of lightweight hikers, and took a bright yellow shelled pile jacket from a hook.

"Let's go," he said.

The two men walked down the stairs and out a back door into the parking lot. Cars dotted the lot and ribbons of yellow crime-scene tape festooned the fire escape from the Senate Finance offices. They crossed a street and mounted a long flight of stairs past a former grade school that had been converted to offices for the legislative bureaucracy.

"What did the troopers want?" Kane asked as they climbed. For some reason, he found it hard to talk and breathe at the same time.

"They wanted to know where I was last night," Hope said.

"If you . . . had . . . an alibi?" Kane panted.

Hope nodded.

"Do . . . you?" Kane asked.

Hope shook his head.

"Where . . . were . . . you?" Kane asked.

"In my office," Hope said. "Then at home. Enjoying my freedom. Alone."

At the top of the stairs, they crossed another street and started up another flight, longer and steeper, that ran between houses. Kane decided to save his breath for climbing. Hope seemed to be doing the same. Their efforts soon brought them to a more level road that led past a few houses, then around the shoulder of a still-higher hill. Ahead lay a seemingly undisturbed valley.

That's Alaska, Kane thought. One minute city, next minute wilderness.

The sun shone brightly through broken clouds. A light wind cooled them as they walked. They followed the road, then turned off to a path that led over a bridge across a partially frozen creek. They found themselves on a well-traveled trail sandwiched between the creek and a steep hillside. Hope led the way in silence.

"I like a good nature hike as well as the next guy," Kane said at last, "but I'm here under the impression that you have some things to tell me."

Hope stopped in the lee of a small stand of spruce, turned, and said, "I'm being advised to tell you about my relationship with Melinda Foxx." He paused. "But I'm finding it hard to do so."

Kane unzipped his coat. The heat of the sun had warmed him too much during their walk.

"Why's that?" Kane asked. "You must have checked by now to see if I'm trustworthy. If you didn't think I was, we wouldn't be here."

A smile flashed across Hope's face.

"It's not you," he said, "at least, not you personally. It's just that . . ."

Hope stopped talking for so long that Kane began to fidget.

"I'm just a simple Indian," Hope said at last. "I have to be careful."

Kane laughed.

"You can forget that 'many moons ago my people' routine," Kane said. "I'm not buying. You've been playing the political game for—what, ten years now? And pretty successfully, too, by all accounts."

Hope opened his mouth to say something, but Kane continued, "But you're making a mistake in dealing with me. I don't care about the politics. I'm here to help you beat this murder charge, as long as you didn't do it. And as long as you don't tell me about any other crimes you may have committed, what you tell me stays with me. And even if I was inclined to blab, I'm constrained by attorney-client privilege because I work for your lawyer. So stop playing coy and tell me."

The two men looked at each other for a handful of minutes.

"Melinda was giving me information," Hope said. "Information about Senator Potter, about what he was doing."

"You mean, like, about his shady contracts and illegal campaign contributions?" Kane asked.

Hope nodded.

"Why was she doing that?' Kane asked.

"I'm not really sure," Hope said. "She said it was because she believes in good government and what he is doing is wrong."

"That's it?" Kane asked. "She was just being a good citizen?"

"That's what she said," Hope replied, "but in politics, there's usually more than one reason that things happen."

"Do you know what other motivations she might have had?" Kane asked.

Hope shook his head.

"I don't," he said.

Kane stood thinking for a while, then asked, "Did you see her the night she was killed?"

"I did not," Hope said. "She sent me an e-mail saying she'd meet me in our usual meeting place, that she had something important to tell me. But she never arrived. I went looking for her, and that's how I found her. Her body."

Kane looked carefully at the other man.

"And that's it?" he asked. "She was helping you for reasons you don't know. She had something to tell you, but she never showed up?"

"That's everything I know," Hope said.

The faint sound of a human voice made the two men look around. High above them, two people in brightly colored coats moved across the hillside. They seemed to be roped together. Kane couldn't tell if they were men or women. Or children, for that matter.

"Why haven't you told anyone about this?" he asked Hope.

"I don't want anyone to know," the senator said. "If my colleagues knew I had a spy in another senator's office, it would cause me a lot of problems."

Kane shook his head.

"So political decorum is more important than saving your neck?" he asked.

"It's more than decorum," Hope said. "Much of what we do is done on faith, because we believe that someone will do what he or she says. And sometimes two people tell each other things that must be kept quiet, at least for a while. So trust is essential, and me having somebody spy on one of my colleagues is not exactly a trustworthy thing to do."

"Did it bother you personally?" Kane asked. "Beyond the chance you'd get caught, I mean? Did it cause you moral qualms?"

He let the silence stretch out until he was sure Hope wasn't going to answer, then said, "Never mind. Did you keep the e-mail?"

Hope shook his head.

"No, I erased it," he said. "I didn't want it sitting around where somebody might find it."

The voice above them grew excited. Kane looked up to see the leading figure stop. Was he kicking at something, or just trying to keep his feet? Suddenly, the spot he was standing on began moving. He scrambled backward. Rocks came loose and bounded down the hillside toward where Kane and Hope stood.

Without a word, Hope pivoted and ran up the trail. Kane was close behind. They could hear the clatter of rocks coming down and the softer, deeper sound of the water-soaked, sun-heated hillside giving way, bringing ice and snow with it. They ran faster. Kane's pulse pounded in his head and the rasp of his breathing mixed with the sounds of the avalanche. Ahead of him, Hope stumbled, twisted in the air, and came down on his feet like a cat. They ran on. Bits of earth and broken rock pelted them, when, suddenly, they turned a corner and the avalanche was behind them. They ran on another fifty yards or so and Hope fell to his knees. Kane caught a tree branch and stood there on shaky legs, bent over, panting. He could still hear the noise of the avalanche crunching down the hillside.

The noise had stopped by the time they caught their breath. The two men walked unsteadily back and looked around the corner. The trail was buried in dirt, rocks, ice, and snow for what looked like a hundred yards.

"Damn," Hope said. "Damn. We could have been killed."

Kane nodded and scanned the hillside. There was no sign of the two figures that had started the avalanche.

He turned to look at Hope. The senator had his head down and was mumbling something that sounded like a prayer of thanks. When he was finished, he looked at the detective.

"Did you see those two men?" he asked. "Are they all right?"

"No sign of them," Kane said. "Either they're under all that or they've gotten out of sight. Too bad. I'd like to know if that was an accident."

Hope looked at him in surprise.

"Do you think they might have caused the avalanche on purpose?" he asked. "That they were trying to kill us? That seems a little far-fetched."

"Far-fetched?" Kane said. He was surprised at the anger in his voice. "Two people are already dead, Senator. This is a serious business. I'd advise you to treat it that way."

Hope was shaking his head.

"An avalanche as a murder weapon?" he said. "I find that hard to believe."

Right then, Kane wanted to take the other man by the shoulders and shake him. Instead, he took his cell phone from his pocket. It told him he had no signal.

"Come on," he said. "We've got to hike back to where I can call 911. They'll have to close the trail, and somebody may want to search for the people who caused this. And if they find them alive, I'll have a few questions of my own to ask."

23

Politics is a profession; a serious, complicated
and, in its true sense, a noble one.

Dwight David Eisenhower

Think we should have tried to find those men if they were buried?"
Hope asked as they trudged back to the city.

Kane shook his head.

"What would we have dug them out with?" he asked. "Our hands?"

Hope nodded.

"Yeah," he said, "and there's no telling how unstable that hillside
still is. We could have started another slide and gotten buried ourselves."

Kane wondered if he was rehearsing his answer, in case some
reporter asked him why he hadn't played hero. Not that it mattered.
They really had no way to be of assistance.

They walked along in silence for a while, each of them with his own
thoughts. Kane was thinking about how good it was to have escaped

the mixture of human stupidity, or malignity, and indifferent nature. When he reached a spot where his cell phone worked, Kane dialed emergency and reported the avalanche. He told the operator about where it was, and that he had seen two people on the hillside before the avalanche but not after. She took down the information, including his name and telephone number, and thanked him.

By the time the call was complete, the two men had reached the top of a long flight of stairs that took them past some houses to a street. The street led downhill some more, past the city cemetery, then up and around, past the governor's mansion, a turn-of-the-twentieth-century structure complete with columns.

"So that's where you want to live?" Kane asked.

Hope stopped and turned to look at the detective.

"Is that so unlikely?" he asked. "Why shouldn't I want to be governor? Why shouldn't a Native be in charge of the state that is so much more important to us than it is to most of you?"

"Whoa, slow down there," Kane replied. "I think anybody who wants to be governor is an idiot, no matter what color he is. Politics makes no sense to me at all."

Hope turned and started walking again.

"Politics is all we have," he said, "the only way we have to shape what our state will become. It's how we sort out our differences and find compromises. It's how we try to decide who we will be as a people and what legacy we will pass on to those who come after us. It's very damned important, and there's no shame in wanting to use it for good ends."

Kane shrugged.

"Everybody thinks their ends are good," he said, "even when they are completely opposed to somebody else's good ends. Take this civil unions bill of yours. Your side says that gays should be able to establish their relationships legally. Your opponents say recognition like that only helps them lose their souls to sin."

"That's just bigotry," Hope said.

"Maybe," Kane said, "but maybe the bigots don't think so. They think they are protecting their own rights and trying to help those who have made a bad choice. And I don't see how all the politics in the world will find an acceptable compromise between that position and yours."

"Civil unions are a compromise," Hope snapped, then walked awhile in silence. When he resumed, his voice was softer. "People have a lot of different ideas about gays, a lot of different ways to look at them. For myself, the way I look at them is as a group being discriminated against. I'm a Native in Alaska, so I know all about being discriminated against. I think discrimination is wrong, and that by allowing it against one group we encourage it against other groups. That's why I'm trying to get the civil unions bill passed, to break people of the bad habit of discrimination."

Kane nodded.

"Okay, fine, if that's all there is to it," he said. "But some people say you're just using the issue to rally the troops for your run for governor."

Hope laughed.

"Those people must think I'm truly stupid," he said. "The people I'm supposedly rallying are already with me. In electoral terms, all I'm doing is rallying my opposition."

"Then why are you doing it?" Kane asked.

They rounded a corner and the Capitol rose in front of them.

"I'm doing it," Hope said as they crossed the street, "because it's the right thing to do."

They stopped in front of the building's main doors. Hope mounted a couple of steps and turned.

"We've all become very cynical about politics," he said, sweeping an arm in a gesture that seemed to take in the whole state. "We come down here and spend money and pass one bad bill after another, beating up on people who can't fight back. But when it comes to standing up against the powerful, or trying to protect the weak, we look the other way. I'm done looking the other way. I'm going to do everything I can to give gays legal protection. I'm done looking the other way."

Kane heard something in the other man's voice that sounded like sincerity. Since setting foot in Juneau he'd heard and seen a lot about how the political machinery worked, and about the calculations of politicians with one eye on the main chance and the other on reelection. These were the first words he'd heard that were at all inspiring, and he found himself admiring the man who spoke them. For the first time, getting Matthew Hope out of a jam was more than just another job.

"Okay, then," he said, "but watch yourself. A lot of people are working pretty hard to sideline you, if not put you away for murder. So be careful."

Hope nodded at that, turned, and walked up the steps into the Capitol. Kane watched until he was out of sight, then continued toward the coffee shop.

Maybe that's the attraction to politics, he thought, the chance to do something noble. When he'd been on the police force, he'd sometimes thought of his job that way, although he never dared say anything out loud. The other cops would have kidded him right off the force. But he knew that he yearned to be part of something bigger than himself, and lots of other people did, too. He could see that was at least part of the attraction of religion and of politics, and he supposed that's why some people became parents, to make their mark on the world and join in the chain of family that reached backward into history and forward past their time on earth.

Religion doesn't work for me, Kane thought. Maybe politics would. But the thought was quickly followed by doubt. Even if he decided to believe in Matthew Hope's noble causes, there were plenty of people like Senator O. B. Potter, Governor Hiram Putnam, and even Chief of Police Tom Jeffords to make politics the soiled and unappealing process it had become. Institutions are no better than the people in them, he thought, and this cast of characters doesn't inspire much confidence.

The coffee shop was full of hippie-looking young people working on laptop computers, playing guitars, or chattering away. He got a coffee and a big cookie and sat down at the only empty table. As he ate, he wondered what one of these youngsters would say if he asked them what claimed their allegiance. Most likely, none of them would have an answer. When you're young, he thought, life spreads out in front of you like a long, long picnic. You've got your youth and your infinite possibilities. You don't need anything bigger than that.

As he walked back to the hotel, he thought about what he needed to do next. Finding out about what Melinda Foxx had wanted to tell Hope might help. And learning whether Ralph Stansfield had been pushed. So talking with the people in Potter's office seemed to be a good idea. And getting his hands on the rest of the autopsy. At least he had an idea about how to do that.

And then there was Dylan.

Sitting on his bed in the hotel, he looked through a little pocket legislative guide and tried Potter's office. No answer. The same was true at Representative Duckett's office.

I guess they knock off early for the weekend, he thought.

He didn't have Dylan's home number. He called Laurie to get it. No answer there, either.

If everybody had already scattered for the weekend, he wouldn't be able to do much. But the last thing he wanted to do was waste a couple of days sitting around in a hotel room. He picked up the telephone directory, dialed the number for the troopers, and asked for Sam. The woman who answered the phone didn't want to tell him anything, but he finally wheedled a cell phone number out of her. Sam answered on the first ring.

"It's Nik Kane, Sam, " Kane said. "I'd like a look at Melinda Foxx's autopsy report." He listened. "That won't cut it, Sam," he said. "I know you've got it." He paused. "You don't need to know how I know. You just need to know that how you handle this request will affect whether I file a complaint against your partner." Pause. "Now, Sam. Blackmail is such an ugly word." Pause. "That's up to you. I'll meet you anywhere." Pause. "Here? Sure." He gave his room number, then: "Twenty minutes? See you then."

Sam arrived with a briefcase and a sour expression.

"This is low, Nik," he said, opening the briefcase. "When I walk out that door, we're quits."

"If that's the way you want it, Sam," Kane replied, "but I'm not the one who saddled you with a political investigation and a bad partner."

Sam took a report from the briefcase and handed it to Kane.

"You've got to read it here," the trooper said. "I'm not making any copies, and neither are you."

Kane sat down at the table. He made a show of reading the front of the report. No sense letting Sam know he already had it. What the coroner found when he opened Melinda Foxx up was routine until he got to the last page. He read the pair of paragraphs closely, then whistled.

"Any idea who the father is?" he asked, looking at the trooper. Sam was standing stiffly with his back to the hotel room door. He hadn't even taken off his coat.

"What you get is what's there," he said. "That's the deal. Nothing more."

Kane took out his notebook and made a few notes. Then he closed the report, got to his feet, and handed it back to Sam, who returned it to his briefcase and turned to go.

"If you're smart, you'll get Harry to retire," Kane said to the trooper's back. "He's just an accident waiting to happen."

"You should know all about that, Kane," Sam said and went out the door.

Kane picked up his cell phone and punched in a number. After listening for a minute, he said, "Doyle? It's Nik Kane. Call me back on my cell. I have something you'll want to know."

He broke the connection, looked at the legislative directory, and dialed Hope's number. No answer. Probably just as well, he thought. I should talk to Doyle first.

Kane sat back down on the bed, propped some pillows behind his head, and stretched out. He tried thinking about the case, pushing the facts around in his head to see if they formed a pattern. But there were too many missing pieces. So he tried instead to think of a way to approach his son.

What was it that Montaigne wrote? Kane got off the bed to get the Frame translation that was never far from his hand. Here it was: "I would try by pleasant relations to foster in my children a lively and unfeigned affection and good will toward me, which is easily won in a wellborn nature . . ."

But when he lay down again to figure out just how to do that, he fell asleep instead.

The telephone brought him to. After all the walking, running, and stair climbing, his legs felt like a couple of sticks of wood. He had no idea of the time, although by the darkness it was late. Oil Can Doyle was talking a mile a minute, sounding like a gerbil on speed. Kane let him wind down and told him what the autopsy report said.

"Why, the minx," Doyle squeaked. "Any indication of who the father was?"

"None," Kane said, "although I think somebody had better ask our client about that. He was having secret meetings with her."

"What do you mean?" Doyle said. "What secret meetings?"

So Kane told him about his conversation with Matthew Hope. When he finished, Doyle said, "Good work. Let me talk to Hope about this other thing. I've got to establish a better relationship with him somehow, and maybe this will help. I'll call him and see what he says, and change my ticket to be back Sunday night. Maybe we should meet. In the bar there at the hotel?"

They set a time and Doyle hung up. Kane lay there for a minute, feeling hungry and slightly disoriented. He heaved himself to his feet, stripped, showered, and dressed again. His hand was on the doorknob when his phone rang again. It was Alma Atwood.

"I've got everything for a pretty good dinner," she said, "if you aren't busy."

Kane didn't have to think long about the offer.

"What can I bring?" he asked.

"Just yourself," Alma said. "And maybe a toothbrush."

"I'll run right over," Kane said. "I'll be there in about thirty seconds."

That brought a laugh from Alma.

"See you soon," she said and broke the connection.

Kane put a few things in his coat pockets and took the elevator down to the lobby. He thought about calling Cocoa, then about all the guff he'd have to take when he revealed his destination. A cab was discharging passengers at the hotel, so he grabbed it instead.

"Where can I get flowers this time of night?" he asked.

The cabbie took him to a supermarket, where Kane picked up a couple of bunches of flowers. Then he gave Alma's address. As they made the drive over to Douglas Island, he found himself smiling.

Careful, he thought. You can't go around with your heart on your sleeve all the time.

Alma opened the door to his knock. She was wearing a big, white apron and had something that looked like flour on the end of her nose.

"You really did run over here, didn't you?" she said.

He produced the flowers, and while she made appreciative noises, he looked over the little apartment. It was spotless, the table in the postage-stamp-sized eating area set for two.

They made small talk while Alma fussed with the flowers, emerging from the kitchen with the blooms arranged in a glass vase that she set in the center of the table. She told Kane to sit, returned to the kitchen, and came back with plates full of a fancy dinner: chicken cordon bleu, rice pilaf, baby asparagus, dinner rolls. They sat and ate, Alma talking almost nonstop about the situation in the Capitol.

"There's a rumor that the oil tax increase will come to the floor soon," she said, "although nobody knows why Potter would let it out of his committee."

"What about the civil unions bill?" Kane asked around a mouthful of chicken.

"The word on that hasn't changed," she said. "Still stuck in Potter's committee. And even if Senator Hope could pry it loose somehow, he'd still have to get it to the floor, get enough votes for passage, and shepherd it through the House. And even if he did all that, the governor would veto it. I'm afraid there just isn't much chance."

"If that's true," Kane said, "why are people trying to keep Hope away from the Capitol?"

Alma shrugged.

"It could be anything," she said. "There are something like eight hundred bills, including some big spending bills, that are in play at the moment. But let's not talk about business. It's so depressing."

Then she launched into a funny story about a fight that had erupted between two women at the legislative bowling league the week before, "over a man, of course."

Kane found her liveliness refreshing. You're spending way too much time in your head, he thought, and right now that's a gloomy place to be.

They finished eating and he helped with the dishes. When they were done, she hung the towel neatly, turned, and put her arms around his neck. For a moment, Kane wasn't sure what to do. Then he decided the hell with it and kissed her. The kiss led to another, and that led to other things. An hour later, they lay naked and pleasantly spent. Alma was pressed against him, one leg thrown over his body.

"That was great," she said.

Kane felt a rush of satisfaction, then chuckled. Oh, vanity, thy name is man, he thought.

"You can cook dinner for me anytime," he said.

They lay there for a while, then Alma stirred, got up, and went into the bathroom. When she returned, she said, "Can you stay?"

Kane smiled at her and said, "I can't think of any reason I'd want to leave."

So they dozed, awoke, and made love again, Kane marveling at how his aging body responded to her. Despite sharing a strange bed with a woman he didn't know very well, he slept like a log. He awoke early to Alma's touch and they spent a long time renewing their acquaintance with each other's body before they lay still again.

"I'm sorry to have to say this," Alma said after a while, "but I've got a busy day today and I've got to get going."

Kane looked at the bedside clock. It read 6 a.m. Odd for her to be in such a rush on a Saturday, but he didn't object. He wanted to get some distance, too, to examine his feelings. So he arose, put on his clothes, and brushed his teeth with the toothbrush she'd advised him to bring along. As he was putting on his shoes, Alma emerged wearing a flannel bathrobe. Without makeup, she looked her years and maybe a few more.

I'm a fine one to be making judgments, Kane thought. I probably look like Methuselah's dad.

When he stood up, Alma walked over and kissed him.

"I had a wonderful time," she said.

"Me, too," Kane said.

"Will I see you again?" she asked.

"You can count on it," he said.

Alma laughed.

"Then you won't mind if I ask you to take out the garbage," she said. She went into the kitchen, rustled the bag around, and handed it to Kane.

"The garbage cans are at the end of the driveway, around the other side of the house," she said.

"Will do," Kane said.

"Do you want me to call you a cab?" Alma asked.

"You're a cab," they said in unison, then laughed more than the old joke warranted.

"No, thanks," Kane said. "I'm going to walk for a while, then I'll call one on my cell."

They kissed again and Kane left, carrying the garbage bag in his hand. A crunching noise came from the bag, so he felt the outside. Some of the contents seemed to be take-out boxes.

I guess she's not a gourmet cook after all, Kane thought.

He found the garbage cans sitting next to a wooden shed. A screen of bushes hid them from the road. He deposited the bag and turned to walk away.

The blond man stepped out from behind the shed, put a stun gun against Kane's neck, and sent 300,000 volts rampaging through his body.

24

Power politics is the diplomatic name for the law of the jungle.

ELY CULBERTSON

Kane's muscles spasmed and he began to fall. The blond man grabbed one arm and his dark-haired companion stepped out to grab the other. They dragged him to a delivery van and dumped him onto the floor. The dark-haired man jumped into the back with him. The blond closed the doors, looked around, got into the van on the driver's side, started it, and drove away.

Kane's muscles felt like pudding. He tried to throw a punch at the dark-haired man and his arm barely twitched. By the time some semblance of control returned, the dark-haired man had taken off Kane's coat, handcuffed him, and sealed his lips with a piece of duct tape. He pulled up Kane's sleeve and tied a piece of rubber tubing around his biceps. When the veins in his arm popped out, the dark-haired man took the covering off the tip of a syringe and, ignoring Kane's attempts to struggle, knelt on his chest and shoved the needle into his arm. In a matter of moments, the world was a tiny place at the wrong end of a long, long telescope. Then it was nothing at all.

Afterward, he had no idea of how much time had passed. His memories were a jumble of voices and dimly seen faces, movements, and noises. He had the impression of an argument, a loud voice barking orders, and under it all, country music. All of his senses were blunted by something, like he was experiencing life from the bottom of a pond. Every time he was about to reach the surface, he'd feel a pain in his arm and start sinking again.

Kane came around to the sound of voices.

"We've got to stop giving him this stuff," one voice said. "He almost stopped breathing the last time."

"I gave him the dose we were given," the other voice replied. "He's a big guy. He'll be all right."

"He'd better be," the first voice said. "I'm not sure I want murder on top of everything else."

"Aw, fuck him," the second voice said, "and that faggot lover he's working for."

Kane lay on something soft, his hands cuffed to something over his head. The duct tape was still in place over his mouth. His head ached like he'd been hit by Muhammad Ali, every single muscle was sore, and he felt like he was going to throw up.

Better not, he thought. Not a good idea to barf while gagged.

He heard footsteps approaching and fought to keep his breathing even and his muscles relaxed. Even through closed eyelids, he could sense someone looming over him. Fingers touched his neck, lay there, then withdrew. Then they grabbed his ear and twisted. Kane ignored the pain. The fingers let go of his ear and the footsteps led away.

"He's still out," the first voice said. "What are we going to do? I'm getting hungry."

"If it was me, I'd cap his ass," the second voice said, "but that's not what we're getting paid for. So let's just throw a blanket over him and go get something to eat. He isn't going anywhere cuffed to that cot. Besides, I'll give him another shot and we'll be back before he wakes up."

"He doesn't need another shot," the first voice said. "He's way under. And the way the stuff seems to be building up in his system, another one might kill him. Our employer wouldn't like that."

"Yeah," the second voice said, "well, fuck him, too. He's got to make a decision about what to do with this guy, and he's waffling around like a teenaged girl trying to pick a prom dress."

"Maybe he's got to check with somebody else," the first voice said.

"Maybe," the second voice said, "but who cares? I say we zork this guy so he can't tell the cops about us, no matter what the big bad boss says. Sooner or later he'll figure out that Mr. Nik Kane can ID us, and that we can ID him. So he'll want the dude dead, anyway."

"Maybe, maybe not. We'll find out soon enough," the first voice said. "One thing I know for sure is that we're not doing anything more until we get our money. Let me make sure this guy's secure and then we can go get some dinner."

Kane heard footsteps approaching and felt a blanket being spread over him. A hand shook his handcuffs. The footsteps left him, were joined by a second set, and trailed off into silence. Kane lay there until he heard the faint sound of a vehicle starting up, then opened his eyes.

It was hardly worth the effort. In the dim light, Kane could see only rock: rock walls that glistened with water, a ceiling hewn by hand out of rock, a rock floor. He tried to lean up to get a better view and pain shot through both shoulders. He swore softly and, gritting his teeth, swung his legs off the cot and walked his feet sideways until he could sit up. The room swam around and his stomach jumped into his throat. He leaned over, got a grip on the edge of the duct tape, and ripped it off. He spent the next couple of minutes retching but didn't have much to bring up.

I must have been out for some time, he thought. I wonder what became of that big dinner I had.

Kane looked around his prison. It seemed to be a cave. He was off to one side. Several feet away, he could see a table and what seemed to be several wooden storage lockers. The faint light was coming from a source he couldn't see. He slid his hands along until the cuffs were at the top of the bunk's metal frame, then stood. His legs gave out and he fell to his knees, retching. The cuffs scraped the skin from his wrists as he went down, and he could feel blood seeping down his left arm. He knelt there for several minutes, waiting for his stomach to stabilize.

Gotta do better than this, he thought. Gotta get out of here before they get back. He climbed slowly to his feet and stood, swaying and drawing deep breaths. When the room quit moving, he tried to drag the cot toward the table. The metal legs squawked across the rock floor a few inches and he stopped, panting. In his condition, even the cot was too heavy to move. He thought about that for what seemed to be a week, got down on his knees, gripped the edge of the cot, and strained. The legs nearest to him left the ground. As the cot rose, Kane twisted and dumped the cot onto its side. Then he dragged it free of the bedding and across the floor. The metal squealed along the rock floor and sparks shot in all directions.

Hope there's no old dynamite in here, Kane thought.

He was tired and sweating by the time he reached the table and sat on one of the metal folding chairs. A couple of water bottles, a big, battery-powered light, and a crank radio sat on the tabletop.

That explains the country music, Kane thought.

He lifted the cot until he could get his hands on a water bottle, twisted off the cap, and lowered his head to drink. When the bottle was empty, he lifted the cot again, arms trembling, picked up the light, and clicked it on. Its brightness dazzled his eyes and he looked away, spots dancing in his vision. As they faded, he looked around. The wooden storage lockers looked to have been handmade, stout and secured with locks and metal hasps. He wasn't getting into them bare-handed. He got up and dragged the cot along the rock floor toward the light, which was coming in around a thick, wooden door that didn't quite fit its opening. The door gave a little when he leaned on it, but then held firm. Locked from the outside.

"This is another fine mess, Ollie," he said aloud.

As he dragged the cot back toward the table, it clinked against something. Kane stopped, dragged the cot around, and saw an old, rusty pick mattock lying against the wall. He got to his knees and dragged it away from the wall with his fingertips. The head still seemed securely fastened to the handle. He fumbled with it until he got it onto the cot springs. Then he got to his feet, stuffed the mattock end between the bed frame and headboard, and heaved.

The mattock jumped out of the opening and the handle fetched him a sharp blow on the right kneecap.

"Jesus," he yelled as he hopped around, only to be brought up short by the handcuffs.

When the feeling returned to his knee, he crouched, grimacing, slid his hands down the frame, and picked up a rock. He used it to tap the mattock firmly into the opening. Then he leaned against the handle, steadily increasing the pressure. The bolts holding the frame together parted, a piece of metal zinging across the cave like a bullet to ricochet from the rock wall, and the frame sagged to the side.

Success, he thought. At this rate, I'll be free in a week or so.

He pushed his way between the frame and headboard, tapped the mattock into the opening, and wrenched. More metal shot across the cave and the frame separated from the headboard, falling to smack Kane's right foot.

As the pain subsided, he thought, Thank God nobody's here to see this. I must look like all three of the Stooges.

Free of the bed frame, Kane picked up the headboard and the mattock and walked over to the storage lockers. He used the mattock to wrench the hasp free from the wood and open the locker door. Inside was dust, cobwebs, and more rusty tools. One of the tools was a hacksaw. Kane thought about trying to cut himself loose from the headboard but decided he didn't have time. He wrenched open a second locker, which held the same things as the first.

Maybe I'd better just try to get the door open and get out of here before my pals come back, he thought. Then he noticed a new lock on the next locker.

Okay, one more, he thought, and wrenched the door open.

His automatic sat on a shelf next to his wallet and his cell phone. Someone had taken the money out of the wallet, but everything else seemed to be there. He checked the automatic, ejecting the clip to be sure it was loaded. He thought about trying to shoot his way out of the cuffs but knew that, in the condition he was in, he couldn't trust his aim.

He dropped the cell phone into his shirt pocket, stuffed the gun into his pants, picked up the pick mattock, and attacked the door.

Chewing through the door with the pick end of the tool was slow going, especially since he had to stop every few minutes to rest. With every chop, the headboard banged him somewhere, and it got in the way of any full swing. Kane was convinced that his captors would return long before he finished. He concentrated on cutting away the wood around the hasp and, when he could see it he dropped the mattock, pulled out the automatic, pointed it at the hasp, and pulled the trigger.

The noise pounded his ears closed. The hasp sagged. Kane hit the door with his shoulder, but all he got for his trouble was another bruise. He put the automatic's barrel back in place and fired a second shot. The hasp parted. He pushed the door open.

Kane stepped out and looked around. He was in the middle of nowhere, at the end of a narrow, brushy road. He had no idea how far he was from the city. He might be on an island somewhere, for that matter. Southeast was lousy with uninhabited islands. He flipped open his cell phone, turned it on, and was relieved to see that he had a signal. He punched in Cocoa's number.

"Cocoa?" Pause. "I don't care what you were doing, pal. Some goons snatched me up, and now I'm standing in the tules handcuffed to the headboard of a metal cot." Pause. "Okay, here's what I can see." He described his surroundings. Pause. "Okay, then get out here as fast as you can. These guys are coming back, and I'm in no shape to receive them. I'll start walking now."

He closed the cell phone and dropped it into his pocket, got a good grip on the automatic, hoisted the headboard onto his shoulder, and set off. A chill wind cut through his shirt and the headboard tried to snag itself on every branch and bush. He fell once and lay there, willing himself to get up. As he looked into the woods, he thought he could see all of his family looking at him and shaking their heads: his parents, his brothers and sisters, Laurie and the kids. All of them filled with pity and disappointment.

"This isn't my fault," he yelled. The figures faded from his vision, replaced by the awful emptiness of the Alaska landscape.

Too much to do before I die, he thought, just as he had thought in the jungles of Southeast Asia and on the streets of Anchorage. He pushed himself to his feet and set off again. I just hope I have a chance to make things right, he thought as he staggered along. Make peace with Laurie and the kids, try to be the father Dylan should have had instead of some bad Xerox of my own father.

Make things right, he thought. Make things right.

His foot hit a tree root and he fell hard. He didn't have the strength to get up again, so he lay there mumbling to himself. The noise of tires crunching along the old snow and ice of the road reached him and grew louder. He tried to get the automatic around to where he could shoot, but the effort was too much. The last thing he saw was his father, shaking his head.

Too bad ninety percent of the politicians give
the other ten percent a bad reputation.

Henry Kissinger

Kane awoke fighting for his life. He thrashed and kicked and bellowed and tried to get to his feet. A pair of powerful hands held his shoulders until, exhausted, he lay back and opened his eyes.

The room was small, its gleaming surfaces all white. Winthrop's broad brown face stood out like a bear crossing a snowfield. He took his hands off of Kane's shoulders and stepped back, leaving behind a faint undertone of expensive cologne that was immediately masked by the smell of disinfectant and body odor.

That must be me, Kane thought. I don't smell too good.

He was lying in a hospital bed cranked halfway up, a needle sticking into his forearm and monitors clipped here and there. A plastic bag hung from a metal pole. Clear liquid dripped from it down a plastic tube, through the needle, and into Kane's arm.

Hospital, Kane thought. I'm in a hospital.

He felt like he should be in a hospital, like he'd been beaten by an angry mob of small boys with sticks. Some of his muscles hurt. The rest ached. His head felt like it had been inflated to twice its size. And his arm hurt like it had been stabbed several times with a hot poker.

"How are you feeling, Sergeant Kane?" Mrs. Richard Foster trilled.

Kane couldn't see her, so he tried to sit up. The minute he tensed his muscles, he thought better of that. Instead, he tried to say hello, but all that emerged was a croak. Winthrop took a plastic glass from a bedside table and held its straw to Kane's lips. He sucked in a little water.

His stomach tried to turn itself inside out. Kane clamped his throat closed until the wave passed, then said, "I've felt better, Mrs. Foster. What are you doing here?"

"Why, when you disappeared," the woman's voice said, "I felt we had to come. I thought my presence might stir the authorities to greater effort, and Winthrop is very handy."

About halfway through, the woman's answer stopped making sense to Kane. The world began slipping away. He closed his eyes and concentrated on breathing. In. Out. In. Out. Slowly, reality stabilized.

"Could you crank me up?" he asked Winthrop.

Winthrop hit a button, the back of the bed began to rise, and Mrs. Foster came into view. The black veil was gone.

"You, I can see your face," he said.

The woman smiled.

"Yes, you can," she said. "My year of mourning has ended. Do you recognize me?"

He'd known her the minute he saw her.

"Amber Dawn," he said.

The woman's smile lit up the room like a searchlight.

"Why, Sergeant Kane," she said, "how nice of you to remember. We didn't see that much of each other before your . . . mishap."

"Once," Kane said. "I saw you once. But you were pretty unforgettable."

The woman bowed her head and something like a blush crept up her neck.

"You're too kind," she said.

Kane remembered the only time he'd seen Amber Dawn, hanging stark naked except for a G-string from a pole in a topless-bottomless place called the Beaver Trap. It was maybe three weeks before he shot Enfield Jessup and began his journey to prison. He'd been in the Trap with a bunch of other cops, celebrating somebody's birthday, when she'd come out to dance. Thirty seconds into her routine, all the bullshit and horseplay in his group had stopped and every man at the table was staring at her like she was his chance at heaven. Every other man in the place was doing the same, even the bartender and the bouncer, who had seen it all. She didn't move so much as she flowed, her eyes closed, arms above her head, dancing for all the world like she was alone somewhere, somewhere much nicer than the seedy bar with its sketchy patrons. As the music went on, Kane could see a line of sweat run out from under her honey-colored hair and trace a line down the curve of her neck, then run up and over one perfect breast. He'd never said anything to anyone, but that one memory, that image, had helped him through a lot after the shooting and during his long stretch in prison.

The body, that nearly perfect body, had belonged to someone far too young to be dancing in such a place. When her dance ended and she'd harvested the bills that littered the stage floor, he'd gone up to her, shown his badge, and demanded to see her ID, telling himself he was only doing his duty. She'd led him backstage and produced it, standing there as he examined it, making no effort to cover her nakedness. The ID was very professional and absolutely phony. But as he handed it back to her, Kane realized that he couldn't stand for another second so close to her without doing something he would regret. So he'd mumbled his thanks and fled, barely pausing to tell the others he was going. And he hadn't gone back to the Beaver Trap since.

"I know why I remember you," he said, "but why do you remember me?"

The woman looked up. Her smile was fond.

"You were very nice, the way you dealt with me," she said. "Other cops weren't nearly so nice. And you were polite. It was almost like you were afraid of me."

"I *was* afraid of you," Kane said. "I still am, although I'm older now so I hide it better."

The woman's smile changed, and as they looked at each other, Kane felt something like an electrical current pass between them.

Easy now, he thought.

"How did you become . . . how did you end up . . . ," he said, then laughed. "See? I told you I was afraid. I can't even finish a sentence."

The woman looked at him for what seemed like an hour, then shook her head as if breaking a spell.

"How did I end up as a rich widow?" she asked. "Richard came into that place I was dancing with a big group. He was celebrating some business coup and, if I remember correctly, had a woman on each arm. The next thing I knew, Winthrop was backstage with an armload of flowers and an invitation to dinner in a private room at the top of a hotel downtown. Six weeks later, Richard Foster and I were married."

"And lived happily ever after," Kane said. Even to his own ears, his voice sounded full of innuendo.

The woman gave him a sharp look.

"Lots of people said lots of mean things about us getting together," she said, "but we were happy. I know it seems odd, me marrying someone old enough to be my grandfather, but Richard was so kind and so full of life and I felt safe with him. Safe and appreciated for who I was. He never judged me."

"I'm sorry," Kane said. "I wasn't really judging, either. More like envying the old goat."

That brought a smile from the woman.

"There was a lot to envy about him besides marrying me," she said. "He had a life. I remember once, just before we got married, I got my courage up to tell him all the things I'd done—I'd had to do—to stay alive. And he just put a finger on my lips and said, 'I don't want to hear it. If you tell me the bad things you've done, then I'll have to tell you the bad things I've done. And we'll be here for a month.' "

She shook her head.

"I miss him," she said. "I don't mean sometimes, I mean all the time. I mean right now."

Kane let the silence lengthen, then asked, "You said before that you came down here when you learned that I was missing. What did you mean?"

"I guess you had arranged to meet Mr. Doyle after he came back from Anchorage Sunday night," she said. "When you didn't turn up, he tried your hotel room. He let it go until the next day, then he called me. We persuaded the hotel to let us look in your room and when we didn't find anything and you didn't turn up, we called the police. They grumbled about how you are a full-grown adult, but they at least went through the motions. We were starting to get really worried, when your cabdriver friend called and told Mr. Doyle he'd found you."

Kane had a hard time following the woman's story. She made it sound like he'd been gone a long time.

"What day is today?" he asked.

"Wednesday," the woman said. "It's very early Wednesday."

Adrenaline shot through Kane's body.

"Wednesday," he said. "What's happened while I've been gone?"

"What's happened?" the woman said. "For one thing, the authorities have rearrested Senator Hope. They say that woman, that Melinda Foxx, was pregnant and that DNA evidence proves he was, is, what-

224

ever, the father. And they also say that there is evidence that the other staff member was pushed off the fire escape. They're trying to say Senator Hope did that, too. So they argued that he is a flight risk and a danger to the community and, on Monday a judge named Ritter let them put him back in jail."

Kane closed his eyes. Four days. He'd been out of commission for four days. He opened his eyes again. It didn't sound like he had much time to lie around.

"I need a telephone," he said to Winthrop, "and a directory of legislative phone numbers."

Winthrop and Mrs. Foster looked at him oddly.

"It's two a.m.," she said. "No one will be at the office."

"Two a.m.?" Kane said. "What are you two doing here?"

Mrs. Foster smiled at him.

"Winthrop is spending the night in case anything happens," she said. "I'm here because I couldn't sleep."

Kane was silent for a moment.

"What else has happened?" he asked. "Anything in the Capitol?"

Winthrop and Mrs. Foster exchanged looks.

"Well, with Senator Hope in jail, they sent the oil tax bill to the Senate floor this morning and Senator Grantham switched his vote without telling anybody," the woman said. "The tax failed. And both his aides quit. At least, that's the rumor in the Capitol."

"Better give me that phone anyway," he said.

When he had it, he punched in a number and waited. He closed it again without saying anything.

"She's not home," he said. "Or she's not answering."

He punched in another number and waited. After some time, he said, "Laurie? It's Nik." He listened. "Yes, I know what time it is. I wouldn't be calling unless it was necessary. I need Dylan's home telephone number in Juneau." He listened some more. "No, it's business. I wouldn't bother him, either, if it wasn't." He listened again. "Why

don't you let me worry about how he'll react. Please. Okay, thanks."
He listened some more. "Yes, I told you. I'll come and get that stuff as
soon as I'm done here. I haven't forgotten. 'Bye."

He closed the phone, opened it again, and punched in another
number.

"Dylan," he said. "No? I need Dylan Kane. This is his father."
While he waited, he said to Winthrop, "I'll need clothes. I'm getting
out of here."

"The doctor said you should have at least a couple of days' rest, to
let the drugs work their way out of your system," the woman said.

Kane grimaced at her.

"Hello, Dylan," he said. "This is your father." He listened. "Yes, I
know what time it is. I need some information." He listened again.
"I don't really have time to listen to you tell me what a son of a bitch I
am, Dylan. What do you know about Alma Atwood? Has anything
happened to her?" He listened some more. "Dylan, this is important,"
he said sharply. "Stop being childish and answer me." He listened.
"What?" he said. He listened some more. "Thank you, Dylan. We'll
deal with your issues before I leave." He snapped the cell phone shut
and handed it to Winthrop.

"Thank God for the Juneau rumor mill," he said. "The woman I
need to talk to quit, and she's ticketed on the ferry that leaves Auke
Bay at eight a.m. "

He looked at the clock.

"That means I've got time to shower, thank God," he said. "They
wouldn't let me on a cattle boat the way I smell. Winthrop, I thought I
asked for clothes."

Wordlessly, the big Native opened the door to the closet section of
the all-in-one piece of furniture that shared the room with the hospital
bed. Kane's clean clothes hung there. The detective reached over,
peeled the surgical tape from his forearm, and slid the needle out of his
flesh. Then he began disconnecting monitors.

"Nurses will come running," he said to the woman. "Would you mind dealing with them? If nothing else, it will get you out of this room before seeing a sight no decent woman should see when I climb out of this bed."

The woman laughed and got to her feet.

"I like the decent woman part," she said and left the room.

"You're not so lucky, big boy," Kane said. "Give me a hand."

Winthrop took Kane by the shoulders and lifted him to his feet like he was a baby.

"Don't worry, I'm not going to look," Winthrop said as he was doing so. "I value my eyesight."

26

Think of a politician's soul as an apartment. Think of lobbyists as renters. Each year, the renters show up, waving wads of cash.

TONY SNOW

The MV *Fairweather* is 235 feet of aluminum twin-hulled ferry, designed to carry 35 cars and 250 passengers at 32 knots. It was set to scoot up the Inside Passage from Juneau to Skagway and Haines in just two hours' time. Once on the road system, the passengers could go wherever their desires and credit cards took them.

Kane walked aboard as the crew was securing for departure, carrying a big cup of coffee. He'd had to talk both Winthrop and Cocoa out of coming with him.

"You keep a close eye on your employer," he said to Winthrop. "These people are idiots, but they're violent idiots." To Cocoa, he said, "Here's what I want you to do," then gave him instructions.

"What if your bad friends are on the ferry?" Cocoa asked.

Kane patted his side, where the automatic hung from his belt in its holster.

"I'll be fine," he said.

He walked through the car deck as the ferry left the dock, sipping coffee and looking for Alma Atwood's license plate. He found it on a battered Subaru crammed with boxes.

"Hey," a crewman called to him, "nobody's allowed on the car deck while we're under way. You've got to go up to the passenger deck."

Kane nodded and waved, found a companionway, and climbed to the passenger deck. The ferry seemed to be about half full. He worked his way from the stern to the bow and found Alma sitting in the observation lounge, ignoring the attempts of a hairy young fisherman to chat her up.

"Ah, there you are," he said to Alma.

She looked up, gave a little squeal, and swiveled her head around as if looking for an escape route. Kane stepped closer to keep her from getting to her feet.

"Thanks for keeping my daughter company," he said to the fisherman.

The young man looked at Kane, at Alma, at Kane again. He opened his mouth to say something, stopped, shrugged, rose, and walked away. Kane sat in his abandoned chair and rested his hand lightly on Alma's arm. She was trembling.

"We've got to talk," he said.

Alma burst into tears. A couple of passengers looked her way, but Kane's stare sent them back to their own business. He waited as the woman's tears became sobs, then labored breathing.

"Look," he said, "I'm not here to do anything to you. I just need information."

Alma looked at him with skepticism in her face.

"How did you . . . ," she said. "How did you find me?"

"Gossip and connections," he said. "Gossip in the Capitol put you on the ferry, and the connections gave me your license plate so I knew for sure."

Alma nodded, dug around in her purse, pulled out a wad of tissues, dried her eyes and blew her nose.

"I didn't know anything was going to happen to you," she said. "He just said . . . he just said he wanted to get you someplace private to talk."

"Who said?" Kane asked.

Alma looked around again, as if expecting that some way out would magically appear.

"I can't—I can't tell you that," she said. "He said that if I ever told anyone, something bad would happen to me."

Kane nodded and sat silent for a moment.

"Let me explain how things sit," he said. "You set me up for a kidnapping. I can make a citizen's arrest and haul you back to Juneau, where you'll have to talk and you'll probably go to jail. Or you can tell me what I want to know and go on your way. You decide."

They sat for a pair of minutes. Rain began hitting the observation room windows, then turned to hail that rapped the windows like BBs. The vibration of the ship remained unchanged as it raced ahead. Kane could feel the weariness in him try to assert itself and fought it back. He didn't have time to rest.

"It was George Bezhdetny," Alma said.

Kane nodded.

"Tell me the whole story," he said.

Alma dabbed at her nose, took a deep breath, and began.

"George has been hanging around the legislature now five or six years," she said. "The gossip is that he came over from the Ukraine, where he did stuff for the Communists before the . . . you know, the change over there. He started out working in the lounge, of all things, like busing tables or something. He got to know some of the legislators, since most of them go in there to hide out from time to time. You know, nobody but legislators and people who work there can go in. Anyway, from there he got a staff job for one of the House members, then, after a couple of years, set up as a lobbyist.

"As a lobbyist, he was kind of a joke. He had weird clients and didn't make much money, just hung around doing errands for legislators and more powerful lobbyists. But at the end of last session, I don't know, he started dressing better and taking people out to fancy meals and just acting more like a player. Everybody thought he'd gotten some hot new client, but I checked his disclosure report and nothing showed up. So we all figured he was getting paid under the table. The law requires lobbyists to declare all their clients, but there's lots of ways besides lobbying fees to pass money around."

She stopped to dab at her nose.

"What's all this got to do with what happened?" Kane asked.

Alma gave him an offended look.

"You said you wanted the whole story," she said. "That's what I'm giving you."

She reached down and rummaged in her purse, came up with a water bottle, and took a drink.

"Then, just before session, our receptionist quit and the senator hired Jennifer," she said. "He told me that George had recommended her."

Alma's voice dropped.

"You probably heard that Senator Grantham and I were . . . well, we were an item," she said. "But we weren't here two weeks and I was out and Jennifer was in. When I asked the senator about it, he acted like it was just some sort of change in staff assignments. The bastard."

She paused to cry a little more. Kane let her. When she stopped, he said, "Why did you do it, Alma? Why did you get involved with him in the first place?"

Alma shrugged.

"I was young," she said. "What did I know? At first, I thought maybe he'd leave his wife for me. Then, by the time I knew that wasn't going to happen, it was just . . . just the way things were. He had power, and I had power over him, and we just seemed to be kind of . . . kind of a team."

The look she gave him was so forlorn that Kane decided to drop it.

"Okay," he said, "back to you and George."

She nodded and continued.

"George knew I was unhappy," she said. "How could he not? Everyone did. I should have left, but I couldn't afford it. These staff jobs don't really pay all that well, and there's the expense of moving back and forth and, if you are a woman, looking good. So I didn't have any money in the bank and I was miserable.

"Then all this stuff started happening. George seemed really happy that Senator Hope was in trouble, although he tried to keep it to himself. When you showed up, he sort of asked me to keep an eye on you. Said he'd pay me for it. Then, a few days ago, he says he has to talk to you and could I get you alone so he could."

She shook her head, drew a deep breath, and continued.

"I said I wouldn't," she said. "He just sort of smiled and took a fat envelope out of his pocket and handed it to me. We were in my office, the day after I got so drunk, I remember. I opened the envelope and it was full of money. It turned out to be ten thousand dollars. 'Drop dead money,' he called it. And . . . and the chance to walk away from it all, to just leave that bastard Grantham and this awful situation, just overwhelmed me and I said yes. I'm so sorry. I didn't mean for you to get hurt."

Alma started sobbing again. Kane sat quietly until she finished, then said, "So George Bezhdetny paid you to help him get me out of the way? Why did he do that?"

Alma shrugged.

"I don't know," she said, "except that he didn't want Senator Hope to get out of his trouble, at least not soon."

"How about his client?" Kane asked. "Any idea who that is?"

Alma just shook her head.

"How about Jennifer?" he asked "Why did she quit?"

"Maybe she just saw through that bastard Grantham a lot faster than I did," she said. "Maybe she was really outraged by his vote on oil taxes. I know I was."

"Alma," Kane said, "that vote wasn't why you did anything. I looked at your car. You must have been already packed by the time the vote happened."

Alma sighed and nodded.

"You're right," she said. "It was just a pretext to get the hell out of Juneau. But it was still the wrong thing for him to do. And I just don't understand why he did it."

She was silent and, when it didn't seem like Kane was going to speak again, she said softly, "What happens now?"

Kane understood that she was really asking what would happen to her.

"I suppose that, as a good staffer, you've got a pen and some paper in that storage locker you call a purse," he said. "I want you to write down just what you told me, sign it, and date it. Every page. Then, when the ferry docks, you can go wherever you want. I'll try to not use your statement unless I have to. But don't kid yourself. There's nowhere you can go that you can't be found."

Alma nodded, took a pen and steno pad from her purse, and began writing. Kane watched the other passengers watch the scenery. They'd passed through the rain, and the sun was playing tag with the ferry through the clouds. The throbbing of the ship's engines and the sunshine and the warmth of the woman next to him conspired to put him to sleep, but he drank his coffee and fought against his weariness until Alma finished. She handed him the statement, prepared just as he'd said.

She was probably a very good staffer, he thought.

He read the statement, tore it from the pad, folded it, and put it into a pocket. On the port side of the observation deck, people pointed over the side and talked excitedly.

"Orcas," one of them called across the deck. "A pod of orcas."

The other passengers hurried over to look, leaving Kane and Alma isolated in their chairs.

"I'm really sorry, Nik," Alma said. "I never meant for anything bad to happen to you. I . . . I like you. A lot. It's just, I had to get out and this seemed like the only way."

"That's okay, Alma, I understand," Kane said as he got to his feet. "It was just politics."

27

As they say around the [Texas] Legislature, if you can't
drink their whiskey, screw their women, take their money,
and vote against 'em anyway, you don't belong in office.

MOLLY IVINS

Kane watched Alma Atwood's car roll off the ferry in Haines, drive up the road and out of sight. He knew he probably should have kept his hands on her, but couldn't see himself dragging her back to a place she wanted to escape so much.

You're getting soft in your old age, he thought. He patted the pocket that held her signed statement, then walked back to the observation deck to sit. He took out his cell phone and was surprised to find he had a signal. He dialed Cocoa's number, talked for a few minutes, returned the phone to his pocket, and leaned back.

Kane was nearly asleep when the ferry vibrated and started moving again, making the short run to Skagway, where it would turn right around for the return trip. He could have saved time by getting off in Haines and seeing if one of the little commercial planes that served the town was flying to Juneau, maybe chartered one if he had to. But he wasn't in that much of a hurry, and he didn't like flying in small planes anyway.

At Skagway, he got off the ship and grabbed a quick sandwich, then hustled back aboard as the ferry was making ready to get under way. Haines had looked like a real town, at least from the ship. Skagway—what he'd seen of it, anyway—was all Gold Rush–era Alaska, a few buildings that had survived for more than a century amid a bunch of faux structures, almost all of them closed. No need to open them, really, until the cruise ships started delivering their thousands.

When he was back aboard, Kane put his ticket in his breast pocket so it was visible to anyone who cared, closed his eyes, and went to sleep. He awakened as the ferry was making its slow way to the dock in Auke Bay in the fading light of late afternoon. He took out his cell phone and called Cocoa, only to find that the cabbie was waiting for him at the dock.

"Who's watching our friend?" he asked as he got into the cab.

"My cousin Ralph," Cocoa said, "and my cousin Cecil."

"They know he might be dangerous?" Kane asked.

"They do," Cocoa said, "but they don't care. They think they might be dangerous, too."

Cocoa put the cab in gear and began navigating the road back to downtown Juneau.

"Where we going?" he asked.

"I think we'll go see if Winthrop wants to join us," Kane said, "while we talk to Mr. Bezhdetny."

"Good idea," Cocoa said. "That's one big white man. Might be smart to have a big Eskimo on our side. How'd you know to tell me to find that guy before you left, anyway?"

"Just a hunch," Kane said. "I knew he'd been hanging around Grantham and that Grantham had done something odd. I thought he might be mixed up in what's been happening."

"You think he killed that woman, that White Rose?" Cocoa asked.

"We'll see," Kane said, then closed his eyes and leaned back against the doorjamb.

Cocoa shook him awake when they reached the hotel.

"You sure you're up for this?" he asked. "You seem a little worn out."

"It's got to be the drugs," Kane said. "I've had plenty of sleep. Let's go talk to some people."

They got out of the cab.

"I'm leaving my bus out there for a few minutes, Bobby," Cocoa said to the bellman as they headed for the elevators.

"No sweat, Cocoa," the bellman said.

They rode up in the elevator with a couple of dazed-looking guys in suits.

"That Senator Dean," one of them said. "She really is the queen of mean."

"Got that right," the other one said.

Cocoa and Kane got out on the top floor. Cocoa led the way to a door and knocked. Winthrop opened the door and ushered them into a suite that was, for the Baranof anyway, surprisingly swank. Mrs. Richard Foster and Oil Can Doyle sat on a big sofa under another massive Sydney Laurence painting.

"Good to see you back, Sergeant Kane," the woman said. "Did you get what you needed?"

Kane took an armchair and said, "I did. I have the woman's signed statement implicating George Bezhdetny in kidnapping. And if I'm not mistaken, he's been engaged in a little extortion, too. I need to talk to Senator Grantham first, though, to be sure about that."

"What about the murder?" Oil Can Doyle squeaked. "That's all I care about. In case you've forgotten, you're supposed to be helping Senator Hope defend himself against a murder charge. Two now."

"I haven't forgotten," Kane said. "I figure it's logical that one bad guy may have done all the bad things." To the woman, he said, "Did you invite Grantham up here?"

"I did," she said, "right after your friend there"—she nodded toward Cocoa—"relayed your instructions. He should be here anytime."

She'd just gotten the words out when they heard the sound of knuckles rapping on the door.

"Make sure he doesn't rabbit," Kane said to Winthrop.

"Teach your grandma to suck eggs," Winthrop replied, opening the door to allow Grantham to step in. The senator looked around the room and turned toward the door again, only to find it closed, with Winthrop leaning against it.

"You can leave if you want, Senator," Kane said to his back, "but that just means you'll be talking to the people who work for the governor instead of us. He'd like that, wouldn't he, your old friend Hiram Putnam?"

Kane watched Grantham's shoulders sag. The senator turned toward the room and said, "I don't know what it is you think I have to say. I'm here at Mrs. Foster's invitation to talk politics."

"Oh, I think we'll be talking politics," Kane said, "as well as some other things. Have a seat."

Winthrop took the senator's coat and pointed to a chair, being careful to keep between Grantham and the door. Grantham walked slowly to the chair and sat. He crossed his legs, tried to smile, and said, "What is it you want?"

"Well," Kane said, "I guess we could start with an explanation for why you changed your vote on oil taxes."

Grantham looked from one face to another before replying.

"I don't know why I should explain myself to you," he said, smiling, "but there are several sound economic reasons not to increase taxation on the oil industry. The state depends on oil for most of its income, after all."

He looked around the room again, but not an expression had changed.

"Let's try this again, Senator, shall we?" Kane said. "I have a signed statement from Alma Atwood that you two were involved in an affair of long standing that ended only because you took up with a younger employee who George Bezhdetny introduced you to."

Grantham's smile faded as Kane spoke.

"Are you attempting to blackmail me?" he asked, trying to sound offended. "In front of witnesses?"

"Nice try, Senator," Kane said, "but there's no blackmail here. Your career is over no matter what you do or say. The only real question is whether you go from the Senate to private life or from the Senate to prison. What you say in this room will go a long way toward deciding that."

"Prison?" Grantham said. "Why should I go to prison?"

It was Kane's turn to smile. His smile wasn't pretty.

"If Bezhdetny bribed you to change your vote, then it'll be prison," Kane said, "but if you changed for some other reason—blackmail, per-haps—then you'll only have to retire."

"And if that's the case," Mrs. Richard Foster said, "I'm sure we could find some suitable employment for you somewhere. No one wants to punish a victim."

That was well said, Kane thought. This woman is no dummy.

Grantham sat silently for a few minutes.

"I'd like to speak to Mrs. Foster privately," he said at last.

"Uh-uh," Kane said. "That's not going to happen. But I'm sure Winthrop, Cocoa, and Mr. Doyle wouldn't mind retiring to the kitchen for a little while."

Oil Can squeaked at that, but the three men left the room to Kane, Grantham, and Mrs. Foster.

"Now, Senator," Kane said, "you must see that it is in your best interest to be candid with us."

The look Grantham gave Kane was full of venom, but when he turned to Mrs. Foster he was all smiles.

"I'm sure we can work something out to make this all go away," he said. "After all, there's a reconsideration vote coming up, and I could be persuaded to change my vote for the right inducements."

The woman gave the smile back to Grantham and said, "You're finished, Senator. Now act your age and do the best you can for yourself. If you don't, I'll make sure that everyone hears about your behavior."

"Bitch," Grantham said.

Kane was on his feet and, before he knew what he was doing, he'd slapped Grantham hard enough to send him sliding out of his chair. Kane grabbed the senator by the lapels and hoisted him back into the chair. He put his nose against Grantham and said, "This is your last chance, scumbag. Start talking or you're going to find yourself in a cell married to the guy with the most cigarettes."

Grantham took a handkerchief out of his pocket and blotted some blood from the lip Kane had split. Her looked like he wanted to cry, but pulled himself upright and said, "I'm in a difficult position. George had some tapes that could cause me a great deal of embarrassment."

Kane returned to his chair and sat.

"About what I thought," he said calmly, "but why don't you tell us what happened."

Grantham looked at the woman once more, but what he saw in her face didn't make him happy. He cleared his throat and began.

"I've always felt sorry for George. He's a foreigner, you know, but he wants to be an American, a successful American, so badly. I don't know why he settled on lobbying, but he did. He managed to make enough to keep from starving. And he was useful in small ways, running errands, providing the occasional support for a wayward member's story to his wife. He was a convenience."

Grantham paused to suck air into his lungs, then continued.

"Then last year sometime, he seemed more prosperous. I was happy for him, if you can believe that. And when I was looking for front-office help, he had this young woman with a wonderful résumé, and she was beautiful in the bargain. Too good to be true, really."

Grantham tried to chuckle at that but came out with a noise that sounded like gears grinding.

"Too good to be true," he said again, sarcasm in his voice this time. He stopped and stared off into the empty distance for a minute or so before beginning again.

"Politics, state politics, has been my life, you know," he said. "I started as a young man, full of optimism and good intentions. But I've seen too much, watched the wrong side prevail too many times, witnessed money and power win out over justice and common sense. I have lost so often, over and over again really, that all I wanted was someone to treat me like I was important, some sign that I mattered. That's why I took up with Alma. She worshiped me—in the beginning, anyway. And then this new woman came along, Jennifer, and she was younger and more beautiful and even more willing."

He shook his head.

"I should have known better," he said. "We'd been meeting in her apartment for . . . well, you know, and earlier this week, right before they arrested Matthew Hope again, George came into my office and told me he had photos and videotape of Jennifer and me together, that she was working for him, and unless I did what he asked he'd see that the pictures would go to my wife and to the Anchorage newspaper and television stations. And if I did what he asked, just changed one vote, he would give me everything and I could destroy it. Jennifer would leave town and no one would be the wiser."

Grantham was silent again, then resumed.

"I should have thrown him out of my office, reported him, and taken what came," he said, "but he showed me some of the pictures. And I looked so . . . so pathetic, this fat old man and this young, beautiful girl. We'd done some things that couldn't be explained away, and there they were on glossy paper in front of me. So I did what he said and here we are."

Kane let the silence lengthen.

"Do you have the tapes and photos?" he asked.

"No," Grantham said bitterly. "I asked George about them this afternoon and he just laughed and said he thought he'd hold on to them, they might come in handy again sometime. I suppose I should have seen that coming."

Kane nodded at that.

"Yes, you should," he said. "Do you know anything about Bezhdetny being involved with Melinda Foxx in any way?"

Grantham shook his head.

"I don't," he said, "but I wouldn't put anything past him. Including murder."

Kane looked at Mrs. Foster and raised his eyebrows. When she nodded, he said, "All right, Senator. I'm going to get some paper and a pen, and I want you to write down what you just told us and sign it."

Grantham shrank back in his seat like he was trying to escape the room through the back of his chair.

"I won't do it," he said. "That would be my political death warrant."

Mrs. Foster gave the politician a smile and said, "You don't seem to understand, Senator. You are already dead politically. Even if word of this never gets out in public—and, frankly, I can't see how it can remain a secret—even if the public never finds out, you are going to announce your retirement as soon as the session ends and you are not going to run for reelection. If you cooperate with Sergeant Kane, he may be able to keep you out of prison, but that's the best you can hope for. That and a job with one of the companies I own. You may not want to take my offer, though. All my companies have strict sexual harassment policies."

Watching Grantham wilt as the woman spoke was like watching a balloon deflate. By the time she was finished, he was just a tired old man. Kane went to the desk and took out a pad of hotel stationery and a pen. Then the three of them sat quietly as Grantham wrote down his tale and signed it.

"Thank you, Senator," Kane said after he'd scanned the statement. "You may go."

Grantham tottered to the door, opened it, and walked through.

"You can come out now," Kane called, and Winthrop entered the living room, followed by Doyle and Cocoa.

"Did you get anything useful on the murders?" Doyle squeaked.

"No," Kane said, "but we've got better ammunition for talking with Bezhdetny. Much better ammunition. What I'd like to do is get some sleep and tackle him in the morning."

"Maybe not," Cocoa said. "While we was in the kitchen, Cecil called. Said the big, white guy was in his car and it looked like he was driving to that mine storage place where those guys kept you."

Kane shook his head.

"No rest for the wicked," he said.

He folded Grantham's statement, took Alma's out of his pocket, and handed both to Mrs. Foster.

"Please put these somewhere safe," he said. "If it's okay with you, and with him, I'd like to take Winthrop along."

"I can see to Mrs. Foster's safety," Doyle squeaked, and only the fact he was so tired kept Kane from laughing.

"You two lock the door behind us, and don't open it for anyone but one of us," he said. He turned to Winthrop and said, "You ready?"

The big man left the room and returned a moment later, smoothing an imaginary wrinkle out of his suit coat.

"Looks like this dude was born ready," Cocoa said, opening the door to allow Kane and Winthrop to precede him.

28

War cannot be divorced from politics for a single moment.

MAO TSE-TUNG

The cab bounced slowly along the old mining road, lights off, Cocoa mumbling curses as he strained to miss the biggest potholes. A man stepped out of the brush and held up his hand.

"That's Cecil," Cocoa said as he brought the cab to a halt. The three men got out and Cocoa nodded to his cousin.

"'Sup," he said.

"Your big white guy is down at the mine," Cecil said. "Couple other white guys joined him a little while ago. Ralph's watching 'em."

"They know you're here?" Kane asked.

Cecil looked at him and shook his head.

"We're Indians," he said.

Kane nodded.

"Oh, yeah, right, I forgot," he said, "that makes you invisible."

Cecil and Cocoa exchanged a look.

"Not your typical *gussik,* is he?" Cecil said.

"Nope," Cocoa said. He walked to the back of the cab, opened the hatch, removed something wrapped in a blanket, and said, "Why don't you show us the way, Cecil?"

The four men walked down the side of the road with Cecil in the lead. Without talking about it, they let space open up among them like they were patrolling in hostile territory. Kane looked for clues that he'd been down this road before, but recognized nothing.

I must have been really drugged up, he thought.

Kane wasn't sure how far they'd walked when Cecil led them into the woods. They moved quietly through the darkness until Cecil held up a fist and motioned them to the ground. They followed him as he began crawling. Kane could see the soles of somebody's sneakers when Cecil signaled them to crawl into a line abreast.

They were at the edge of a big clearing. On the opposite side of the clearing was a rock face with a door in it. Kane wouldn't have been able to see the door if it hadn't been hanging slightly open, spilling light into the evening's semidarkness. The light shone on two cars that were parked nearby.

Guess nobody's had a chance to fix the door, Kane thought.

Cocoa and Ralph squirmed around until their heads were near Kane's.

"Three of 'em," Ralph whispered. "Heard some shouting, but nothing else."

Kane nodded.

"I guess somebody's going to have to go in there," he said.

He could see in the men's eyes that they didn't like the idea. He didn't either. Crossing open ground in the presence of the enemy was no way to stay healthy. But if they waited until the men came out, they could have a running gunfight on their hands and who knew what would happen. He wanted Bezhdetny alive. Better to get them when they were all in one place.

"If there's going to be trouble," Ralph said, "me and Cecil have got to go. Cocoa's our cousin, but if we take another charge we'll never see the outside again. Besides, we got no guns. Felons and firearms, you know."

Kane didn't like that, but he understood it. Nobody who'd been inside wanted to go back. Nobody sane, that is.

"You'd better go, then," Kane said. He looked at Cocoa. "You, too?"

Cocoa shook his head.

"I'm good here," he said.

Ralph crawled over and touched Cecil on the shoulder. The two men crawled off.

"What's in the blanket?" Kane asked.

Cocoa unwrapped the blanket to reveal an old, well-kept AK-47. The barrel seemed longer than Kane remembered. Cocoa unfolded a pair of legs from the barrel and set their ends on the ground.

"My dad's," Cocoa said. "Him and my uncles brought it back in pieces from that old war."

"Okay," Kane said. "That means you stay here to provide cover. If that door opens while Winthrop and I are crossing the clearing, we'll be sitting ducks. So I want you to put fire on it. But aim high. I don't want to be picking pieces of your lead out of my hide, or to get all three of those guys shot to pieces before I can talk to them."

"Yes, sir, sir," Cocoa said, giving Kane a mock salute.

Kane crawled over to Winthrop to tell him the plan. When Cocoa had his weapon set up and loaded, the other two men got to their feet and began moving across the clearing. Kane had the automatic out and hanging at his side. Winthrop was carrying what looked like a .44 Magnum.

Well, he's big enough to shoot it, Kane thought.

He and Winthrop moved in a curve, trying not to get between Cocoa and the door, which would be a very unhealthy place to be indeed if anything happened. Although, Kane thought, with all this rock around, a ricochet could get you from anywhere.

Days passed as they moved across the clearing, or so it seemed to Kane. He was sweating and he had that peculiar itch between his shoulders that he'd always gotten on patrol.

How do I get myself into these situations? he thought. I'm too old for this shit.

They reached the door without incident. They could hear voices. Kane put his lips next to Winthrop's ear.

"I want you to pull the door open," he said. "Try not to make much noise."

Winthrop gave him a disgusted look, ghosted across to the other side of the door, nodded at Kane, wrapped a hand around the edge of the door, and pulled it open. The door creaked loudly.

Kane looked around the edge of the doorway. All three men were standing, looking at the doorway. The blond one brought a pistol out from under his coat and fired. A bullet made a familiar stuttering noise as it cut the air next to Kane's ear. Kane had his automatic up. He leaned into the opening and aimed along the barrel, feeling loose and confident. He pulled the trigger three times, then rushed through the doorway, staying low. The blond one began to fall. On his way down, he pulled the trigger again. Kane heard the bullet crack into the rock floor and something struck his leg, knocking it from under him. He hit the floor and rolled, bringing his automatic up to cover the dark-haired one, who was struggling to get something out of his pocket. He really should have bought a holster, Kane thought, but some people never learn. He put a bullet into the wooden storage locker next to the dark-haired one's ear.

"Freeze," he shouted, "or the next one blows your brains out."

The noise from the gunshot had deafened him to the point that he could barely hear his own shouts. He hoped the other man could hear better.

The dark-haired one stopped moving.

"Hands where I can see them," Kane shouted. "Now."

The dark-haired one lifted his hands to show they were empty, then raised them above his head. Kane rolled himself into a sitting position and looked for Winthrop.

The big Native was half standing, half crouching. His left hand was wrapped around Bezhdetny's right wrist. His right hand rested on the big Ukrainian's shoulder. Bezhdetny's left hand grasped Winthrop under the arm. Both men were straining, their lips peeled back to show their teeth. As he watched, a pistol dropped from Bezhdetny's right hand. Both men ignored it. Kane was certain that if he could hear, all he would hear is the two men's breathing.

He thought about shooting Bezhdetny somewhere nonfatal, but didn't think Winthrop would appreciate the help. Besides, he didn't like the idea of more metal flying around. His own leg was starting to hurt, and he snuck a peek at it. Blood was seeping from his thigh. When he looked back, the dark-haired man had his hands at waist level. Kane gestured with the automatic and he raised them again.

Kane had no idea how long the two men grappled. At some point, Cocoa came through the door, gun barrel first. He surveyed the situation, looked at Kane, and jerked his head toward the wrestlers. Kane shook his head, then nodded toward the body on the floor. Cocoa walked around Winthrop and Bezhdetny, knelt, and put his fingers on the blond man's neck. He looked at Kane and shook his head.

The two men were still locked in their private struggle. It's like watching an epic battle, Kane thought. Hercules contending with Apollo. Or maybe good versus evil, but with the conventional colors reversed. But we can't watch this all night.

Kane was about to tell Cocoa to hit the Ukrainian with his rifle butt when Bezhdetny's left leg buckled and he let loose a scream Kane had no trouble hearing. Winthrop let go of him and the big, white man fell to the floor, where he rolled around clutching his left knee. Winthrop shook his head like a man coming out of a fog, looked around, walked over to the dark-haired man, and pulled his hands behind his back.

"Pick up the weapons, Cocoa," Kane called. "Get the one in that one's pocket as well. And the last time I looked, they both had ankle holsters."

When Cocoa was finished, he had an armload of handguns.

"Dump them outside," Kane said.

When the other men's weapons were all outside the rock room, Kane limped to the door, took out his cell phone, dialed 911, and told the dispatcher what he needed. He used Tank Crawford's name liberally. When he finished, he limped back to a chair and sat. Cocoa took out a Buck knife, knelt next to him, and cut open his pant leg, revealing a jagged hole surrounded by black-and-blue tissue that leaked blood. He took a not-too-clean-looking handkerchief out of his pocket, folded it, and laid it on the wound. Kane put his hand on the handkerchief and pushed. A bolt of pain shot through his thigh, but he kept the pressure on.

"Good thing you called for an ambulance," Cocoa said. "That's going to need looking at."

Kane nodded.

"I don't know how long it will take for the cops to get here," he said, "but if you want to hold on to your toy, you'd better stash it somewhere."

Cocoa smiled and left the room.

Winthrop had finished tying up the dark-haired man. The big Ukrainian lay as he had, his hand wrapped around his knee. He was no longer howling, but had his teeth set in a way that said he was in real pain.

"We should talk before the cops get here, George," Kane said. "It would be in your best interest."

Bezhdetny shot him a hard look.

"Fuck your mother," he grated.

"That's no way to talk, George," Kane said. "You should know that I've got written evidence that you were involved in blackmail and

MIKE DOOGAN

kidnapping, and I'm sure that your pal here"—he nodded toward the dark-haired man—"will be only too happy to talk as well. So maybe you should tell me why you murdered Melinda Foxx. You know, sort of practice your story before the authorities arrive."

Bezhdetny's expression seemed to contain real surprise.

"Murder?" he said. "I murdered no one. I didn't even know this Melinda Foxx. And I know nothing of blackmail or kidnapping."

Then he closed his mouth and didn't utter a sound until what seemed like the entire Juneau police force arrived, guns drawn.

29

Force is all-conquering, but its victories are short-lived.

ABRAHAM LINCOLN

Kane was staring morosely at a bowl of Jell-O when Tank Crawford walked in.

"This is what they call lunch," Kane said. "Can you believe it?"

"If you're looking for sympathy, bubba, you'll find it in the dictionary between shit and symposium," Crawford replied.

Mrs. Richard Foster looked up from the magazine she was reading. Crawford's face reddened.

"Sorry, ma'am," he said. "I didn't see you sitting there."

Kane was in the hospital again, with a thick wrapping around his throbbing thigh and a slightly thick head from the anesthetic they'd given him before digging around in there. The room looked exactly the same as the previous one. For all he knew, it was the same as the previous one. Mrs. Foster was here keeping him company, while

Winthrop was at the courthouse watching Oil Can Doyle trying to use the Ukrainian crime wave to pry Matthew Hope out of prison.

"The language doesn't bother me," Mrs. Foster said, "but the sentiment does. Sergeant Kane was wounded apprehending dangerous criminals."

The red in Crawford's face grew brighter. He opened his mouth, but Kane intervened.

"I think the two of you should know who you are talking to," he said. "Mrs. Foster, this is Juneau Police Detective Harry Crawford. Tank, this is Mrs. Richard Foster, the widow of *the* Richard Foster."

The two nodded to each other.

"Pleased to meet you, ma'am," Crawford said. "But what I meant was, if Kane here and his pals had just let the police do what we're trained to do, he wouldn't have gotten shot."

"I didn't get shot, at least not technically," Kane said, trying to change the course of the conversation. "It was a piece of rock they dug out of my leg, not lead."

The woman was not deterred.

"Detective Crawford," she began.

"Tank," Crawford said. "Just call me Tank, ma'am. Everybody does."

"Tank, then," the woman said, "what do you think would have happened if Sergeant Kane had gone to the police? Did he have enough evidence for a warrant? Could you have gotten a warrant at that time of night? How long would it have taken to round up your SWAT team, or whatever you call it here? Would those men still have been there by the time all that happened? Would you have been able to creep up on them if they were, as Sergeant Kane and Winthrop did? Or would you still be out there trying to get them out? As I understand it, the cave or room or whatever it is they were in would have been difficult to remove them from. How many police officers do you think might have been injured, or even killed, in the process?"

By the time she was finished, Crawford was holding his hands out in front of him as if to stop the flood of rhetorical questions.

"Whoa, whoa, whoa," he said. "You might be right, ma'am, but Nik here will tell you that civilians taking the law into their own hands makes cops nervous."

The woman gave him a sweet smile.

"Is it a job-security issue?" she asked.

Crawford's face got so red Kane was afraid it might explode. Then Tank began to laugh.

"Maybe so," he said, "maybe it is. But we like to think we're here to keep citizens safe, not the other way around."

He turned to face Kane.

"Anyway, I've got good news and bad news for you," he said. "The good news is that the City and Borough of Juneau is recommending to the DA that you not be charged with a crime in connection with the events of last night. Your story matches those of the other witnesses and the forensic evidence, so it's pretty clear the other guy shot first. Lucky for you, one of our techs found his first bullet in a tree way the hell and gone on the far side of that clearing. Guys don't usually get off a shot like that after taking three in the pump."

"That's good enough news," Kane said. "What's the bad news?"

"Your pal Bezhdetny swears he didn't have anything to do with Melinda Foxx getting killed," Crawford said, "and he's sticking to that story like glue. He's denying everything, of course, but he's got a darn good alibi for the night she was killed, since he was wining and dining some members of the Putnam administration, including the Commissioner of Public Safety."

"That is bad news," Kane said. "What about Frick and Frack?"

"Believe it or not, their names really are Smith and Jones," Crawford said. "Until recently, they'd been working security for an oil field service company, Dorian or Delorean or something like that. Left there last month. Who they've been working for and what they've been doing since then is a little murky, but the one you didn't shoot says they were in Anchorage that night and he's got the credit card receipts to prove it."

Kane lay there thinking.

"Maybe you should find out why the state DAs kicked them loose," he said. "That might tell you who they were working for."

"And it might not," Crawford said. "You didn't hear this from me, because telling you would be very wrong, but after you had them arrested for that little fracas in your hotel room, the DA got a call from the governor's office, said to let them."

"That's interesting," Kane said. "Where did you hear that?"

"One of the trooper investigators told me when I asked him," Crawford said. "He was nice enough about it after I let him know I'd be going to ask the DA myself if he didn't. The other one, though—is he an asshole or what?"

Crawford's face reddened again.

"Sorry again, ma'am," he said, then to Kane: "I got to get going. Thought you'd want to know first thing about the charges, and about the White Rose Murder still sitting there. Take care, bubba. Ma'am."

When they were alone, Mrs. Foster put her magazine down and said, "This is so irritating. Matthew Hope did not kill that woman. Even though I am very upset with him, I know that."

Kane looked at the woman for a moment, then said, "Perhaps now would be a good time for you to come clean about your relationship with Senator Hope."

"I've already told you," the woman replied calmly, "I don't have a relationship with Senator Hope."

Kane rolled his eyes and sighed.

"You know," he said, "I'm getting tired of being lied to by all and sundry. In case you haven't noticed, Winthrop isn't around to protect you, so there's really nothing to keep me from turning you over my knee and spanking you. In fact, I might like it."

The woman showed him a wicked grin.

"I might like it, too," she said, "but aren't you afraid you'd reopen your wound?"

Kane didn't say anything, and after several moments the woman said, "My husband was quite ill there at the end. Senator Hope came to visit him several times and was always so nice and considerate, asking me if there was anything I needed."

The woman was quiet again for so long that Kane thought she had thought better of talking. But, finally, she continued, "He was so sweet. And he is a very handsome man, and I—God forgive me— began to wonder if, maybe, after Richard died we'd . . ."

Again she was silent before resuming. "Isn't that awful? My husband lying on his deathbed and me having lustful thoughts about another man? I thought it was awful. I've done some things that are condemned by polite society, but that was the first thing I'd done— thought, I guess, since I never really did anything—that I'm actually ashamed of."

Kane wondered if he should say something, but he wasn't sure if her story was done, so he held his peace.

"Then—it wasn't a week before he died—my husband asked me to bring him his wallet," she said. "He could barely open it, but he took out an old piece of paper and said, 'I'm leaving you everything, Amber, but I want you to promise me that if any of the people on this list needs help, you'll give it to them.' Then he handed the paper to me. I've got it right here in my purse. There were eleven names on it. Three had been crossed off. Of those that are left, Matthew Hope's is number seven.

"I didn't know exactly what to make of it then, but I gave him my promise and I'm keeping it. And something about that—about the way Richard sounded when he asked, or about Matthew Hope's name being on the list—it changed the way I felt about the senator. No more lustful thoughts. But I continued to support him politically, and when his name turned up as a suspect—*the* suspect—in the White Rose Murder, I knew I had to do something. I'd promised my husband. So I hired Mr. Doyle and you."

Kane let the silence stretch out before saying, "You think Hope is Richard Foster's son, don't you? That the list is the names of his children?"

The woman sighed.

"I guess I must," she said, the words coming in a rush, "because when I tried to figure out why my feelings toward him had changed, all I could come up with is that if he is Richard's son that would mean . . . would mean any sort of physical relationship between us would be somehow a betrayal. And I just couldn't do that. I won't do that. I won't betray my husband's memory. It's all I have left of him."

The woman fell silent. Kane lay there thinking about fathers and sons and all the complications those relationships created. He'd never run into one quite like this, but he recognized that fathers and sons and issues like sex were just a bomb waiting to go off. He must have dozed then, because the next thing he heard was the squeaky voice of Oil Can Doyle.

"That Ritter is a disgrace to the bench," Doyle said, throwing his coat on the floor and knocking his toupee cockeyed in the process. "The old fraud is a tool for whoever has power."

Kane started to say something, but his lips were stuck together. He drank from the cup on his bedside table and said, "I take it the judge didn't buy your arguments for letting Senator Hope out on bail."

Doyle went and sat in the other chair in the room. That left Winthrop and Cocoa, who must have arrived while Kane dozed, standing, Doyle and Mrs. Foster sitting.

"Maybe if we got a couple more people in here, we could set a record," Kane said.

"No, the pompous fraud didn't buy it," Doyle said. "Claimed that nothing was proven about Bez-whatever-his-name-is and his pals, and that even if they'd done it there was no way to connect them to the White Rose or the other aide, and that even if there was, there was plenty more evidence against my client. So I guess I should congratulate you, Kane. You have apparently solved a mystery, but not the freaking mystery you were hired to solve."

The little lawyer closed his mouth with a click and cupped a hand under his chin.

"Feisty little fella, ain't he?" Cocoa said. "Anyway, I just came here to see when they're going to let you out, Nik, and whether you're going to need a ride when they do."

"Don't know, Cocoa," Kane said. "I haven't seen much of anybody on the staff. Maybe I'll have to check myself out again."

The minute the words were out of his mouth, a nurse came in followed by a doctor who looked maybe eighteen.

"What's this, a convention?" the nurse said. "I'm going to have to ask you all to leave so we can examine the patient."

"Come back when they're done, Oil Can," Kane said. "I've got something to tell you that you'll want to hear."

After everyone left, the nurse unwrapped Kane's leg and the doctor poked and prodded for a while, following every painful noise Kane made with an even more vigorous thrust. When he was finished, he said, "I'm told that back when you were my age, doctors kept people like you in the hospital for several days. But I want you on your feet walking by tonight, and if that doesn't open anything up, I'll send you home tomorrow."

While the nurse rewrapped Kane's leg, the doctor made some notes on the chart that hung at the end of the bed. The two of them left together and everyone but Winthrop returned.

"He's bringing the car around," Mrs. Foster said. "I'm going back to the hotel for a while. What did the doctor say?"

"He said I could get out tomorrow," Kane said. "So I'll call you, Cocoa?"

The cabbie nodded and he and the woman left the room. Ignoring the fact that the little man's toupee now seemed to be on backward, Kane told the lawyer what Tank Crawford had said about the governor's office intervening on behalf of the two criminals. By the time Kane was finished, Doyle had a big grin on his face.

"Oh, I hope I can get to a reporter or two with that before they've finished their stories," he said. "This blackmail and kidnapping and shooting is so hot right now that everyone's pretty much forgotten about the White Rose for the moment. If I can tie this around that idiot Putnam's neck, it'll help when I show that he's been messing around in the White Rose case, too."

Kane thought about what he'd told Alma and Grantham about trying to keep their statements quiet and decided he didn't care. They'd each had a chance to choose between right and wrong, and they'd both chosen wrong.

The lawyer picked his coat up off the floor.

"So what you've done so far isn't really a complete loss," he said. "You might not have proved that Hope is innocent, but you've given me plenty of the kind of skulduggery juries love."

Doyle bustled out of the room. Kane lay there thinking. If Bezhdetny wasn't involved in the murders, he would pretty much have to start from scratch. And he wasn't going to get very far until he talked with the people in O. B. Potter's office.

He could feel his eyelids trying to close. Being drugged and shot really takes a lot out of you, he thought.

His mind wandered until he was standing in the doorway of the rock room again, aiming along the barrel at the blond man. He felt the shock of the automatic firing run through his arm. Breathe normally, he thought. Level the barrel. Squeeze. The gun went off again, then again, Kane firing until the blond man went down, the way he'd been trained to. Now he was looking down at the lifeless body, searching inside himself for how he felt. Once, he had promised himself that he would never kill anyone again. He expected to feel guilt, and disappointment in himself. Instead, he could hear his lungs working and the blood rushing in his veins, and he felt alive and happy to be that way. In the doorway, in the moment, he'd had no choice. Someone was going to die, and he was elated that it wasn't him.

He opened his eyes. The white room was gray in the late-afternoon light, the shapes of the chairs blurry and indistinct. I'm alive, he thought, and the next thought came unbidden: And I have a job to do. I should be figuring out how to do it. Instead, images flowed through his head in an unchanneled stream: Letitia Potter, Alma Atwood, Melinda Foxx, Mrs. Richard Foster, the woman—what's her name—with the streaked hair, Dylan's friend. With that, he was asleep, dreaming that Dylan was shooting at him with an AK-47 and shouting something important. But he couldn't quite make out what it was.

30

It is my settled opinion, after some years as a political correspondent,
that no one is attracted to a political career in the first place
unless he is socially or emotionally crippled.

AUBERON WAUGH

Kane was easing his way out of Cocoa's cab when his cell phone rang.
It was Dylan.

"Why didn't you tell me you were in the hospital?" he asked.

Kane leaned back against the cab to take the pressure off his
wounded leg. A clump of men in suits came through the hotel's
glass doors, turned right, and headed up the hill. A misty rain, or
maybe fog, hung in the air, which was fresh and sharp with the joy of
spring.

"I didn't know you'd be interested," Kane said.

A long silence ensued. Kane couldn't believe how tired and weak he
felt. All he'd done that day was listen to the doctor tell him to take it
easy, get dressed, ride a wheelchair to the cab and the cab to the hotel,
but he felt like he'd been wrestling bears for a week.

"What happened?" Dylan asked. "Did you fall down again?"

Kane laughed at that. More proof, he thought, that I am ridiculously happy to be alive.

"Which time?" he said.

"Which time?" Dylan asked.

"You're going to have to pay closer attention if you want to keep track," Kane said. "I've been in the hospital twice since you threw a fit and walked out of the restaurant. The first time, I was kidnapped and drugged. The second time, I was shot."

The silence was longer this time.

"I'm sorry about the other night," Dylan said. "I behaved badly. I didn't want to, but I couldn't help myself."

He was quiet again.

"I'd love to continue this conversation, Dylan," Kane said, "but I'm standing in the rain on one good leg. Maybe you could stop by the hotel at lunch?"

"Maybe, if I have the time," Dylan said.

"Good," Kane said. He gave his son the room number, then added, "How did you find out? That I was in the hospital?"

Dylan snorted.

"This is Juneau," he said and hung up.

Leaning on Cocoa's arm, Kane hobbled through the lobby, into the elevator, down the hall, and into his room. He sank thankfully into the chair. Cocoa tossed the plastic bag that held the remains of Kane's change of clothes on the bed.

"Now what?" he said.

"Now I rest," Kane said, "until I can muster the strength to go out and buy some more clothes. The ones I'm wearing haven't been washed in I don't know how long, and those"—he gestured toward the plastic bag—"are trash."

"You're as trashed as they are," Cocoa said. "Why don't you give me some money and some sizes and I'll go buy the clothes."

Kane looked Cocoa up and down. The cabbie was dressed in a flannel shirt, jeans, and motorcycle boots.

"Maybe I should ask Winthrop to do it," he said, shifting so he could get at his wallet, "considering he dresses so much better than you do."

A broad smile split Cocoa's face.

"Yeah, that's one Native knows how to dress all right," he said. "'Course, I'd be dressing fine, too, if a rich white lady was buying my clothes."

Kane handed Cocoa an ATM card, then rattled off the PIN number and his sizes. The cabbie left. Kane was dozing when his phone rang.

"Dad?" Dylan said. "Something's come up. I can't make lunch. How about if I come by after work."

"That's fine," Kane said and Dylan hung up.

Kane thought about shifting to the bed, but it seemed like a lot of work.

I probably ought to take off my coat, though, he thought, so he got to his feet, removed the coat, hobbled to the table, and hung it over the back of a chair. He went into the bathroom, drank a glass of water, and made it back to the bed. He took the automatic from the plastic bag and threw the bag on the floor. He set the gun on the bedside table and lay down. I should get rid of these shoes, he thought, and went to sleep.

Pounding on the door awakened him. For a moment, he had no idea where he was. Then he looked at the clock. He'd been asleep for all of fifteen minutes. The pounding continued.

"I'll be right there," he called.

Groaning, he got to his feet, limped to the door, and opened it to find Oil Can Doyle standing there.

"We've got to talk," the lawyer said, scooting past Kane into the room.

Kane closed the door, went back to the bed, and lay down, propping his head up on the pillows so he could see Doyle. The little man was hopping around like a cat on a griddle.

"We've got a situation," Doyle said. "We need to figure out what to do."

"Why don't you stop bouncing around like a demented bunny rabbit and tell me what's going on?" Kane said.

Doyle threw himself into the chair and immediately started bouncing on the seat.

"Bezhdetny's lawyer called me," Doyle said. "He said his client wants to see you."

"So?" Kane said.

"It's unusual—it's very unusual," Doyle said. "Someone who is accused of crimes wanting to see one of the witnesses? It's not done. I think I should go with you."

"Stop bouncing," Kane said. "You're making me seasick. Have you been using illegal substances to pep you up?"

The lawyer stopped bouncing, stood, and pulled himself to his full height.

"I do not use illegal substances," he said with dignity. "Although I have had a lot of coffee this morning."

Then he began pacing. Kane sat thinking, then said, "What does Bezhdetny want?"

Doyle paused in his pacing to say, "His lawyer claimed not to know. Said he'd advised his client that such a meeting was unwise but that his client insisted."

"Okay," Kane said. "I'll do it." Doyle started to say something, but Kane held up his hand. "It's not that much of a problem. I'm not really a witness against the guy; Alma Atwood and Grantham are. And who knows? Maybe he wants to confess to killing Melinda Foxx."

So Kane found himself limping into the hospital again, leaning on Cocoa's arm. The detective was wearing fancy gear that Cocoa had purchased at the outdoor store across from the hotel.

"It breathes," the cabbie had said as he dragged it out of the bags. "It repels insects. It will probably do your taxes if you let it."

Salmon and balsam aren't really my colors, Kane thought, but at least the stuff is clean.

A uniformed cop sat on a chair outside of Bezhdetny's room.

"I'm going to have to pat you down," he said, and did so. When he was finished, Kane went into the room. Bezhdetny lay like Gulliver, strapped to a bed he came close to overflowing, his left leg raised above the bed by a cat's cradle of wires. Tubes and wires ran from machines and disappeared under his hospital gown. His hair was a mess and there were deep lines in his face. Kane moved slowly to the chair beside the bed and sat.

"You look like I feel," he said.

Bezhdetny gave him a wan smile.

"I apologize for the shooting," he said. "There should have been no shooting, but those men had no training and no discipline."

Kane shrugged and said, "I suppose there's no reason criminals should have better luck getting good help than anyone else." When Bezhdetny didn't reply, he said, "Why did you want to see me?"

"My lawyer is negotiating now with the authorities," Bezhdetny said. "He is trying to make a deal. I will name my employer and testify against him for certain considerations in charging and sentencing. Therefore, I cannot tell you the name of my employer, although I can tell you everything else."

"Why would you do that?" Kane asked.

"Why would I not?" Bezhdetny said, surprise in his voice. "Someone killed those people, that White Rose and the other. Maybe something I say will help you catch that killer."

Kane thought about that for a while, then said, "Okay. Start talking."

Bezhdetny reached over and took a cup from the table that was positioned next to the bed. His hand shook. He managed to corral the straw with his lips and suck down some liquid. He put the cup back and began.

"I am from Kiev," he said. "My parents were not important, so I didn't have many opportunities. But I did well in school and was accepted by the state security service. That is where I learned English. I had a good life in Kiev by the standards of the time. But I had rivals, too, in my job—office politics, you know? They are everywhere—and when one of them was promoted over me, he sent me to Magadan, in the Russian Far East. Magadan is not so nice as Kiev. Not so nice as Hell, really. But there were opportunities and compensations for a man in my position, so I made the best of it.

"Then the Communists gave up. Can you believe it? It was like I had been cursed. I did not get paid and life in Magadan got worse. I thought about going back to Ukraine, but why? So I came here, to Alaska. I had met some people on cultural exchanges, and everyone was so happy about the change in relations that I had very little difficulty getting the necessary permissions."

Bezhdetny took another drink, sighed, and continued.

"I thought perhaps my luck had changed. I studied those around me and decided that politics offered the fastest path to success. So I came to Juneau and got a job working in the lounge, and I watched and I learned. Perhaps no one in history paid such close attention to the Alaska State Legislature and how it worked and how someone could make money from it. It was obvious that of all the people associated with the legislature, a lobbyist made the most money. So I became a lobbyist.

"At first, I thought my lack of success was due to the fact that I was new and did not know the task well. Then I thought perhaps it was because I was an outsider and did not have the connections necessary to succeed. But as time went on I realized that history was my handicap. I had grown up in a much different society, with different standards and rules, and no amount of study and hard work would give me the . . . reflexes . . . I needed to succeed here."

The Ukrainian stopped to stare off into the distance for a while.

"Once I realized that, I didn't know what to do. I am getting older and I have the same concerns as anyone: What happens if I get sick? What do I live on when I retire? I began to feel that I had wasted my life and my opportunities and that the curse had defeated me.

"Then, near the end of the last legislative session, the man I will not name came to see me. He owns a company in the oil field service business. He told me he knew that the legislature would attempt to raise taxes on the oil industry. This, he said, would slow down oil development and cost him a lot of money. He needed my help to prevent it.

"I knew who this man was. I knew he could afford many lobbyists much more successful than I. I asked him why he was talking to me then. He said that with oil prices so high, regular lobbying could not defeat this bill, that the House was impossible, and that he had counted the votes in the Senate and was one short. He said that he knew something of my past, and that he thought perhaps I had learned some things in state security in the Soviet Union that would help him prevail. He said he would pay me much money, but that I would be hired—how did he put it?—off the books.

"I asked him for time to think. I didn't know what he meant. Americans have this strange idea of the old Soviet Union, one that perhaps made him believe I had spent all my time in state security making people do things against their will. The truth is that all I pushed around was paper. I spent my time drinking tea with my comrades and standing in lines and maybe enjoying too much vodka at night.

"But I looked at his list of names and how they would vote, and I saw Senator Grantham's name and I had an idea. I knew that he was having an extramarital affair of long standing with his aide. Such a man is subject to pressure. I thought about asking his aide, Alma, to help me bring that pressure but decided she would not. Then I asked myself, What does such a man as Grantham want? And the answer came to me: A younger, more beautiful woman. I knew his receptionist was quitting, so I found such a woman who would do what I asked for money, helped her compose a résumé that would get her hired, sat back, and waited."

Bezhdetny tried to adjust himself in the bed and winced.

"This knee is very painful," he said. "They did much surgery on it and say they must do more. I had no idea how powerful that man was, that such a powerful man existed. It is the curse working, that I should encounter this man who is more powerful than I."

He shook his head, then picked up the thread of his story.

"As I thought, Senator Grantham was attracted to the younger, more beautiful woman and I soon had what I needed. I told my employer to arrange for the bill to advance and that I was certain there were not eleven votes to pass it.

"Then Melinda Foxx was murdered and Senator Hope arrested. And I became greedy. I blame myself, although I had been working around greedy people for so long I can understand completely my failure. I thought that if I could just keep Senator Hope off the scene, I could save my information on Senator Grantham for another time, another client. So I asked this man I cannot name for some help and he sent me those two amateurs."

"I don't understand," Kane said. "How could you expect to manipulate the criminal justice system to keep Hope out of the Senate long enough to do what you wanted?"

Bezhdetny shrugged.

"I wasn't sure that I could," he said. "But I knew that others, some for the same reasons as I and some for other reasons, would want Senator Hope to be out of the picture. And I only needed three days: One to get the bill to the floor, one for the vote, and one for the reconsideration vote.

"My plan was good, but it did not allow for Senator Potter 's ambition. He wanted to hold the bill in his committee and win the support of the oil companies for his candidacy for governor. So the bill did not move. I needed to keep Senator Hope in jail longer. I thought perhaps to take his attorney captive, but feared that would stir up the authorities too much. Then the man who I cannot name told me that you were coming to investigate. Even in the Soviet Union, lawyers are dependent on investigators, so I knew that removing you would slow the proceedings. I sent those men to see you, but you bested them. Then Senator Hope was released, so I decided to abandon that strategy.

"I went to Senator Grantham and told him about the evidence I had of his infidelity, and he reacted as I thought he would. But before I could do anything more, I heard about the report of Melinda Foxx's pregnancy. And the other aide was murdered, and I knew Senator Hope would be arrested once more."

He raised a fist and pounded weakly on the hospital bed's metal railing.

"Again, I was greedy," he said, "greedy and stupid and proud. I should have continued as I did, in the end, with Grantham. But I wanted to keep that information for later. And you had insulted me in the restaurant by declining my hospitality. I knew that Alma wanted to leave, so I arranged your capture. I told myself that without your help Senator Hope would be less likely to be released, but really I was only trying to salvage my pride. But it was all for nothing. The bill moved more quickly to the floor than I anticipated, and I was unable tell Senator Grantham he could vote as he wished. Then you escaped, and now here we are."

He waved vaguely at the room and was silent.

"You had me kidnapped because I insulted you?" Kane said. "Really?"

"It is so," Bezhdetny said. "Since coming to Alaska, I have swallowed many insults many times. I saw an opportunity for revenge that seemed to coincide with my goals and I took it."

Kane sat trying to digest that. A smart man would have ignored his emotions, wouldn't he? That's what he'd always thought: Don't let your emotions interfere with your work. But was he doing so well that he could look down at the Ukrainian for trying to get a little of his own back?

"So your efforts were all about the oil tax bill?" Kane said. "And you had nothing to do with Melinda Foxx being killed?"

Bezhdetny nodded.

"That is correct," he said.

"Might your employer have had it done?" Kane asked.

"Why would he?" Bezhdetny asked. "She was not a problem on oil taxes, and that is all he is interested in."

Kane sighed. If Bezhdetny was telling the truth, and he seemed to be, then he was probably right. His efforts to defeat the oil tax bill and Melinda Foxx's murder weren't connected.

"Do you know anything about that murder that might help me?" Kane asked.

Bezhdetny smiled.

"That, really, is why I asked you here, to see your face when I told you this," he said. "As I said, I watched everyone very carefully. I do know something about Melinda Foxx that might help you. But I will not tell you what it is. I will not tell anyone, unless I need the information to trade with the authorities."

The Ukrainian laughed unpleasantly.

"You have ruined my life," Bezhdetny said. "I will not help you with yours. We are like your country and my country, Nik Kane. You have won a battle but not the war. You may leave now."

31

A king, realizing his incompetence, can either delegate or
abdicate his duties. A father can do neither. If only sons could
see the paradox, they would understand the dilemma.

MARLENE DIETRICH

The bastard," Doyle said when Kane called to tell him about his
interview with the Ukrainian. His voice was so revved up with
anger that it was practically ultrasonic. "He knows something that will
help us and he won't spill it because, why, he's pissed at you?"

"Says he knows something," Kane said. "We don't know that he
actually does."

In the silence that ensued, Kane looked around his hotel room. He
needed to finish with the lawyer, take a shower, and get some sleep.
He wanted to be more alert when Dylan arrived.

"So did you believe him?" Doyle asked.

"I believe most of his story," Kane said. "It had just the right mixture of intelligence and incompetence to be a true criminal story. But

knowing something about the murder? He might just be trying to mess with me to get even. I don't know what to believe."

"Yeah, me either," the lawyer said. "We could tell the cops and see if they can get anything out of him. But it might be handy just to file that piece of information away until we need it. This Bezhdetny seems like just the kind of villain juries love to pin things on. With him in the mix, Matthew Hope skates out of trouble."

"I thought about that," Kane said. "You might be able to keep Hope out of prison, but the only thing that saves his political career is establishing his innocence."

"Saving his political career is not my problem," Doyle squeaked.

"You may not think so," Kane said, "but I'm sure your client, and the woman who is paying you, would both like that to happen. So I reckon I'll just keep snooping around."

"I'm not sure I like that," Doyle said. "If you continue investigating, you might turn up information that hurts our case rather than helps it."

"Risk you take," Kane said and closed his phone.

He took a while getting out of his clothes, then examined the bandage on his leg. No blood showed. He'd had Cocoa stop at the grocery store on their way back to the hotel and buy a roll of plastic wrap. Now he covered the bandage in several layers of plastic, got into the bathtub, and turned the shower on as hot as he could stand it. He let the water wash his thoughts away, until his mind was blank to everything but the pounding of the spray. He didn't know how long he had been standing there when he roused himself, shampooed his hair, washed his body, rinsed, and got out of the shower.

Toweling himself off was a logistical nightmare, and the calf of his wounded leg was still wet when he dragged himself out of the bathroom and flopped onto the bed. He had just enough energy left to leave a wake-up call before his eyes closed and he was gone.

The telephone woke him. A recorded voice told him to wake up. The pain that shot through his thigh when he swung his legs out of the bed nearly made him faint.

Maybe lying down and stiffening up wasn't the best idea, he thought.

He gritted his teeth, levered himself to his feet, and more or less hopped into the bathroom, where he splashed cold water on his face. He dried himself, ate some prescription painkillers the doctor had given him, and made it back to the bedroom, where he tried vainly to dress without hurting himself some more.

This is stupid, he thought. I'd have as much luck throwing the clothes into the air and running under them. So he put up with the pain it took to get dressed, then hopped around making the bed and picking clothing wrappers and tags off the floor. When he was satisfied with the condition of the room, he sat in the chair to wait. He opened Montaigne and found himself at an essay called "Of Judging the Death of Others." He read along until he hit a quotation from Pliny: "A quick death is the supreme good fortune of human life."

Is that so? he thought. Maybe if you are old or in bad health. But for a young and vital person like Melinda Foxx, was that really good fortune? And what about the man he had shot? Certainly, his death was quick. But didn't he regret, even in that moment, all the life he might have had if he'd behaved differently? Or are the young so sure of their immortality that they never consider death, even when they are looking it in the face?

And he himself, Nik Kane? He could feel the breath of age on him. Would a quick death be a blessing? Since he'd gotten to Juneau, he'd had nothing but aches and pains and injuries, his pleasant, happy moments, like the night he'd spent with Alma Atwood, only setting him up for more unpleasant, unhappy ones.

No, he decided, putting the book down. I'm not ready to die. I have too much to do, too much damage to repair, too many flaws to overcome, to welcome a quick death. I am, as Montaigne says, like every-one else, too full of myself to contemplate death: "Whence it follows that we consider our death a great thing, and one which does not pass so easily, nor without solemn consultation with the stars."

That's me, he thought. Too important to die.

He found he'd been sitting there for some time, thinking what Lau-rie would have called "morbid thoughts," when a knock at the door brought him to. He got to his feet with difficulty and let Dylan in. He offered the young man the chair and perched on the bed.

"This is easier on my leg anyway," he said.

Dylan picked up the book and looked at the cover.

"Montaigne," he said. "I read some of this once."

"What did you think?" Kane asked.

"It was for a class," Dylan said. "Why are you reading it?"

Kane shrugged.

"I guess because it helps me figure things out," he said.

"Is figuring things out important to you?" Dylan said. "Is that why you're a detective?"

"I suppose it is, at least partly," Kane said. "Why are you asking all these questions?"

Dylan looked around the room. His movements reminded Kane of Laurie, too. He's really his mother's son, Kane thought.

"I guess because I don't know you very well," Dylan said. "I was still pretty young when you left, and what I remember is that you weren't around much even before that. It made me mad, that you didn't pay more attention to me."

"Are you still angry?" Kane asked.

Dylan shrugged, his thin shoulders coming to points under the white shirt he had worn for work.

"I guess I am," he said. "I don't want to be, but I am. And I don't know what to do about it. There were times when I really needed a father, and you weren't there."

The truth of what Dylan said, and his honesty in saying it, made Kane flinch.

"I could be a father now," he said.

Dylan nodded as if he'd expected Kane to say that.

"I know," he replied, "but I'm not sure I need a father now. Besides, what good does it do to have someone in your life if you're mad at them all the time?"

He got to his feet and walked around the room, looking at the furniture like he'd never seen anything like it before.

"You got anything to eat?" he asked.

"No," Kane said, "but we could call room service. Let's look at the menu."

They did, and Kane called and ordered. As they waited for the food, Dylan chatted about school and his job. It was as if, in talking about his anger, he had walked up to the edge of a cliff and, now, he wanted to back away from it in a cloud of inconsequential noises.

The food arrived and they sat at the table. Dylan began eating the French fries from his fish and chips and Kane took a bite of his steak sandwich. Dylan broke off a story about a party he'd been at and said, "Why did you leave us?"

Kane swallowed his food and said, "I was put in prison."

"I know that," Dylan said, "but Mom always said that you went to prison because you'd made bad choices. Why did you make bad choices?"

That's the $64,000 question, Kane thought. He took another bite and chewed and swallowed automatically, then drank some water.

"I could give you a lot of reasons for that," he said. "I could tell you about my difficult childhood and about the fact that I'm an alcoholic. But I've come to think those are just rationalizations. I think the real reason I made bad choices was that I wasn't thoughtful."

"You mean you were, like, impulsive?" Dylan asked. "People say I'm impulsive."

"Not exactly, although I was impulsive at times, too," Kane said. "I mean I didn't think about my life, about what it was and what I wanted it to be. It was like I just accepted everything about myself without question, without judgment. So I never really saw the bad parts of myself. No, that's not quite right. It's more that I never really saw that I could or should do something about those bad parts. I just thought I was who I was and there was nothing to be done about it. And since I was, by my reckoning, a better man than my father, I didn't really see the need to try to improve. Until it was far, far too late."

Both men ate for a while in silence.

"What do you think now?" Dylan asked.

"I think Socrates was right," Kane said. "'The unreflective life is not worth living.' Now, I'm trying to figure out why I am who I am, and what I can do to be a better person. That's why I read Montaigne, I guess, and sit in church. It's hard, though, two steps forward and one step back. Sometimes three steps back. I'm beginning to wonder if I have enough time left to get where I'm going."

Dylan reached out and put his hand on his father's.

"It might be too late for us to be father and son," he said, "but we could still be friends. I could work on my anger and you could work on your bad habits and things might improve."

"I'd like that," Kane said. "I would certainly encourage you to be thoughtful about your life, and to judge who you are and what you do by whether it makes you happy, not by whether you are doing well in the eyes of the world. It's a better way to live, even if it doesn't solve all your problems."

"What do you mean?" Dylan asked. "I thought that's what you were talking about, solving your problems."

Kane ate silently for a few minutes, trying to get his thoughts in order.

"I think what I mean is that changing yourself takes a lot of time and effort," he said. "I'm not sure that I could have made myself a better father even if I'd known I needed to. I love you and your sisters, but I never really had the patience to spend much time with you. I was too demanding and critical and, frankly, the things you enjoyed when you were younger bored me. I'm not sure there was any way I could have overcome that."

"What should you have done, then?" Dylan asked.

"If I'd known myself well enough, I would have not become a father," Kane said, "at least until I'd managed to change myself."

They finished their meal in silence, both of them considering what Kane had said.

"How do you change yourself?" Dylan asked when they'd finished. "There are some things I don't like about myself, either."

Kane shook his head.

"I'm not sure I know, really," he said. "About all I've figured out is to change my behavior and hope my instincts fall into line with it. I'm trying that with a few things now, like drinking, and it seems to be working. Sometimes."

Again they were silent, until Dylan said, "Pretty heavy conversation. I've got a lot to think about now."

He got up and walked around the room again.

"I've got to get going soon," he said, "but tell me how your case is going. The Capitol gossip is all crime all the time. Hardly any work is getting done."

So Kane told him about the Ukrainian, the plot to defeat the oil tax, the kidnapping and the shooting.

"Wow," Dylan said, "it's like a Harrison Ford movie or something."

"Not much like a movie," Kane said, shifting to make his leg more comfortable. "And none of it seems to be much help in figuring out who killed Melinda Foxx."

"The White Rose," Dylan said. "Is that over the top, or what? Maybe I could help you with the case. I know a lot about what goes on in the Capitol."

"I'd be grateful for information," Kane said, "but I don't think you should get involved in any other way. Two people are dead, so we know the situation is very dangerous."

Dylan laughed and got to his feet.

"I'm sure you're right," he said. "I've got to be off. I'm going to meet Samantha down at the Alaskan Hotel. They've got a band tonight."

He went to the closet for his coat.

"Dylan, are you really sleeping with that woman?" Kane said.

"Why do you ask?" Dylan said.

"Because I was in the Triangle the other night and saw her making out with another woman," Kane said. "She's gay, isn't she?"

Dylan stood quietly, like he was thinking.

"I'm not sleeping with her," he said at last. "I just said that to sound, you know, older. I like hanging out with Samantha and everything, but she doesn't like men that way. She's a lesbian. One of the reasons she lets me hang around, she told me, is that it gives her cover."

"Why does she need cover?" Kane asked.

"My American studies prof would say it's because the legislature is very chauvinistic," Dylan said. "Its culture is based on male values like dominance and aggression, and it is also deeply homophobic, as a matter of culture as well as politics. So a lesbian, well, she just screws everything up."

He paused for a moment.

"Man," he said, "that sounds deep, doesn't it? All I know is that it's only okay to be gay if you don't flaunt it."

"Dylan, are you . . . ," Kane began, then thought better of what he was going to ask. "So why do you hang around with her?"

Dylan shrugged again, and when he spoke his voice sounded forlorn.

"I don't know," he said. "I'm not good with girls. She's safe and there's no pressure. I'm still trying to figure stuff out."

"It's worth the effort," Kane said. "Figuring stuff out. It's hard, and sometimes you don't like the answers, but it's still worth it."

Dylan put out his hand and Kane took it, then pulled the boy into his arms. The strength of his hug surprised Kane. Then they both let go and Dylan opened the door.

"You know, Dad," he said, "right after they found Melinda Foxx's body, Samantha told me that they'd been friends last year. Samantha's kind of friends, that is. And that Melinda had a new friend this year. Maybe I can find out more about that."

"I think you should let me do that, son," Kane said. Dylan gave him an unreadable smile and left.

Kane thought about putting on his coat and going to find Dylan and Samantha and questioning the woman. But he was sore and found that the conversation had drained him.

I'll do it first thing tomorrow, he thought, and started getting ready for bed.

It is true that the politician, in his professional character,
does not always, or even very often, conform to the
most approved pattern of private conduct.

FREDERICK SCOTT OLIVER

Y ou look like you're about to go on safari," Mrs. Richard Foster said
as she opened the door for Kane.

The detective had to admit she was right. Kane had gotten some of
Cocoa's purchases back from the hotel laundry, and everything but the
underwear had some sort of loops or epaulettes or little squares of Vel-
cro on it.

"This is what I get for sending the fashion impaired out to buy me
clothes," he said, shooting a look over her shoulder at a laughing
Cocoa. "Where's Winthrop?"

"He's in the kitchen making mimosas," the woman said. "Please
come in and help yourself to the croissants. The kitchen here baked
them special."

Kane sat down at the big table, poured himself a cup of coffee, and tasted it.

"This isn't the usual dishwater they call coffee here, either," he said.

"If you have a choice between being rich and poor," Mrs. Foster replied with a smile, "pick rich."

Winthrop came in and set a tray of mimosas in delicate-looking flutes in the center of the table, then went to answer a knock at the door. Oil Can Doyle came in, removed a paper from under his arm, handed it to Mrs. Foster, took off his coat, tossed it to Winthrop, patted his toupee into place, and sat.

"Listen to this," Mrs. Foster said. "The headline says, 'Governor's office aided alleged criminals.' It's the big headline, too, on the front page."

Doyle was grinning like a crocodile.

"That's today's paper," he said. "It should give Hiram Putnam and his minions heartburn. Here's yesterday's."

He took a folded paper from his inside pocket and handed it to Mrs. Foster. She unfolded it and said, "It's the main headline again. It says, 'Blackmail, kidnapping in scheme to defeat oil tax.'"

"Yes, yes, yes," Doyle said. "Somehow that reporter, Cockerham, got his hands on copies of Miss Atwood and Senator Grantham's statements, plus a lot of information on what happened to you, Kane. I can't imagine how he did that. Or what the jury will make of all this if Senator Hope comes to trial."

Instead of replying, Kane took a bite of croissant. It practically melted in his mouth. He swallowed and said to Mrs. Foster, as if Doyle hadn't said a word, "That's good advice. Be rich. I'll have to remember that. Why doesn't everyone sit and we can get started."

Before going to bed the night before, Kane had made a round of telephone calls to set up this meeting. Then he'd gotten up early and hobbled up the hill to sit in the back of the church during the early mass. The old priest had given a vigorous sermon against what he called "unnatural acts" and the civil unions bill "being considered down the street," using as his text Romans 1:26: "For this cause God gave them up unto vile affections; for even their women did change the natural use unto that which is against nature."

A pair of middle-aged women got up in the middle of the sermon and walked out, talking loudly about "closeted old queers" and "mixing religion and politics." Kane followed them out, thinking about what Dylan had said the night before. How have we gotten to this place in America where people glory in looking down on other people? He knew that religions weren't perfect—the Roman Catholic Church has plenty to answer for, God knows—but expected them to resist the impulse to condemn people, not encourage it. No wonder Dylan's friend Samantha was careful not to tread on convention.

When everyone was seated, he began, filling in the group on his dealings with George Bezhdetny.

"So you think he isn't involved in the murders?" Mrs. Foster asked when he'd finished. "Where does that leave us?"

"I'm not sure," Kane said. "But last night my son told me that a woman he knows named Samantha was once involved romantically with Melinda Foxx, and that Melinda may have had another woman lover this year. I think my next step is to find this Samantha and get her to tell me what she knows. But I don't even know her last name. I tried calling Dylan just before coming here, but he wasn't home. All I did was wake up his roommate again."

"I'm sure I can find out," Mrs. Foster said. "Let me make a few calls."

Cocoa cleared his throat. Kane looked at him and raised an eyebrow.

"I know where she lives," he said. "I can take you there."

He looked at the surprised faces around the table and said, "What? All the cabbie can do is drive? I've driven Samantha home plenty of times. Like I already told Nik, I expect I know where everybody in the legislature, and everybody who works there, lives."

"Okay," Kane said. "Then I guess I'll go talk to her. Does anybody have anything they want to say before I go?"

"I do," Oil Can Doyle said. "After I left you yesterday, I went out to talk with my client, and he actually told me some things."

"What things?' Kane asked.

Doyle looked around the table.

"I'm not sure how much I can say," he said. "The rest of these people could be subpoenaed."

Kane gave the little lawyer a disgusted look. Mrs. Foster opened her mouth, but the detective held up his hand to silence her. Everyone looked at Doyle until he actually began to squirm.

"I need something to drink," he said, looking at Winthrop. "Could I have some just plain orange juice?"

Winthrop got up and went into the kitchen.

"Too early for you, Counselor?" Mrs. Foster asked, amusement in her voice.

"He doesn't drink," Kane said.

Both the woman and the lawyer looked at Kane in surprise.

"But his reputation . . . ," Mrs. Foster began.

Kane nodded.

"He pretends to drink," Kane said, "but it's all part of his act. He wants people to think he's strange and flawed and repugnant. He wants them to underestimate him."

Winthrop returned with a glass of orange juice and handed it to Doyle. The lawyer took a drink and said, "I'm not sure about repugnant. How did you know?"

"You stuck me with the bar tab, remember?" he said. "The night I got here? All that was on it was ginger ale."

Doyle smiled, a real smile this time, not the horrible rictus he usually employed.

"I guess I can't be both a deadbeat and a pretend lush," he said. "I'll have to remember that."

He looked around the table.

"Melinda Foxx called Senator Hope when he was in Anchorage last fall and asked to meet him in an out-of-the-way bar," he said. "He thought it was odd, but she said it was important.

"When she arrived, she seemed to be both troubled and afraid. She said she had proof that her employer was breaking the law. She said that she was willing to give the proof to Hope but that he had to keep her identity a secret. He said he started out suspecting she was part of some sort of scheme to discredit him but her sincerity convinced him otherwise. Still, he was reluctant—the whole one-senator-spying-on-another problem—but she told him that they both had an obligation to expose corruption. He couldn't argue with that, so he agreed.

"She gave him the information about the no-bid contract. He handled it carefully, he said, and when the information turned out to be good, he was happy to meet with her again when she called. This time, she insisted on a hotel room. She was very excited when she arrived, he said, and even more afraid. He tried to comfort her and she was, by his account, more than willing to be comforted. At the end of their . . . encounter . . . she gave him the information about the illegal campaign contributions."

Doyle swigged orange juice and looked around the table.

He likes being the center of attention, Kane thought. I suppose that's one of the things that make him a good trial lawyer.

"He saw her frequently after that, always at the same hotel," Doyle said. "She said she was still looking for information, but mostly they met to have sex."

Kane looked at Mrs. Foster. Her face was deadpan. He realized that she had never actually said how she felt about Hope now that her husband was dead, and thought about trying to get Doyle to stop talking about the sex he was having with another woman. But he decided that it was too late for tact and that she was going to have to protect her own heart.

"They continued to meet here after the session started," Doyle said. "About a week before she was murdered, they met at their usual spot. She was very excited. She told him she was pregnant with his child and asked him what he wanted to do about the baby. He said he'd have to think about it. They agreed to meet again the night she was killed. As she was leaving, she said, 'We make a good team,' and that's when he knew she wanted him to marry her."

Doyle stopped talking and looked around the table.

"That's it?" Cocoa said. "What happened?"

"What happened is that she sent him an e-mail a couple of days later saying she had some information that might help him get his civil unions bill passed, that she'd give it to him at their next meeting. Their usual meeting place was a hotel room out by the airport. But she didn't keep the appointment," Doyle said. "So Hope went to her apartment, didn't find her there, and returned to the Capitol to look for her. And found her dead."

Silence reigned for several minutes.

"Did Senator Hope say what he planned to do about the pregnancy?" Mrs. Foster asked. Kane could tell from her voice that she had been harboring something for Hope.

"You mean, might it have been a motive for killing her?" Doyle asked. "No. He said he had decided to do the honorable thing and marry her. I don't know how much luck I'd have selling that to a jury, but I believed him."

Kane watched Mrs. Foster's face for a moment without learning anything more.

"So does he think she honey-trapped him?" he asked Doyle. "Do you?"

"He said he wasn't sure, that she seemed sincere about everything," Doyle said. "But, really . . ."

Kane let the silence stretch out.

"Yeah," he said. "Me, too." He paused, then said, "Did he have any idea what the new information might be?"

"No," Doyle said, "but if it was something on Potter, that might have been a motive for murder all by itself."

"Maybe," Kane said, "but everyone around here keeps telling me people don't murder for political reasons."

"And they do blackmail and kidnap?" Doyle said, his voice squeaking like he'd suddenly remembered it was supposed to. "That's a pretty fine line."

Kane nodded.

"You're right," he said. "It is."

He got to his feet, wincing as the stitches in his thigh pulled.

"I think I'll go talk with Samantha," he said. "Maybe she knows something, maybe she doesn't. But the only other thing to do is sweat Potter, and I don't like my chances of getting in to see him, let alone get the truth out of him, without something to hold over his head."

He reached down, picked up his coffee cup, and drained it.

"Ready to go, Cocoa?" he asked.

As the two of them headed for the door, Mrs. Foster said, "I think Winthrop and I will return to Anchorage. With those men in custody, I don't see why we should stay."

Sure, Kane thought. What sort of threat is a double murderer? But at least you won't have to see Hope if he ever gets out.

"You'll keep me informed?" she went on.

Kane nodded.

"I will," he said. "Have a good trip."

Cocoa opened the door and Kane limped through it.

"Keep your guard up," Winthrop said.

Good advice, Kane thought. Damn good advice.

33

Politics makes strange bedfellows.

CHARLES DUDLEY WARNER

The day had turned fine, with all the blue skies and sunshine and hundred-proof air that spring could provide. Ice won't be a problem again until next year, Kane thought. Cocoa pulled up in his cab and Kane got in.

"Let's go see Samantha," he said.

Samantha lived in what was called the Highlands, a hilly area of single-family homes just north of downtown. With Cocoa driving, the trip took five minutes. She lived in an apartment at the top of a big, white place with green trim, up a long set of white steps that ran beside the structure.

"Great," Kane said, starting up the stairs, swinging his bad leg behind him at each step.

"Jeez, you look just like Chester," Cocoa said from behind him. "You know, the guy on the old TV show?"

Kane saved his breath for climbing. The staircase creaked and groaned with each step.

She gets plenty of warning of visitors, Kane thought.

When he got to the top, Samantha was standing in a bathrobe in the open door. Behind her was a small kitchen. A young woman wearing a large football jersey sat at the tiny table, drinking coffee.

"Mr. Kane," she said as he reached the landing, "what are you doing here?"

Kane stood for a moment catching his breath.

"I'm investigating the White Rose Murder," he said, "and I was hoping you could give me a little information."

"Her name was Melinda, not Rose," Samantha said. "She was a real person, not some sort of character in a sensational story."

"Sorry," Kane said. "I know better. Anyway, I have some questions and I'm not sure you want your friend"—he inclined his head toward the woman at the table—"to hear them or not."

Samantha looked at the woman, who glanced up from her coffee cup and smiled, then back at Kane.

"What makes you think I'll answer questions?" she asked. "You don't have any standing to compel me."

"I have reason to believe that you have information material to a murder investigation," Kane said. "You can talk to me, or I'll be back here within the hour with a police officer and you can talk to him."

"Reason to believe," she said. "What reason to believe?"

She stood looking at Kane for a moment, then snapped her fingers.

"Dylan told you, didn't he?" she said. "The little weasel."

She looked at Kane some more, then shrugged and stepped back.

"I should have known better than to trust a man with a secret," she said. "You'd better come in." She looked at Cocoa. "Him, too, I suppose." She turned to the woman. "Meg, honey, I think you'd better go. I have to speak to these gentlemen."

The woman got to her feet, giving Kane a view of a fine set of legs and what lay above them.

"Better go?" she said. "Something's come up and the piece of ass better go?"

She stormed out of the room. Samantha followed. Kane could hear soft voices, one pleading, the other hissing. Then the woman came back out fully clothed, burst past Kane and Cocoa, and flew down the stairs. Samantha came back into the kitchen with a rueful smile on her face.

"Young people." She said. "So impetuous. Can I give you coffee? No? Well, we better go into the living room where we can be more comfortable."

When they were seated, Kane said, "I know that you knew Melinda Foxx. Could you tell me the nature of your relationship?"

Samantha laughed.

"The nature of your relationship," she said. "I like that. We were lovers."

Kane opened his mouth to speak, but she held up a hand.

"This will go faster if I just tell you the story," she said. "You can ask whatever questions you have afterward. Is that okay?"

Kane nodded, and she began.

"I met Melinda last year, when she first got to Juneau," Samantha said. "She was quiet and seemed nervous in a new job, but she was beautiful and I was attracted to her. If this were a TV show, I'd say my gaydar went off, but the truth is, my gaydar isn't all that good. But I decided I'd give it a try anyway. So I made excuses to see her and to take her out for drinks after work. I thought I was scheming on her.

"Then, one evening, we were sitting in the Baranof just having a drink and she said to me, 'You're trying to seduce me, aren't you?' She didn't sound scandalized or offended, just curious. I denied it, of course, but then she proceeded to tell me that she had had a couple of boyfriends in college and the sex was fine, but she was hoping that I was interested in her because she wanted to try it with a woman, an experienced woman, to see if that didn't suit her better.

"We came right back to this place and made love," Samantha said. "She seemed to like what we did, and me, and we carried on for the rest of the session. We were careful when we were in public. I took her to Vegas over Easter break and bought her a few things. We were happy, I thought. Then, the last day, at lunch, she thanked me and told me that it was over."

"Just like that?" Kane asked.

"Just like that," Samantha said. "I thought it was odd, but I didn't mind so much. With the life I lead, I've more or less given up the idea of a permanent relationship."

"Why did you think it was odd?" Kane asked.

"Well, I'd gotten to kind of like Melinda, as a person I mean," Samantha said. "She seemed sweet and full of ideals, but the way she broke it off was so . . . bloodless and clinical that I began to wonder if it was all just an act."

"Was it?" Kane asked.

Samantha looked out the window for a minute or so.

"I don't know," she said. "I just don't know. If it was, she was a first-class schemer. Anyway, I didn't see her again all during the interim, but a couple of weeks after the legislature reconvened I ran into her and we had coffee. She acted like I was an old friend, and she seemed nervous and happy at the same time. I asked her about her love life, and she gave me this smile and said, 'I've decided there's no such thing as love. Only sex and politics.'

"So I asked about her sex life, and she laughed and said I was the only one she knew who would ask such a question. I kept after it, and finally she said, 'Active.' So you're seeing more than one person? I asked her. Men or women? And she just laughed and didn't answer.

And then, without saying this was related to the rest of the conversation, she asked me what I thought of Letitia Potter. Gorgeous and bloodless, I said, and she said, 'You'd be surprised' and wouldn't say any more. That was the last real conversation I had with her."

"So that's what you were talking about when you told Dylan that Melinda had a new friend?" Kane asked.

"It is," Samantha said. "She didn't come right out and say it, but I got the strong impression she and Letitia Potter were lovers."

Kane thought for a moment and said, "So, when Melinda Foxx turned up dead in that . . . that obviously sexual way, why didn't you tell the authorities about this?"

Samantha looked at him like he'd grown a second head.

"You mean, why didn't I suggest that the Senate Finance chairman's daughter was gay and right in the middle of a spectacular murder?" she said. "I make my living as a lobbyist, Mr. Kane. How long do you think my clients would have stuck with me if I'd done that? Besides, I didn't really know anything, did I? And her father said they were together at home at the time of the murder. And the police arrested Senator Hope so quickly. I thought the whole thing had been solved."

Kane got to his feet. He thought about saying something about how weak her rationalizations were but realized it would be a waste of time. It seemed that if you couldn't rationalize iffy things, you didn't belong in politics.

"Well, thank you for your time," he said.

"You're welcome," Samantha said as she followed him out through the kitchen to the door. "Perhaps you could answer a question for me."

"What's that?" Kane asked, turning on the landing to face her.

"Why didn't you just ask Dylan about all this?" she said. "I told him the same story."

"You did?" Kane said. "When?"

"Last night," she said. "At the bar. He came in all pumped up about how you and he were getting along better, and how he wanted to help you. So I decided I should tell him, probably because I'd been drinking shots with some people before he got there. Then he left, saying he was going to crack the case, and Meg sat down at the table and one thing led to another and I forgot all about it until you showed up."

"You know where the Potters live?" Kane asked Cocoa.

The cabbie nodded.

"Then let's get there," Kane said. "Fast."

He ignored the pain and took the stairs three at a time going down. When he got to the bottom, he limped quickly to the cab, pulling his cell phone from his pocket as he did so. He slid into the cab and punched in Tom Jeffords's private number.

"It's Sunday morning," Jeffords barked. "This had better be important."

"And a good morning to you, Chief," Kane said cheerfully. "Have you seen the paper this morning?"

"Oh, it's you, Nik," Jeffords said. "I did see the newspaper. It looks like bad news for Hiram Putnam."

Jeffords didn't sound at all sorry that his political ally was in the soup.

"Well, between that and two murders in O. B. Potter's office—not to mention the other scandals around these guys—you should be a happy man," Kane said.

"Why would you think that, Nik?" Jeffords said. "The governor, the senator, and I are political allies."

"Yeah, I've seen how that works," Kane said. "I figure the reason you wanted me to come down here was because you wanted Putnam and Potter to be in as much trouble as possible so your mayor had a clear shot at the nomination for governor."

"I have no idea what you are talking about, Nik," Jeffords said. "If Governor Putnam and Senator Potter are in trouble, I don't see how that affects me. I'm just a local police chief."

Kane laughed.

"It would be fun to fence with you for a while, Tom", he said, "but I need something fast. I'm doing your dirty work now, so there's no reason you shouldn't help. I need you to talk to whoever you need to and have a Juneau Police detective named Crawford meet me in thirty minutes at the Silver Bow coffee shop."

"Can't you just ask him yourself?" Jeffords said. "You know my reluctance to become involved in this affair."

"I could," Kane conceded, "but I'm not sure he would come. He's been warned off the White Rose Murder by his boss, at the behest of your political pals. The only way his boss would let him get involved is if some other political heavyweight asks. And that's you."

"Look, Nik," Jeffords began, "I'm afraid you have an inflated—"

"It's Dylan, Tom," Kane interrupted. "I'm afraid he's in trouble and that I'll need official help. So just do it, please. Thirty minutes. Crawford. Silver Bow."

"I—" Jeffords began, but Kane overrode him.

"If you need any more incentive," he said, "I think this will take Potter off the board completely. Your guy will have a clear run."

There was a brief silence.

"I was going to say that of course I will help," Jeffords said, his voice thick with frost. "Not everything is politics."

Maybe not, Kane thought as he put his cell phone away, but I never thought I'd hear Tom Jeffords say so.

34

No man, however strong, can serve ten years as schoolmaster,
priest, or Senator, and remain fit for anything else.

Henry Brooks Adams

Cocoa pulled into the curb. They'd gone just three blocks.

"What are we stopping for?" Kane asked.

"You wanted Senator Potter's place," Cocoa said. "This is it."

The house, a ranch-style painted pea green, looked deserted—no
car in the driveway and the curtains on the big picture window pulled
tight. Kane got out of the cab, limped to the front door, and pounded
on it.

"Open up," he yelled. "Police."

"Police?" Cocoa said from behind him. "You ain't the police."

"I want in there, Cocoa," he said. "I'm afraid something might have
happened to my son."

He pounded again, but there was no response.

"Guess I'll have to break it down," he said.

Cocoa pushed him out of the way. He had two thin pieces of metal in his hand. He inserted them in the lock and twitched them around. Then he straightened and turned the knob. He saw the look on Kane's face and said, "I just said I never been in prison. I didn't say I don't have criminal skills."

Kane took the gun off his hip and went through the door, stopping to listen. He heard people whispering.

"Police," he said. "Come out. Now."

Senator O. B. Potter walked from the back of the house clutching a terry-cloth bathrobe around him. His white hair stood up at all angles and sweat ran down his flushed face.

"What's . . . what's the meaning of this?" he asked.

"Where's your daughter?" Kane asked.

"Who are you?" Potter said. "Why do you want my daughter?"

"I'm the guy who is going to shove this gun about three feet up your ass if you don't answer my questions," Kane said. "Where is Letitia?"

"I—she's not here," Potter said. "I'm not sure where she is. The office, perhaps. She's a very conscientious worker, and now, with two empty staff positions, we're very busy. She worked very late last night, and I suppose she's at work again now."

"Hear him?" Kane said to Cocoa. "Two empty staff positions. As if murder was just another personnel problem."

He looked around the living room but saw nothing of interest.

"Where was your daughter the night Melinda Foxx was killed?" he asked.

"What?" Potter said. "Why, she was here, at home with me."

He straightened his shoulders and tried to puff out his chest, but his robe slipped and he had to grab it again to keep it closed.

"Who are you?" he said. "What right do you have to break into my home and ask questions? Do you know who I am?"

Kane laughed.

"I love it when they ask that," he said.

"If you are the police, where is your warrant?" he said. "I want to see your warrant. And some identification."

Kane put his hand in the middle of the senator's chest and pushed. The old man stumbled backward and fell into an armchair, his robe flying open.

"I'll be a monkey's uncle," Cocoa said. "Would you look at that?"

Beneath the robe, Potter wore a leather halter and tight leather shorts with a black leather codpiece. The leather was studded with copper rivets.

Cocoa took a cell phone from his pocket and opened it.

"Who are you calling?" Kane asked.

"I ain't calling anybody," Cocoa said. His voice sounded like he could barely contain his joy. "I'm taking pictures."

The senator scrambled to his feet and clutched his robe around him. He was making noises, but no words came out.

"Who do you suppose he's dressed up like that for?" Cocoa said. "Maybe we should go look."

Pushing the senator before them, Kane and Cocoa went out of the living room and down a hall, past the bathroom, and into a bedroom with an open door. The mousy receptionist from Potter's office was struggling to untie her right hand from the post of a four-poster bed and sobbing. Her ankles were still tied to the bed, and it was clear that she'd been spread-eagled across the end of the bed. She was naked, and her back, buttocks, and thighs were pink and ridged with welts. A leather-handled whip lay on the floor near her.

"Why, you kinky old devil," Cocoa said, snapping away with his cell phone, "and you a conservative Christian."

"I'm not . . . we're not breaking any laws," the senator said. "This is completely consensual."

Kane walked over and untied the woman's hand, then knelt to remove the ties on her ankles. The material used to tie her was soft, and there weren't any difficult knots in it.

"I'd guess that this was okay with both of them," he said. "She needed to be punished, and he needed to feel powerful, and somehow in this cockeyed world, these two crazy kids found each other."

Once she was free, the woman scrambled into the bed and under the covers.

"Why are these men here, Orestes?" she said. "What do they want?"

The old man sank down on the bed next to her and patted her hand.

"This is consensual," he said again. "And heterosexual. And legal. We'll be all right."

His voice sounded like even he didn't believe that, and the woman began sobbing again.

Kane knew he should feel revolted by the two of them, but his stomach was tied in a knot of apprehension.

"I'm only asking one more time, Senator," Kane said. "Where was your daughter the night Melinda Foxx died?"

"She was," Potter began, but Cocoa waved the cell phone at him and he stopped. "I don't know where she was. I was at Anita's and we were doing . . . this."

"Why aren't you at her place now?" Cocoa asked. The cabbie really seemed to be enjoying the situation.

The woman mumbled something.

"What was that?" Cocoa asked. "I can't hear you."

"I said my mother is visiting," the woman spat. "We couldn't do this in the same apartment with her. That would be sick."

"And this isn't?" Cocoa said softly.

"Enough, Cocoa," Kane said. "We don't have the time. The night Melinda Foxx was killed, Senator?"

Potter ran his hand over his hair, but it sprang right back up.

"As I said, Anita and I were together at her place. And I could hardly use that as an explanation for my whereabouts, so I said my daughter and I were home together. Letitia swore that she was at home, alone, and I believed her."

"And, of course, she offered to alibi you, so you were anxious to believe her," Kane said. "She must have seen the advantage to that right away. Neat. Did you believe her when she said the same thing about the night Ralph Stansfield died?"

He could see doubt creep into the old man's eyes. He'd been a politician too long to really believe anything he hadn't seen with his own eyes.

"Yes, I did," he said. "But what if she wasn't? What reason would she have to kill those people?"

"I don't know that yet," Kane said, "but I think she was in a lesbian relationship with Melinda Foxx that went wrong somehow."

The old man looked baffled, then outraged.

"Lesbian? Letitia? How could that be?" he said. "She was—she is—the most devout person I know. She would never engage in that wickedness."

"You're a fine one to be talking about wickedness," Cocoa said.

Kane tapped the cabbie on the shoulder and said, "Let's go. We've wasted enough time with this old fraud. We need to find his daughter."

Kane hobbled quickly through the house and got into the cab, Cocoa right behind him.

"Well, at least we've got the goods on the old hypocrite," Kane said.

"What goods would those be?" Cocoa asked, putting the cab in gear.

"The pictures," Kane said. "The ones you took with the cell phone."

"Don't tell the senator," Cocoa said as he accelerated down the street, "but my cell phone don't take pictures."

35

Of what does politics consist except the making of imperfect decisions,
many of them unjust and quite a few of them deadly?

LEWIS LAPHAM

Kane was out of the cab before it was completely stopped. He limped
around it and started across the street toward the Capitol.

Cocoa rolled down his window.

"Want me to go with you?" he asked.

"No," Kane said. "Go down to the Silver Bow. You should find
Tank Crawford there. You should know him; he's a Juneau cop. Tell
him if he wants to catch the White Rose killer, he'll race right up to the
Senate Finance office."

"You could wait and make it legal," Cocoa said. "The Silver Bow's
just down there."

Kane shook his head, crossed the street, and mounted the steps. He
wanted to race up the five flights, but didn't think his leg would take
it. He punched the button for the elevator and the doors slowly opened.

"Not many offices occupied on a Saturday," the security guard said.

Kane ignored him and punched the button for the fifth floor. The elevator seemed to crawl upward. As it rose, Kane did his best not to think about what might have happened to Dylan. The boy wasn't strong. Why did he have to get involved?

The elevator stopped on the third floor and a couple of guys in tennis outfits started to get in. They saw the look on Kane's face and backed right out again.

"It's going up," one of them said to no one in particular. "We don't want to go up."

When the elevator opened on the fifth floor, Kane limped rapidly down the hall, passing a janitor who was polishing the drinking fountain and doing a tightly controlled dance to the music coming through his earphones. The floor seemed to be empty otherwise, all the office doors closed and no lights showing. Kane pushed open the swinging doors to the Finance Committee, walked across the big hearing room, and tried the door to O. B. Potter's offices. It was locked. He pounded on it hard enough to make the frosted glass rattle in the frame.

"Open up," he called. "Police."

No response.

"Open up now," he called, pounding again, "or I'll break it down."

He heard a muffled response, the sound of doors closing, then the sound of the lock being turned. The door opened a crack.

"What is it?" a woman's voice asked.

Kane hit the door with his shoulder and bulldozed it open, pushing the woman's body backward. Then he was in the outer office, watching Letitia Potter rubbing her forehead. There was a red mark where the door had hit it.

"That hurt," she said. "Who are you? Oh, Mr. Nikiski. What are you doing?"

"Several things," Kane said. "One is looking for my son."

The woman dropped her hand from her forehead and made a show of confusion.

"Your son?" she said. "Who is he? Why would he be here?"

Kane looked at her face and saw the striking beauty there. She's like a Greek goddess come to life, he thought, but her eyes are as empty as a panhandler's pockets.

"If he's not here," Kane said, "I'm sure you won't mind if I look around."

The woman shrugged.

"Whatever," she said.

Kane opened the door to the staff office. It was an even bigger mess than it had been. Stacks of folders and what looked like office supplies covered the desktops. Kane saw a key hanging from the handle of one of the metal cabinets and started forward.

He sensed rather than saw the blow coming, hunched his shoulders, and half-turned. Too late. Whatever the woman was swinging made contact with the back of his head and he was down, stunned. He landed on his side. Hands scrabbled at the automatic on his belt. He tried to pin one of them, but they got away, taking the gun with them. He rolled over and looked up at Letitia Potter.

She held the gun on him, a slight smile on her lips.

"You lose," she said in the little-girl voice Kane had heard at the bagel place.

She reached up with her free hand, grabbed the lapel of the blue work shirt she wore, and pulled. Buttons popped and the shirt gaped open to reveal creamy skin and a lacy, pale blue bra.

"You forced your way in and tried . . . tried to do things to me," she said in the same voice, "but I—we struggled and I got your gun and shot you."

She unbuttoned her jeans and pulled them down around her hips. Then, before Kane could move, she raked the automatic's sight across her exposed abdomen, leaving a livid welt that seeped blood at one corner. She shivered and laughed, her eyes now glistening pinpoints.

"Naughty man," she said. "Naughty man must die."

All Kane could think was, Stall. Stall.

"Where's my son?" he asked.

Letitia's eyes flicked to the locked cabinet, then back to Kane. She smiled but said nothing.

"Why did you kill Melinda Foxx?" he asked.

Letitia's finger whitened on the trigger.

Wrong question, he thought.

"No," he said. "Killing me won't help you. Too many people know."

He watched as she eased off on the trigger.

"Too many people know what?" she asked. There was something ghastly about the singsong little-girl voice coming from a grown woman.

"Too many people know you killed Melinda," Kane said. "And Ralph Stansfield."

"That was an accident," Letitia said, shaking her head from side to side. "You told me he knew something and I waited to talk with him about it and we were the only two left in the office and he went out to smoke a cigarette and I went with him and he said something that made me mad and I pushed him and he fell over the . . . over the railing and he died."

"What did he say?" Kane asked.

The woman silently raised the gun again.

"He said he knew you and Melinda were lovers," Kane said quickly. "He said he would tell your father if you tried to have him fired."

Letitia looked at him wide-eyed.

"How did you know that?" she asked, lowering the gun again. "What else do you know?"

"I know that you and Melinda were being very careful," he said. "I know that if you'd been found out, it would have been a scandal. You couldn't have that, could you? A scandal?"

"We were careful. So careful," she said. She stuck out her lip and stamped her foot. "Daddy would be so mad if he found out. He thinks I'm his little angel. That's what he calls me. But when he's angry, he beats me."

A leer chased the child's smile off her lips for an instant, and her voice became a woman's, deep and sexy.

"I like to be beaten as much as that little slut Anita," the woman said, "but I'll never tell him that."

She looked down at Kane and she laughed.

"You're just stalling, aren't you?" the woman said. "You think somebody is coming to save you."

Got that right, Kane thought, and said, "If you were lovers, why did you kill Melinda Foxx? Did you find out she was betraying you? Did she tell you she was pregnant?"

The woman took a step back and brought her left hand to her mouth.

"She was pregnant?" Letitia said. "Melinda was pregnant? How could she be pregnant?"

Kane opened his mouth, but Letitia held her finger to her lips and listened, as if she'd heard something, then relaxed.

"How could Melinda be pregnant?" she asked again, raising the gun.

"She was seeing Matthew Hope," Kane said. "They were lovers, too."

Letitia shook her head as if denying what she'd heard.

"I never knew," she said. "I knew she was betraying me—Daddy and me—but not that way."

Her voice took on another timbre, neither the woman nor the girl, someone in between.

"I was a virgin," she said. "I had boyfriends but didn't really like them that much. They just wanted one thing, and the thought of all that bumping and stickiness made my skin crawl.

"Then Melinda came to work. She was smart and efficient and so good-looking. I liked being around her. Then, this summer, she started being really nice to me. And one night we were working late, going over the draft of a bill, and she just leaned down and kissed me. Just once.

"And I fell in love with her," the woman's voice said. "I chased her and she ran until, just as the session started, she stopped running. It was wonderful. The sex was wonderful, and the playacting, pretending we were just coworkers, that was wonderful, too. At first we'd meet at her place, but then she suggested we do it at the office, and that made it even better. Doing it there on my father's desk, the desk he pounded when he yelled about dirty faggots, made it so good.

"But I guess I was suspicious, because a little voice in my head told me to watch her."

Letitia stopped to listen again, and when she went on, it was the little girl speaking.

"This voice told me. I knew we were doing dirty things, and that meant she was a dirty person, to do those things with me. So I watched her, and one day, she left her computer unlocked and I read her e-mail. One of them was to Senator Hope, about how she knew something that would make my father let out the bill about dirty faggots getting married."

She stopped talking and raised the gun again.

"Why am I talking to you?" she asked. "I should just shoot you."

"Don't you want to tell me how you killed her?" Kane asked. "You knew she was in cahoots with your father's political enemy, that she was sharing office secrets with him, that if she told people about your relationship your father would have no choice but to send you away to try to salvage his political position. You couldn't have that, could you?"

"I have nowhere to go," the little-girl voice said. "I didn't plan to kill her. It was just, we were in my father's office, doing stuff, and I was sitting on his desk and she was kneeling there making me feel so good, and when I was finished feeling good, it was just so easy to pick up that stupid award and hit her with it and she fell down and died. I was just so mad at her."

Letitia stared into the middle distance, but her eyes focused quickly when Kane tried to move.

"That's it?" Kane said. "It was an impulse? You were smart enough to pour cleaner in her mouth to destroy evidence of your lovemaking. Where did you get that? The janitor's cart? And you were certainly able to take advantage of your father's weird sexual practices to provide yourself with an alibi. None of that jibes with your story that you killed Melinda on impulse."

The woman looked at him and raised the gun again. Her eyes were like shiny pebbles, made hard by the certainty of Kane's death.

"When they arrested Senator Hope, I thought I'd gotten away with it," Letitia said, her voice back to normal now. "But then there was Ralph, and that stupid boy who found me here last night and started asking me questions. When I got tired of that, I hit him and put him in that cabinet. It was all so easy, just like this is going to be. And then maybe people will quit asking me questions and let me go back to my life. Good-bye."

She gave him a smile and her finger tightened on the trigger and a groan came from inside the metal cabinet. Her eyes jerked up and the gun barrel lifted, and using his good leg, Kane kicked her in the knee. She screamed and started to fall, and the office was full of the noise of the automatic firing. Something punched Kane in the left side, but he was already moving, rolling up her legs. He tried to grab her gun hand, but his muscles wouldn't answer, so he flopped his left arm on her right one. The automatic went off again and again and the bullets hit metal somewhere. Letitia was screaming like a little girl and hitting him in the head with her left fist and he knew he was going to lose this fight and that he would die and something flew past his right ear and hit Letitia Potter in the forehead and her eyes rolled up and she was still.

"Mister, are you okay?" a man's voice asked. "I heard what she said. She was an evil lady, and I tried to help you."

Hands grasped his right side and helped him to his feet. The wreckage of a portable CD player lay next to Letitia Potter's head.

"I threw it—my CD player," Baby Santos said. "It was all I had."

Kane could hear feet pounding across the floor of the big hearing room. He felt like passing out.

Not yet, he told himself, not just yet.

He shook off the janitor's hands and stumbled to the metal cabinet.

"You're shot," the janitor said.

"Nik, what the hell . . . ," Tank Crawford's voice said. He sounded a thousand miles away.

Kane leaned against one side of the cabinet, put his right hand on the key, and turned. Then he grasped the handle and turned it to open the door. But he'd seen the three big holes that the bullets from the automatic had punched low down in the door. He knew what he would find. He fell to his knees and pried the door open and in his chest his heart turned to stone.